THE
HAWK'S FLIGHT

BOOK TWO OF THE THREE BROTHERS TRILOGY

ELIZABETH R. JENSEN

Printed in the United States of America
First Printing, 2022
ISBN 979-8-9856474-2-6

Gryphon Publishing
Jefferson, GA 30549
www.gryphon-publishing.com

Editor: Pam Elise Harris
Cover & Interior: Melissa Stevens

The Three Brothers Trilogy

Book 1: The Wolf's Den
Book 2: The Hawk's Flight

Tales of Etria (coming soon)

*To my husband for supporting all my crazy dreams
and conversations about them.*

THE HAWK'S FLIGHT

I

FALL 604

Fourteen-year-old Borus Wolfensberger is yawning and struggling to stay awake, swaying slightly in the saddle. The last thing he wants to do is topple off his horse in front of all the knights he's with. Borus, along with the long double column of knights and infantry, streams through the gate at Southwind Fort in Etria. Lord Commander Urich Stone salutes Sir Gregory before turning his attention to the officers approaching him.

While the lord commander and other officers take over getting the knights and men-at-arms settled in the barracks, Sir Gregory and Borus, his first-year squire, go inside the fort.

"C'mon, I'll show you to your room," says Sir Gregory, motioning for Borus to follow. Sir Gregory leads him up the stairs and to the first room on the left, then opens the door. "This one is for you. I'll be just down the hall on the right."

They both step into the room and Borus looks around. It has a couple of stuffed chairs by the fire, a desk with a small chair, and a large bed.

"Thank you, sir," says Borus, hesitating.

"Is there something else?" asks Sir Gregory.

"Yes. Do you know how long we'll be here?" replies Borus.

Sir Gregory shakes his head. "Nope, we just go where the orders tell us. I'm going to go to my room. I'll let you know when I need you."

Borus nods in understanding and then shuts the door when Sir Gregory walks out. With his grandfather, the Wolf—the famous General Burchard Wolfensberger—in the north at Alderth Castle, his time here at Southwind Fort will be a chance to finally be taken seriously by others for his own actions, not those past or present of the Wolf.

Sighing, Borus drops his pack on the ground. With King Renard's declaration of war against King Bokur of Wanonia in the north and Ruschmann Blackwell in the south, all the new squires from his class are assigned to knight masters who will be near the upcoming battles. Which means Borus and his friends may see battle firsthand.

Borus remembers four years ago when he left home to become a page. Four years ago, his fear was not being prepared to become a knight because Etria had been at peace for twenty years. Now, he can only hope his friends will return home in one piece. As Sir Gregory confirmed, until they get orders to return or go somewhere else, Borus will be at Southwind Fort. He sets down his pack and sprawls out on the bed to test it out.

There is heavy pounding on the door. Borus opens his eyes and looks around him. There's morning sunlight streaming through his window. Muttering to himself, he rolls out of bed and yanks open the door.

Sir Gregory is outside getting ready to pound on the door again and almost hits Borus on the head. "Grab your gear! Hurry!" he yells and rushes down the hallway and out of sight.

Borus's stomach rumbles. He realizes if it's late morning, then he slept through dinner, the meeting he was supposed to attend, and likely breakfast. Borus growls in annoyance at himself. *The great first impression I was hoping to make is now that I am a slacker. Just great. Freaking great.* He glances in the mirror, runs his fingers through his blond hair, and shrugs. Then he grabs his pack, fixes his scabbard with the sword, and heads out of his room, shutting the door behind him.

A couple of knights rush past him on the stairs. Their urgency causes Borus to pick up his pace. He follows them outside and down the steps. Sir Gregory is on his horse, Borus's horse is saddled and waiting, and the rest of the squad is mounting up. After Borus mounts, Sir Willet, one of Sir Gregory's squad members, sidles his horse closer and hands Borus something in a napkin. Borus takes it, then realizes it's food and smiles gratefully.

"You'll learn soon enough to eat at the meals just in case something like this comes up," Sir Willet says knowingly. Borus looks over at Sir Gregory. Sir Gregory surveys his squad. Once it is clear everyone is ready, he gives the signal and leads them out at a gallop.

Borus almost drops his breakfast, having not expected the speed of the departure. He hastily tucks the meat pastry into his tunic and settles himself better on his horse. Still feeling somewhat out of sorts, Borus follows the rest of the squad.

As the squad reaches the forest, Sir Gregory slows down to a walk. Borus takes advantage of the slower speed and hastily eats the meat pastry Sir Willet gave him. They slip into the forest along a deer trail. A way down the trail, they can hear sounds of a fight. At the signal, everyone in the squad draws their swords and sets their shields if they have them.

The squad comes to a halt. Using hand signals, Sir Gregory orders the knights to split up. Half of the men, including Borus and Sir Gregory, dismount. The plan is to surround the fight and hopefully cut off the enemy from escaping.

The knights on horses melt back into the trees. The knights on foot fan out and quietly slip closer to the sound of fighting. They pause, hidden, but taking in the fight before them.

Borus shakes from nerves. He takes a deep breath to steady himself. *I have been training for this. I must trust myself and my training. Sir Gregory trusts me; otherwise, he would not have chosen me as a squire,* he thinks. Two more deep breaths and Borus quells the shaking.

There are five Etrian knights fighting against twice as many enemy axmen. Several knights are on the ground, wounded or dead. There are many more dead axmen, but it is clear the knights are tiring and beginning to make mistakes. Borus tilts his head. There is a strange whispering sound. He looks around, not sure what it is—then he sees the other half of the squad slowly materializing in the trees behind the axmen.

Sir Gregory glances to his left and right with a grim smile. He puts two fingers to his lips and whistles, then leads the charge.

Borus hesitates for a split second, then runs, sword ready, a step behind the line of running knights. The mounted knights charge and slam into several of the axmen. Blood sprays everywhere. Borus wipes sweat out of his eyes and hastily whips his sword up to parry the axe coming straight for his skull. Thankfully, Borus's training and title of junior sword master have taught him how to quickly size up an opponent. The axman is fast, but not creative. He has two different strikes. After his fourth strike, Borus feints with the sword in his right hand, swaps it to his left, and sweeps his sword at the man's neck. Borus's sword hits its target, and the enemy falls to the ground dead.

Borus takes a deep breath to steady himself and is about to change position when another axman comes out of the trees running toward him. This one is swinging two axes. When the dual-wielding axman is about halfway to Borus, he throws one of the axes. Borus dodges and rolls, coming up to the side. He strikes at the back of the axman's legs, hamstringing him. The axman stumbles, then pivots, striking wildly. The axe slices through Borus's armor and into his right forearm. Borus shudders in pain. He switches his sword to his left hand, a trick he learned as a second-year page when he broke his right arm, and takes a step back. Blood is streaming down his right arm. Borus sways. The axman grins and steps closer, swinging down with a chopping motion. Borus skips to the side and steps behind the axman; using an upper cut, he strikes at the man's torso. His sword gets stuck and the axman falls over, taking it with him. Borus struggles to singlehandedly remove his sword from the enemy's body.

Sir Gregory comes up beside Borus and shakes his head. "Here, let me help you." With a deft yank, Borus's sword is free.

Borus takes the sword and awkwardly puts it in his scabbard with his left hand. "Thanks," he mumbles. His face is white. Borus tries to take a deep breath to steady himself. He takes a second deep breath and then starts to cough. He dashes over to a tree just in time as he retches up his breakfast. Borus takes a few more deep breaths and, using the tree to steady himself, stands up. Keeping his eyes on Sir Gregory and averted from the dead men, he makes it back to the knight.

Sir Gregory quirks an eyebrow at Borus. "This isn't your first time in combat," he comments quietly. Before Borus can answer, he feels bile rise in his throat and dashes behind the tree to retch again.

Borus returns shakily. "It's my second. Last time, I was rescuing Kass and Prince Richard at the Sapphire Coast."

Sir Gregory nods in understanding. "It takes time to train your stomach to not rebel after a kill. Even now, after over thirty-five years, there are rare occasions I can't control mine."

Sir Willet walks over to them. "We got here just in time. I don't think Captain Dorian's squad would have made it much longer without our help." Eyeing Borus, Willet reaches into his pack and pulls out some supplies. He sits Borus down and rolls up his sleeve and chain mail to examine the wound. After cleaning up the arm with water and a clean cloth, Willet looks at Sir Gregory. "I can stitch him up here, if we have time," he says, not sure what other orders they had been given.

Sir Gregory nods. "Yes, that would be best."

Willet hands Borus a flask. "Drink some of this. I'm going to stitch you up, and it is going to hurt."

Borus takes the flask and takes a big gulp, then gasps. "What was that?" he asks in shock.

Sir Gregory laughs. "Never had anything that strong?"

Borus shakes his head.

"Willet makes it himself—a mix of herbs and other things. It will help numb the pain," Sir Gregory informs him.

In the middle of Etria at Burmstone Palace, Julien Wolfensberger, eleven, the first page in many years to want to become a mage-knight at the Trinity Page and Squire School, looks around, searching for his thirteen-year-old brother, Kass—a fourth-year page. All the pages are supposed to be together in the dining hall for breakfast on the first day of school. Finally, he sees Kass slipping in through the doors. Jules sighs in relief. He's sitting at a table with Lewis Vale, one of Kass's year-mates, and a few other pages he only knows in passing. Lewis waves to Kass, trying to catch his attention. Kass sees them and grins, snagging a tray of food and slipping into a seat next to them.

"I thought you were going to get in trouble!" hisses Jules.

Kass shrugs. "I got sidetracked. But I'm here now, so no need to worry about me, brother…"

Kass is about to say something else when Sir Waldorf walks to the front of the dining hall to address the pages.

"To those of you who are new to the palace and don't know me, I am Sir John Waldorf, headmaster of the Trinity Page and Squire School. I have served as headmaster for over twenty years at the behest of King Renard and his father, King Roland. I have seen war and peace and know firsthand the importance of training each generation to be able to defend not only the royal family, but the entire country from enemies of any kind. As you know, we are at war in the north with the country Wanonia and in the south with the traitor Ruschmann Blackwell. This makes what you are learning here even more critical. Any of you who have an affinity for magic will be given some training starting your second year. However, our primary focus here is on creating knights who know how to use all the tools at their disposal, not on making mages. First years will follow me to the training yard. Everyone else, you know where you should be, so go."

Lewis looks at Kass, who is hastily shoveling his food into his mouth. "Want me to wait for you?"

Kass shake his head, causing a piece of food to fly out of his mouth and onto Jules's ear.

Cringing, Jules swipes at his ear. "Ewww, that is so gross, Kass!" Jules grabs a napkin and wipes off his face, then picks up his tray. "I'm going to go, I don't want to be late. See you two later!"

Kass just blinks at his brother, trying to avoid repeating what just happened. Jules follows the pages out of the dining hall toward his first class of the day, logistics with Lord Felix.

A medium-build, sandy-haired, fourteen-year-old squire looks around his new quarters in disgust. The whole room is filthy, covered in a layer of dirt; it's going to take ages for him to clean it off. He sets his pack down on top of the trunk with his belongings and turns around to face his knight master, Sir Lars.

"Roger, I know this is not where you hoped to end up, but I will once again remind you that I do not have control over where I am sent. As my squire, you must go where I go. For the time being, that means we will be here in the far north of Etria at Camp Tooth. One thing I do know for sure is that we will see action. It is critical you continue to train regularly, even if I am not around to oversee it."

Sir Lars turns to walk out of the room when Roger sighs and mutters, "At least we're away from the Wolfensberger brats."

The knight spins back around. "What did you say?"

Roger looks at Sir Lars, unsure. "I said Wolfensberger—"

"What would you know of them?" replies the knight harshly.

"The three Wolfensberger brothers are why I failed at one of my fourth-year training tests as a page. I thought you knew about them," Roger says quietly.

Sir Lars opens his mouth and then closes it, considering his next words. "I forgot about the three boys. The Wolf"—he spits the name—"and I have butted heads many times on the battlefield. However, he is a general, and I am merely a knight, so it has always been his word against mine. I try to avoid him if I can." Lars is about to say more but stops. Afraid to let this fourteen-year-old know too much, before he has had sufficient time to get a real measure of the boy.

Jules is heading out to the training space that has been set aside for his mage lessons when he looks over and sees Kass and the other fourth-year pages practicing archery. He steps over to the fence and leans against it.

Kass's target is set up double the distance. Jules watches in awe as his brother shoots not just one, but three arrows into the dead center of the target. Mouth gaping in surprise, Jules jumps straight up in the air when someone touches his shoulder.

"Whoa there, Jules," Master Brixx says with a chuckle. "I wasn't trying to scare you, but we do have a lesson…"

Beet red in embarrassment, Jules follows Master Brixx over to their training area and turns his back on the fourth-year pages. Twice a week, since becoming a page a year ago, Jules takes mage lessons with Master Brixx or another mage from Onaxx Academy School for Mages. Unlike traditional mage students attending classes at Onaxx Academy, Jules's instructors come to him at the palace. This year, his mage studies are being split into units. Jules will spend four weeks working on a unit with one instructor, and then the unit and instructor will change.

Jules concentrates on the circle of rocks in front of him. The circle fills with water but does not spill over the edges. Instead, it creates a dome. When the dome is full of water, it turns to ice. A second circle of rocks behind the first fills with thousands of tiny lightning bolts. This circle is also contained with an invisible dome. The lightning bolts bounce around, sending off sparks. The top of the dome over the lightning bolts disappears, and the bolts begin to jump higher and higher. The half sphere of ice floats above the ground and settles like a cap over the lightning bolts, slowly sinking to the ground. The sphere of ice absorbs the bolts. By the time it settles on the ground, the ice is a puddle of water and the bolts are gone.

Master Brixx stands up and walks over to Jules. "I admire your creativity when interpreting the assignment, Jules. That wasn't quite what I had in mind, but you did meet all the objectives. As we have previously discussed, each mage is a unique individual, making every magical endeavor unique to the mage performing it. The primary purpose, as you know, was to ensure you can control two separate spells at the same time without using visible magic. Next week we will try three."

Jules bows. "Thank you, Master Brixx. I will see you next week."

Jules walks back toward the page quarters and is running the exercise through his mind. He doesn't see the rock until it's too late. He trips and falls right into a big muddy puddle. Laughter sounds from nearby. Jules slowly picks himself up, muddy water streaming down his face. Kass, who just got done with his training session, walks over, chuckling.

"Are you OK?" he says, offering Jules a hand.

Jules takes the hand and tugs. Kass, not expecting the tug from his brother, drops like a rock into the puddle. Removing his hand from Kass's, Jules steps out of the way as Kass tries to grab his legs.

Shaking his head, Jules looks at the equally muddy Kass. "This is what happens when you think it's funny."

Kass rolls his eyes and steps out of the puddle. "Now we both need to change before dinner."

General Burchard Wolfensberger, famous one-eyed Etrian general, sword master, and grandfather of Borus, Kass, and Jules Wolfensberger, is the officer in charge at Camp Tooth, one of the camps in the north where troops are stationed for the war with Wanonia. The Wolf pushes his chair back hard, causing it to topple over.

"Why on earth would you send a patrol there?" growls the Wolf.

Lord Roman takes a step back. "Sir Gregory said…"

The Wolf snarls, "Sir Gregory is *not* here! He left two months ago. Those men are dead because of your mistake."

There is a quiet knock on the door, and Sir Charles slips in and salutes the Wolf. "General, the men are ready, awaiting your command."

The Wolf nods and glares at Lord Roman. "We are not done with this conversation. When I get back from cleaning up your mess, I will deal with you then." Before Lord Roman can respond, the Wolf departs.

"My horse is ready?" the Wolf verifies as they head down the stairs.

"Yes, General."

Sir Charles and the Wolf walk out into the yard where the knights, including Sir Lars and his squire, are waiting.

"Gentlemen, let's go get us some Wanonians!" the Wolf yells before mounting. He spurs his horse into a rear with his sword raised before leading the way at a gallop out of the gate. The knights stream out behind the Wolf.

About a mile down the road, the number of knights triples as they are joined by other camps. Lord Roman's mistake was costly to Etria. But it also serves as a much-needed diversion. While King Bokur's focus is on maintaining his tenuous hold just across the border, he has left the bulk of his troops without an experienced leader. The Wolf is heading straight for those troops.

Although the Wanonians outnumber Etrians two to one, they are like sheep without a seasoned commander. As soon as the Wolf's troops, flying his banner, come within view, the Wanonians lose their courage and try to scatter. A few Wanonian squads struggle to maintain their position. The Etrian knights slam into the Wanonians from three sides and slaughter them. The battle is quick and bloody. Several thousand Wanonians fall.

Prior to engaging, the Wolf ordered the men to ensure that three of the Wanonians are permitted to run away. King Renard does not want prisoners. Other than allowing the three to run back to King Bokur, the Wolf's orders are to kill all Wanonians. The plan is these three will return to King Bokur with news of the huge loss and encourage their king to end the war.

A month after the defeat of the Wanonian troops at Etria's northern border, the Wolf is sitting in his office at Camp Tooth. A stack of papers awaits his attention. He is about to grab one when there is a knock at the door.

"Come in!" he calls.

Sir Lars, an Etrian knight originally from the northern country Sneg, walks into the office. The Wolf motions for the knight to sit down.

"Thank you for coming, Sir Lars. I have received another complaint about Squire Roger from the camp staff. It is imperative you get your squire under control, or I will have to punish him," the Wolf growls.

Lars looks at the Wolf in annoyance. "I told you last time, I will take care of it."

"It's obvious you didn't 'take care' of it last time; otherwise, I would not have received another complaint. While I understand that fourteen-year-old boys want to test boundaries, I will not tolerate Roger bullying any of the staff of this camp to perform tasks that do not fall within their service contracts. Make sure the message comes across this time, or the next complaint I get, he will be on latrine duty for a whole month." The Wolf glares menacingly at Lars. Lars ignores him and walks out.

An hour later, Sir Lars finds his squire alone in the training yard running through sword drills. The knight waits for his squire to finish before grabbing his arm and dragging him into the shadows of the training equipment shed.

"Roger, whatever it is you're up to, you need to make sure you are much more discreet. People are talking. This is the second time the Wolf has spoken to me. Next time he's going to give you latrine duty for a month," Lars says in a deadly quiet voice to Roger.

Wrinkling his nose in disgust, Roger looks at his knight master and sighs. "I will be more discreet. When do we get to leave this nasty place? No one around here knows how to have fun."

Lars shrugs. "We get to leave when we get orders to leave. However, with the majority of the Wanonian troops dead and the rest retreating…it's possible the Wolf will be recalled to Burmstone Palace. The sooner we can get away from his command, the better. Until then you cannot afford to draw more attention to yourself. The bullying must stop."

Roger sighs in annoyance. "Fine, I will do as you ask for now."

Lars nods. "Good. I have another meeting to attend. I'll see you after dinner." The knight turns on his heel and walks away briskly.

Sir Waldorf sits down at the head table in the dining hall after announcing the details of the annual page camping trip. This year they will stay within the royal forest. Jules is sitting at a table with Kass and Lewis.

Kass shares a look with Lewis before speaking. "I was wondering if the king was going to even let us go on our trip. I guess we have the answer now. Hopefully it won't be too boring."

2

SUMMER 605

Kass settles his yew bow in his hand. The yew bow was a gift from his grandfather, the Wolf, from almost five years ago. To this day, Kass still feels guilty about attacking his little brother, even though if he had never attacked Jules, his brother might never have learned that he is a weather mage. That fateful choice led to Kass being sent to Southwind Fort with his grandfather to learn how to control his emotions and rely on himself, not on Borus.

Drawing the arrow back, Kass aims and lets the arrow fly. *Thud*. The blue-fletched arrow lands in the center of the target twenty yards away. Kass smiles before setting a second arrow; it too lands dead center.

Sir Waldorf clears his throat, and Kass looks at him expectantly.

"Now that you have demonstrated the same level of skill as the other fourth-year pages, you will demonstrate your abilities with targets that are more appropriate to your skill level." Sir Waldorf waves his hand and two of the palace servants uncover a series of targets farther in the field. "Kass, you will put two arrows into each target, starting with the one closest to us and progressing. Begin when you're ready."

Kass repositions himself so that he is aligned with the first target. It's about thirty yards away. Pulling out two arrows from his quiver, Kass quickly shoots them, again into the center of the target. Next, Kass walks over to the position for the second target, at forty yards. The small group of people watching begins to whisper. It is rare to see any one even the royal archers successfully shoot targets at forty yards. Once again, Kass shoots two arrows into the center of the target.

Finally, Kass moves to the last target, at sixty yards. A hush falls over the crowd as it eagerly awaits. Kass sets his feet and adjusts his hands properly on the bow, then takes a deep breath. The first arrow flies true, but lands on the edge of the target, not anywhere near the center. Kass takes a deep breath and rolls his shoulders, then sets himself up again. Drawing the arrow back, he aims, and then looses the arrow. This one lands dead center. Kass sets down his bow and looks to Sir Waldorf for instruction.

The headmaster walks over. "Well done, Kass, well done. You have now passed all the fourth-year page tests and are officially a squire." Sir Waldorf looks over Kass's shoulder and sees Kenric Wolfensberger trying to catch his eye. He raises his hand indicating Kenric should come over. "Your father wants to see you," he says, and with that, Sir Waldorf walks off.

Kenric Wolfensberger walks up to his second son, Kass, and claps him on the shoulder. "Good job successfully completing your fourth-year page tests. I have someone I'd like you to meet." Kenric leads Kass over to a group of men. "Sir Alane of Tarnton Stronghold, I introduce to you my second son, Kassandros Wolfensberger."

Sir Alane offers Kass his hand to shake. "Nice to finally meet you, Kass. I have been talking to John Waldorf and your other instructors about you. It has been decided that you are to be my squire for the next four years."

Kass bows formally. "I appreciate your interest in me, Sir Alane."

"We will need to get to know each other on the road. I have been given orders for us to report immediately to Knight Commander

Andre Emberwood at Port Riverdale. Emberwood believes my years in Wanonia will be of use to him. King Bokur has pulled most of his troops from the northern border and is focusing on using his navy to attack the small, vulnerable towns on Etria's coast that are difficult to defend due to their distance from Port Riverdale and Sapphire Coast Fort. These towns are responsible for a large portion of the fish we get from the ocean."

The first few weeks Kass is with Sir Alane, the knight puts him through a series of tests. Sir Alane is well informed on Kass's adventures from the year before he became a page and as a page. However, seeing his squire's skills firsthand allows him to determine how Kass can be best utilized.

"Since archery is your specialty, I would like to make sure you have a chance to further enhance your skills. Have you tried shooting a target from a moving horse yet?" Sir Alane asks. Kass shakes his head no. "Then you will definitely learn. Just like you did when you first learned how to shoot, we will start with simple targets at short distances, then lengthen the distance, shrink the target, and finally work on all those things with the horse moving at various speeds. Our ultimate goal is that by the time you become a knight, you will be able to shoot an arrow from horseback at a full gallop as accurately as you can from the ground at a target at least forty yards away," declares Sir Alane.

Kass looks at him, surprised. Most knights consider a mere twenty yards as an acceptable target. He smiles at his knight master, excited to begin his four years as squire to a knight who truly wants him to improve his best skill.

The whole trip to Port Riverdale, Kass has trouble containing his excitement for the assignment. Two of his friends are at or near the port. Prince Richard is at the Sapphire Coast Fort, less than a half-day ride from the port, and Theo, a second-year squire, is at the port.

Finally, Sir Alane, curious at Kass's constant good mood, speaks up. "Kass, can you enlighten me on your excitement? Most new squires are terrified, especially when the country is in the middle of not one, but two wars. You are clearly not worried."

Kass laughs. "Sure! Two of my friends are going to be there. My grandfather told me that as a squire and knight it can be lonely because often you are not with your friends. I'm just glad this is not the case."

Sir Alane looks at Kass in surprise. "Just remember that orders change. Do you mind telling me who your friends are? I might know their knight masters."

Kass shrugs. "Theo and Richard."

Sir Alane looks at Kass uncertainly. "I have heard of the second-year squire, Theo, but I do not know of a squire named Richard."

Kass's face turns pink. "Uh…I meant Prince Richard. We have been close friends since we saved each other in the pirate attack at the fort in 601. It's the attack when King Bokur declared war on us."

Sir Alane looks at Kass with interest. He did not realize Kass was the page who had been separated with the prince. "I did hear about that attack, but I was still in Wanonia at the time. As you can imagine, I quickly returned to Etria. My only piece of advice to you is to remember that when it comes down to it, Prince Richard is heir to the throne, and his loyalty is to the crown and country before any individual. Sometimes being close friends with royalty makes friendships extremely challenging at times. Particularly when a decision is in the best interest of the country, but not for the individual," Sir Alane warns Kass.

Kass listens quietly. Sir Alane's words are not new to him. The Wolf and his mother have engaged Kass in similar discussions.

For almost a year, Borus and Sir Gregory have been stationed in the far south of Etria at Southwind Fort under the command of Lord

Commander Urich Stone. Since the first skirmish where Borus got wounded, Sir Gregory's squad has engaged numerous times with Ruschmann Blackwell's forces.

Thus far, all attempts to rebuild the five camps surrounding the fort have been thwarted. Changing tactics, the lord commander has given up rebuilding the camps and instead built fortified watchtowers on all four sides of Southwind Fort, allowing for additional visibility against any attacks. Unfortunately, Ruschmann Blackwell is using bandit-style fighting, engaging the squads on patrol, instead of a full-scale battle.

Although troop losses are on the decline since the completion of the watchtowers, the lord commander is still concerned about having enough men to defeat Blackwell once and for all. Much to the surprise of the lord commander and Sir Gregory, King Renard decides to send the newly knighted, eighteen-year-old Prince Geffrey with additional troops to aid Southwind Fort. The prince arrives just in time to celebrate Borus's fifteenth birthday.

As Blackwell's tactics have changed, so have Urich Stone's. Now instead of sending a single large squad to patrol, he sends three at staggered intervals on the same route. They are close enough to reach each other if there is an attack. If scouts are needed the light cavalry goes with a squad of knights not too far behind, disguised as light cavalry for extra protection.

Jules still can't believe how fast his second year as a page has flown by. His twelfth birthday is in three weeks. It seems like just yesterday it was his first day as a page. He is excited for his birthday, but sad that he will be going home for the summer and will not be able to see his close friend Princess Ellandre for almost three months.

Smiling, Jules quietly enters the queen's garden. He finally spots the queen and princess sitting on a bench near the center. He keeps his walk steady, not wanting to appear too eager to see his friend in front of the queen. When he reaches the bench, he bows. "Your Majesty, Your Highness," he says formally.

The queen smiles and nods. "It's wonderful to see you again, Jules. The two of you can walk around if you would like. I will be sitting here for a bit." Jules bows again, and Ella gives her mother a big hug before bouncing off the bench and down the pathway. Jules hurries after her. When they think they are out of earshot of the queen, Ella slows her pace so they can talk.

"How did training go today with Master Brixx?" she asks.

Jules shrugs. "The same as it usually does, although he mentioned changing things up tomorrow. I'm only going to be here another week before heading home for the rest of the summer."

Ella flashes him a huge smile. "Then we'd best spend as much time as we can with each other until then! Race you to the end!" she says and grabs her skirt to keep from tripping on it, then takes off running down the path. Rolling his eyes, Jules chases after her.

The next day, Jules stands in the training yard listening to Master Brixx explain the exercise. Sir Waldorf is there holding two practice swords. "Today we are going to try incorporating your weapons training with magic. Sir Waldorf is here to help since he has some experience fighting against warrior-mages. Don't worry, I have shielded him so he will not get hurt from your magic."

Jules looks at Sir Waldorf and gulps.

Sir Waldorf hands Jules the second practice sword. "We will start with a basic warmup drill without magic. When you get into the rhythm, you will then charge your sword with lighting."

Seeing Jules's confusion, Master Brixx explains further. "To charge it, you will fill it up with lightning and then use the practice sword as you normally would. The idea is the sword will then pulse with your magic, sending blasts at each strike. As you gain more experience with this technique you will be able to determine how strong of a charge you should put in a particular weapon for a particular opponent. However, for today I just want you to charge it and get the feel of using a charged weapon. Learn how to sense when the charge is running out, and recharge it without stopping using the weapon. We will see how far we get before trying the last step. Ready, begin." Master Brixx takes several steps back.

In the training yard at Camp Tooth, Sir Lars and Roger are practicing archery when Sir Charles finds them. "Pardon the interruption, Sir Lars, but the Wolf is requesting that you go as part of the protection detail for the supply wagon returning to Alderth Castle. You have an hour to pack before the wagon leaves."

Sir Lars stares at Sir Charles. "Only an hour?"

The knight nods, "Yes, they were supposed to be leaving right now, but the knights originally assigned have all come down with a stomach bug."

Sir Lars growls in annoyance.

"You should be grateful you do not have the stomach bug too," Sir Charles chides. "Don't be late!" Wisely, the knight leaves before Sir Lars can say anything they'll both regret.

Roger looks at his knight master and unstrings his bow. "I guess I should go pack?"

Sir Lars nods. "Yes, go pack, quickly."

An hour later, Sir Lars and Roger are mounting their horses near the supply wagon. Much to the knight's surprise, there are only two other knights assigned to the guard detail. He exchanges a look with Roger. *Originally there had been a full squad of twenty knights assigned and now there's only four? How odd.*

The two other knights ride in front of the wagon with Sir Lars and Roger picking up the rear. The supply wagon has a two-horse team and is heavily loaded. The journey between Camp Tooth and Alderth Castle that typically takes a day is now going to take three or four days because the wagon can't go any faster.

As the sun is setting, the supply wagon and its small protection detail make camp for the night. After some debate, Sir Lars finally agrees that they can make a small campfire.

Roger finally notices his knight master's unease. He takes a piece of bread and sits down next to him. "What's wrong?" he asks quietly.

Sir Lars scowls at his squire. "You haven't seen them?"

Roger gazes at Sir Lars in confusion. "Seen who?"

Sighing heavily, Sir Lars looks at Roger. "There are at least five people following us. They have been for at least two hours, probably waiting for us to stop and drop our guard. Given we only have four people capable of using a sword and a fully loaded supply wagon, we are sitting ducks…"

"What are we going to do if they attack?" Roger asks, uncertain.

"What we have sworn our oaths to do: follow orders. Today that is protecting this wagon, so we will do our best."

The knights and George, the wagon supply leader, sit around a small fire talking quietly. No one has brought up the bandits following them. Lars clears his throat before casually saying, "We're being watched."

George, eyes bulging, replies in a shaky voice. "We're not, I would know if we were…I paid good money for a mage to make protection and warning spells for my wagons."

Lars rapidly blinks and shakes his head. "Then you wasted your money on junk. There are at least five people that have been following us and are now out there waiting." Lars peers at the other knights in the firelight, expecting them to confirm his words, but they just sit there glaring at him instead.

"There is no one out there, Lars," Sir Luca says quietly. "But if it will make you feel better, I will do a quick check." Lars nods, and Luca stands up and nonchalantly walks over to his horse as though to check its bags, when he's really trying to see if he can catch sight of the so-called bandits. A few minutes later Luca returns, clearing his throat. "I didn't see anything. The horses aren't acting as though anyone is out there, either."

21

Lars tugs at his lip. "I think one of us should be on watch throughout the night, just in case I'm right."

Luca hesitantly nods and elbows Sir Hugh, before Hugh smiles tightly in agreement. "Fine...I'll take first watch. Lars, you'll take second? Hugh can take the third." Luca confirms.

When everyone is done eating and settled into their bedrolls, Luca sits with his back to the fire, peering out into the darkness. Fighting the sleepiness that's threatening to overwhelm him, Luca pinches his arm hard, regretting his offer of taking first watch.

Hours later, the sky is dark with no clouds out, the fire is down to only a few embers, Sir Lars is asleep, in his bedroll, with his hand around his sword hilt.

Crack.

Sir Lars's eyes fly open, and he scrambles out of his blanket just in time to block a knife coming for his throat. His attacker howls as the sword connects. Roger jumps up and draws his sword, looking around groggily. He sees the other two knights, but they aren't moving.

Warily, Roger walks over to them. "Wake up!" he hisses, trying not to draw attention to himself. Still Sir Hugh and Sir Luca don't stir. When Roger is close enough, he kneels and puts his face in theirs. They still don't respond. Finally, he touches their face and gasps when his fingers come back sticky with blood. He checks both knights and then turns, looking for Sir Lars.

Sir Lars walks up to Roger. "They're dead?" he asks, wanting confirmation.

"Yes, throats cut," Roger says quietly. "What about the wagon?"

Sir Lars stirs up the fire some and tosses another small log on it to create more light to see. He walks over where the wagon was. Deep ruts in the ground, but it's nowhere to be seen. The horses are missing too. Rubbing his face, Sir Lars walks back over to Roger.

"The wagon is gone. So are the horses, which means we're walking back to Camp Tooth. Might as well start now," Sir Lars says quietly.

Roger wants to say something but thinks better of it. They gather the few remaining supplies and start their trek back to Camp Tooth.

Two days later, filthy, hungry, and tired, Sir Lars and his squire finally make it back to Camp Tooth. The Wolf is on the wall and sees them walk through the gate. He rushes down the stairs to meet them.

"What happened?" the Wolf growls quietly when he gets to Sir Lars.

Sir Lars looks at the Wolf sharply. "This is on you, old man, not me. I had three knights and one squire to protect a heavily loaded supply wagon. What did you think was going to happen? Bandits are not stupid. They live for opportunities like this, which you gave them on a silver platter. Sir Luca and Sir Hugh are both dead."

The Wolf, glares at Sir Lars, furious. "I sent a full squad...not three knights and a squire. If you thought something was amiss, then you should have come to me before leaving."

Sir Lars, stares at the Wolf in disbelief. "You cannot blame me for what happened. I did everything in my power to keep them safe." With that, Sir Lars—motioning for Roger to follow him—turns and leaves the Wolf.

Toward the end of the summer of 605, two months after Prince Geffrey's arrival at Southwind Fort, Borus is sent with the prince's squad on patrol. Prince Geff is officially leading the squad, but he often defers the leadership to Sir Vincent of Shauram Summit. Sir Vincent is a seasoned knight who grew up in these southern mountains. The prince doesn't feel he is qualified to lead anyone into battle yet. With the losses the country has already suffered from this war, the prince does not want his inexperience to be the reason they lose more men.

The squad is on a week-long patrol near the ruins of Camp Eagle. They are following the strategy of one squad in the lead with two shadowing the same route. Since the implementation of this strategy, the southern troops have been successful in capturing more of Blackwell's men.

Geff, Borus, and the knights ride in silence. Borus keeps his eyes to the trees. The sun is high overhead.

"I think we need to have someone scout for us from a tree," Sir Vincent suggests, deferring to the prince for the official decision.

The prince nods. "Borus?"

Sir Vincent shakes his head. "You don't send your best man to scout," he explains quietly.

Borus listens in shock. *I'm…the best man in the squad? When did that happen?*

The prince sighs. "Point taken. Who would you send, then?" Borus stares at Geff, eyes wide, as his friend and prince agrees with Sir Vincent in front of an *entire* squad of knights with years of service under their belts.

Sir Vincent considers for a moment. "If we had another squire… but since we don't…your best bet is to just pick someone who is nimble and can easily climb a tree. Sir Nicco, take the spyglass and scout for us in a tree."

Sir Nicco glances at Borus and shrugs before quickly dismounting. He grabs the spyglass Sir Vincent is offering and climbs the tree.

Borus looks up. Nicco is almost at the top of the tree. Borus shifts his gaze to the forest around them. *Thud, thud, thud.* The sounds startle Borus and he accidentally digs his heels into his horse, causing him to spin and rear. Sir Vincent's horse screams and collapses underneath him, throwing the knight hard into a tree. *Snap, crack, crunch!* Another scream and a crash as Nicco falls from the tree, covered in arrows. The squad, following protocol for protecting royalty, immediately forms a protective circle around the prince. Borus is on the outside of the circle struggling

24

to get his horse under control. Small throwing knives fly all around them. Borus gives up on controlling his horse, worried that he will compromise the prince's safety even more if the horse were to interfere with the protective circle. In one smooth motion, he grabs his shield, unsheathes his sword, and jumps off his horse, which collapses as one of the small knives hits its artery.

"Shields!" Borus shouts. Most of the squad hesitates at Borus's order. Two shields go up, but the rest stay down. Borus growls in frustration. He looks at the prince. Geff gives him a slight nod. Borus clears his throat and tries again. "Shields up!"

This time the knights put their shields up. There's another scream, and axe-wielding attackers come flying at them from the trees. Borus glances at the prince again, still unsure about taking the lead. *This is the prince's squad. He needs to lead us.* Geff has his sword out and shield up, waiting. Borus's gaze goes to the unmoving Sir Vincent. He takes a deep breath. *Sir Vincent has faith in me. Geff has faith in me. I must have faith in myself.*

"One, two, charge!" He lets out a roar and takes off, sword slashing through the axmen. The knights and prince follow Borus's lead, picking off the enemies trying to get out of Borus's path. Suddenly the remaining axmen disappear, melting back into the trees.

Borus stops his charge and surveys the area. He shudders and takes a deep breath. There are a lot of dead axmen and a lot of blood. He turns around, worried, and walks over to the prince. "Are you OK?"

The prince lifts his visor, revealing a pale face, sweat-matted dark brown hair, and warm brown eyes. "Yes, thanks to you. I am worried about Sir Vincent and Sir Nicco."

Borus swallows hard and looks over toward the two fallen men before shaking his head and reminding himself to focus on what needs to happen next. "We should not stay here long; what if the axmen come back? I want to know where the other two squads are that should have come when they heard us fighting. The purpose of the lord commander's strategy with three squads is to prevent an attack like this from being successful." Borus walks over to the path they had been following and where they left Sir Vincent and Sir Nicco. He kneels by Sir Nicco, checking his pulse. Nothing. He stands up and walks over to Sir Vincent; no pulse for him either.

Shakily, Geff comes up behind Borus. "Are they OK?"

Borus shakes his head sadly. "Neither one made it. We should round up the horses and get going."

Borus and a couple of the other knights walk around collecting the remaining horses. One of the knights rummages through a few packs and finds some cloth and ropes. They wrap the two bodies and tie them onto two of the horses. They all mount up.

"We should come across the other two squads on our way back," the prince says, hoping the other squads are just too far behind to hear the fighting.

They ride in silence, straining to hear anything in the forest, but it's quiet. Too quiet. The knight in front stops and jumps off his horse to investigate something at the side of road.

"It's blood," the knight announces.

"Is there anything there other than blood?" asks the prince.

The knight shakes his head but continues scanning the ground for a few more minutes. "It's just the one spot here." The knight gets back on his horse and the group continues.

As they continue their route, they come across additional small puddles of blood, but nothing indicating the fate of the other two squads. Geff considers the new information—a blood trail, but no bodies or survivors. He looks around the forest warily. Although he has seen combat, this is the first time he has felt unsure about how to proceed. The loss of Sir Vincent is forcing the prince to take the position he's doesn't feel ready for.

Hesitantly, Geff makes the decision for the group. "We should go back and report to Sir Gregory. We don't have a magic mirror or any pigeons with us. I don't feel comfortable sending one of us ahead to scout."

26

Borus, Geff, and the rest of their squad are almost within view of the watchtower on this side of the fort. As they round the bend, they can see the base of the tower but are still hidden from its view by the forest. Much to their surprise and horror, the road is awash in blood. Bodies of both knights and horses are strewn across the area. The two missing squads have been demolished.

Gasping at the sight, tears streaming down his face, Borus lifts his visor to clear his vision and to gather himself. *Now is not the time to mourn the fallen, not with the enemy so close*, he reminds himself. Looking at the prince for guidance, he sees that Geff is just as heartbroken as he is.

Taking a deep breath, Borus clears his throat, and the knights turn toward him reluctantly. "We need to go, now. The fort will send a crew to get the fallen later. We are not safe." As soon as the words are out of his mouth, Borus hears rustling in the trees. "Now! Go! Go!" he shouts.

When the knights and prince don't immediately obey, Borus reaches over and swats the prince's horse with the flat of his sword. The horse shoots forward, and the rest follow suit. Borus's horse struggles against his hand, wanting to run home too. Shaking his head, Borus takes a firmer hold on the reins, turns the horse, then draws his sword and sets his shield. "This is our job—protect them, so the prince is safe," he murmurs. The horse snorts and then settles.

Axmen pour out of the dense forest. Wanting to buy the prince time, Borus urges his horse into a gallop and slams into the line of axmen, chopping his way out the other side. His horse whirls. One of the axmen reaches out to grab Borus's leg. His horse rears, striking the axman in the head, then surges forward for another pass. Borus knows he's killing many, but they just keep coming.

On the edge of his vision, Borus sees a couple of enemy riders trying to sneak past them. Blackwell's men ride small, nimble ponies, making them excellent at outmaneuvering the larger and heavier horses favored by Etrian knights. Borus debates with himself. *Do I try to catch the riders, to make sure they don't overtake the prince, or do I assume the watchtowers will take care of it and continue fighting the axmen?*

Borus decides to go after the prince and have faith that the men in the watchtowers will have his back. He gives his sweat-lathered horse a quick pat of encouragement, then murmurs, "Let's go protect the prince. Then you can have some nice oats." His horse whinnies and takes off at a gallop. They race around the bend in the road and into something from nightmares. The watchtower is in flames. The prince and the three remaining knights with him are being driven back into the flaming watchtower. Far in the distance, Borus hears a battle horn, but he knows the reinforcements likely won't get there in time.

For a split second, Borus hesitates, until it dawns on him: this, this is the dream. Fighting against enemies and protecting the prince are what being a knight is. Being a knight is not all glory—sometimes it's even boring. But he has to be willing to step up when he is needed, no matter how terrifying the situation is. *The Wolf is right. This is not an easy path.* Borus shakes out his arm and grins. "For Etria!" he shouts, urging his tiring horse on even faster.

The distance between Borus and the axmen on ponies is rapidly decreasing. "I'm sorry," Borus whispers to his horse as they run right into one of the ponies. Borus takes huge leap off his horse and lands on top of one of the enemy riders, knocking him out of the saddle. The pony spins and starts bucking, trying to dislodge Borus. Borus unstraps his shield and throws it like a boomerang at the nearest axman. The pony gives one final buck and tosses Borus. Borus uses the momentum and lands on top of one of the other axmen. His sword lodges in the enemy's back.

Borus gives his sword a twist and it comes free, just in time to block a strike from another mounted axman. He switches his sword to his left hand and swings, catching the axman's leg and causing him to topple out of the saddle.

Arrows sail through the air and two axmen drop. Momentarily distracted, Borus doesn't see the axe flying through the air toward

Prince Geff until the last moment. He throws himself sideways to block the prince and the axe hits Borus squarely in the chest. Borus falls to the ground.

More arrows sail through the air. A battle horn is blown again, much closer this time. There's a third volley of arrows and then the clanking of metal as hundreds of armored knights sweep in and put an end to the remaining axmen.

Someone removes Borus's visor and helmet.

"Borus?" He can't place the voice, but it sounds familiar.

"Borus," the voice repeats. Sir Gregory is afraid to move Borus too much since he can't tell the extent of his injuries. "Borus, can you hear me?"

Borus groans and whispers, "There are more axmen."

"We know. It's being taken care of. The prince is safe, Borus," Sir Gregory tells him.

Borus sighs and passes out. Sir Gregory curses. "Where is the healer? We need to get him inside *now*!"

Geff is sitting at Borus's side, peering into his face. Borus has been asleep for two whole days. Borus's eyes flutter open. Geff grabs his hand and squeezes. "Borus, it's me, Geff. Don't be alarmed. You're in the healing suite."

Borus opens his eyes all the way and looks around before trying to get up. Geff tsks him. "You can't get up yet." Borus still doesn't speak, so Geff continues his monologue. "You've been asleep for two whole days. I'm sure by now you can feel the bandages around your chest. You have a couple of cracked ribs and a crazy-looking bruise, but no internal bleeding or punctures. We got lucky."

Geff offers Borus a cup of water. Borus takes a sip and sighs gratefully. "You're alive…" he says quietly.

Geff looks at him, uncertain. "Yes, I am alive."

Borus gives him a pained smile. "That's all that matters." Borus's eyes droop, and he falls back asleep.

The healer walks over. "How does he feel?"

Geff shrugs. "I think he's still in a lot of pain, but knowing I'm alive seems to have reassured him. How long do ribs normally take to heal?"

"Typically, a couple of weeks for full recovery. It's possible he is just mentally exhausted too. You did lose a ton of men, and Borus is only fifteen, and he single-handedly held off the axmen until Sir Gregory arrived. That much will take a toll on even a full-fledged knight."

Sir Gregory pokes his head into the healing suite. "Geff, there's someone who wants to see you."

Geff looks at Gregory, his interest piqued. "Who?"

Gregory shakes his head. "You'll see," he says mysteriously.

Geff takes one last look at Borus before following Gregory to his office. Geff gets tackled from behind. Surprised, he drives his elbow back and tries to throw his attacker. The attacker laughs. Geff whirls around. "Kristoff?"

Kristoff grins. "You've been practicing that move, I see. It almost worked this time." They grip arms.

"It's good to see you. Did Sir Gregory tell you about Borus?" Geff says, slipping back into the more formal titles. During the time he's spent in the south this year he has become close friends with the knight, but he doesn't think Kristoff has ever met him.

Kristoff nods. "Yes, I am hoping to see him. Your brother asked me to come down here to make sure you stay out of trouble. It looks like Borus could use the help."

"I have not been trying to get into trouble," Geff growls defensively.

"Just your presence is enough to stir things up. How often do our enemies get royalty handed to them on a platter?" Kristoff reminds him.

"The lord commander didn't have an issue with it…" Geff starts.

Kristoff raises his eyebrow. "Tsk tsk. Lord Commander Urich Stone is a professional. He's not going to tell you if you are making his job more difficult. He will just continue in the best way possible."

Geff glances at Greg, who is still in the room, and draws him into the conversation. "Greg, do you agree? That I am a liability?"

The knight considers the question carefully. "I think you are to some extent because, as Kristoff pointed out, you are royalty and are now within easy reach of Blackwell. However, you are also a trained knight with combat experience. Personally, I think the skills you will gain by being here far outweigh the added risk. It is difficult to be accepted as a leader if you don't have any experience in the field or leading. Here you can get both. You are also slowly earning everyone's respect. These men will tell others how it is to rub elbows with a prince. Answering important questions such as: Is he a sissy? Does he get his hands dirty? Can he use a sword? Is he fair?

"War is inevitable. With the experience you will gain here, you will be on your way to becoming an extremely valuable asset to the crown. How do you think the Wolf became a general? It was because he knows how to lead, and people *want* to follow him. Experience he has gained from years and years in the field, but you have to start somewhere."

Kristoff whistles and grins. "See, Geff, you are important and worth determining if adding water will make you grow."

Geff looks at him annoyed. "Now I am a plant that needs to grow? Really?" He takes a swing at Kristoff.

Greg steps between them. "If the two of you want to catch up more, please do so out of my office."

"Sorry," Geff and Kristoff mumble together. Greg opens the door and pushes them both out.

3

FALL 605

A towel in his hand, Jules dries off his face and straightens his tunic. Peering into the mirror, he studies himself. There are some days where Jules can hardly believe that he is a third-year page *and* training to become a mage. He shakes his head ruefully before gathering his practice gear and heading out to the training yard to meet Master Brixx and whomever he is sparring with today.

"I hope you know what you're getting into by agreeing, Armand," Sir John Waldorf repeats for the third time.

"It will be fine. This is not my first rodeo, John." Lord Armand and Sir Waldorf walk into the training yard where Master Brixx and Jules are waiting for them.

"Thank you for agreeing to help, Lord Armand." Master Brixx bows. "Think of it as a normal sword drill with some 'extra.' As a sword master you have excellent skills with a sword, giving you a stronger advantage against most opponents. My goal here is for Jules to move beyond the basic drills. He needs to get experience using the skill of imbuing his sword with magic more representative of real combat."

Lord Armand nods; John had already informed him of what they would be doing before he agreed.

Lord Armand faces Jules. They are using wooden practice swords for the time being.

"Ready, begin," announces Sir Waldorf.

The agreement made beforehand is they will start with the basic drill. When Lord Armand feels he is comfortable with the feeling of sparring with Jules, he can then change into a non-drill by using a simple strike.

Jules settles into the rhythm, noticing that unlike Sir Waldorf, Lord Armand is comfortable going against an imbued weapon. It only takes a few minutes before they switch out of the prescribed drill and into a free choice sparring session. Jules struggles to keep up for a while before he realizes that he does know the appropriate counterstrikes for the moves Lord Armand is doing. Tiny lightning bolts come off of the wooden swords as Jules sends a burst of power with a combination move. Lord Armand smiles before parrying.

Master Brixx checks the clock. "Time!" he shouts, making sure they can hear him over the sound of the swords. Jules withdraws his magic from the sword as he steps back. Master Brixx offers him water and some crackers.

Sir Waldorf offers Lord Armand water too. "I swear it looks like you were having fun." he says in disbelief.

"I *was* having fun," Lord Armand chuckles. "I'd love to take him on as a full-time student." Sir Waldorf stares at him in stunned silence. "What? He is pretty good already with his sword, and I know I can help him become even better and develop methods of using his magic with the swordwork. Master Brixx hasn't had weapons training and you…I think you're afraid of Jules's magic," he says in puzzlement.

Sir Waldorf sighs. "Have you ever been in combat against a mage that can use lightning?"

Lord Armand frowns and shakes his head.

"I would highly recommend not ever being in that situation," Sir Waldorf warns.

"I am not planning on fighting Jules in the field," Lord Armand replies.

"You do remember there are other countries outside of Etria that have magic, right? Just because Jules is the only living weather mage in Etria doesn't mean others don't exist somewhere else."

Kass sits down at the desk in the room he shares with Theo, a few pages of paper and a quill in hand. He writes:

Borus,
I have no idea how long this letter will take to reach you. But here it goes.
Being in Port Riverdale is different, but I think I like it. Sergeant Corning leads training exercises for everyone, and I mean EVERYONE, four days a week. Usually, we just run the exercises in drill lines, but occasionally he'll mix it up so that we're in groups of two on two, or two on three. I have been told he also does the groups with mixed fighting styles, but I have yet to experience one of those sessions.
Sir Alane, my knight master, wants to teach me how to shoot my bow from horseback at long distance targets. We will start the training tomorrow.
I have seen Richard once since our arrival. He is supposed to make monthly visits to the port to meet with Knight Commander Emberwood. Hopefully, his next visit is soon.

I am enjoying Theo's company, but I wish more of us were here. I am beginning to understand what the Wolf was talking about when he described being a knight as lonely.

I hope all is well for you in the south. Please write back.

Miss you bunches,
Kass

Kass folds the letter and puts his seal on it. Then sets it aside and grabs another piece of paper.

Grandfather,
I just wanted to let you know that I was assigned to Port Riverdale. As you probably know, Sir Alane was living in Wanonia a few years ago. I am glad to have a knight master who is interested in helping me further my archery skills.
Thank you for believing in me.

Yours,
Kass

Kass folds the letter and seals it, then stands and stretches. His original plan was to also write a letter to his mother, but now his stomach is rumbling. Kass smiles ruefully. It seems like he's always hungry lately.

Kass walks out of his room into the dining hall. The room is quiet with only a few people scattered around the table eating. For many, it is too early to eat dinner. The kitchen supplying the mess hall always has some sort of food available. If you time your appearance close to normal mealtimes, then there are always two hot options. Kass sniffs the air and smiles. Fish stew and fresh bread.

He heads over to the serving area and fills up a tray, then looks for a seat. Scanning the room for anyone he recognizes, Kass almost drops his tray when he sees Richard. The prince is trying his best to blend in; he's wearing shabby pants and a stained shirt, and his hair is tousled. Steadying his hands, Kass slowly makes his way over to Richard, trying not to draw attention.

"Hello, Richard," Kass murmurs as he slides onto the bench across from the prince.

Richard is staring into his stew and jumps, splattering it on the table and his face. Cursing, he grabs the napkin and wipes his face.

"Sorry," Kass says quietly.

"Oh, it's you," Richard replies, just realizing that Kass is sitting across from him.

"Finding any answers in your stew?" Kass teases.

Richard doesn't reply right away. "I was thinking about the discussion I had with Emberwood and the plan we're working on to attack King Bokur's navy more directly."

Kass raises his eyebrow. "Ah, say no more. I can just eat in silence if you want to go back to your thoughts."

Richard looks at Kass in surprise. "I appreciate the offer, but I truly would prefer the distraction for now. How was your day?"

Kass smiles and launches into the story of his day.

Kass yawns and stretches. His hands scrape the wood beams on the ceiling of the room he shares with his friend, second-year squire Theo. Kass climbs down the ladder at the end of the bed and glances at Theo, who looks back at him.

"G'morning!" Kass says cheerfully.

Theo groans. "Why are you in such a good mood this morning? Oh wait, I remember. Your friend is coming for a meeting with Emberwood."

Kass grins. "He actually got here last night. I found him in the dining hall." He pulls on a pair of dark brown breeches, a tan shirt, and a navy-blue coat. Fall mornings in the port can be cold, especially if there is wind coming off the sea as there has been the past couple of days.

Theo grumbles some more before copying Kass. As squires assigned to knights in Port Riverdale, both young men have duties that rotate weekly. The weekly rotation ensures the squires have the opportunity to learn various skills they will need as knights, including working with the blacksmith, cooking, healing, and falconry. Theo enjoys the blacksmith work the most and often spends his free time at the smithy. Kass, on the other hand, uses his free time to learn more about falconry. As the extra hours add up, they are taught more difficult tasks.

That afternoon, Kass is sitting on his horse, arrow nocked, aiming at a large target twenty yards away. As eager as Kass has been to learn how to successfully shoot from horseback, his horse has had other ideas. The first time Kass tried, as soon as he loosed the arrow and the bow made the *twang* sound, his horse started bucking. Kass fell off in his struggle to regain control and maintain his hold on the bow. Over the past several months he has slowly, with Sir Alane's help, gotten his horse to tolerate the sound of the bow.

At a halt, Kass shoots three arrows into the first target to warm up. His horse stands quietly. At Kass's signal, the horse walks in a straight line. As they get within range of each target, Kass fires a single arrow. They go down the line of ten targets. At the end, using his legs only, Kass signals the horse to trot and trots a big circle then turns back down the line. He repeats the same exercise, a single arrow going into each target, but at a trot. Kass makes a third pass, this time shooting two consecutive arrows into each target. As he's about to turn around for a fourth and final pass, he hears clapping behind him. He pivots the horse on the spot to see who it is. Kass grins.

"Richard!" he yells and urges his horse into a canter. They slide to a stop in front of the prince and Kass jumps off and just stands there grinning, not really sure how to greet him. The prince offers a hesitant smile and takes a step back. Kass looks at him in confusion. "Did something happen?"

The prince hesitates, not sure how much he is permitted to tell a squire. "The news I got in my meeting is not good. There have been more Wanonian attacks on the coastal towns and pirate raids. It is going to be intense for a while as we set some plans in motion to attack over the next few weeks."

Richard slides his hands into his pockets. "The information is on a need-to-know basis. But I wanted to let you know before I leave. Knight Commander Emberwood wants me to go back tonight instead of in the morning. I'm sorry we won't be able to hang out more like we were planning."

Before Kass has time to respond, the prince grabs his horse's reins and mounts back up, kicking the horse hard into a gallop, allowing his frustration at ditching his friend affect his riding. The prince's horse rears in protest before shooting forward and out of the training yard.

Jules is sitting on a bench in one of the courtyards at Burmstone Palace, letting his mind drift, when he hears footsteps on the gravel path. Eyes flying open, Jules calls a ball of lightning to his hand before he sees Ella.

Giggling, Ella waves her hand to indicate the ball of lightning. "Do you think I am going to attack you, oh mighty page-mage?"

Jules makes the ball of lightning disappear and smirks. "Page-mage?"

Ella, still giggling, holds up her basket. "Are you hungry? I brought some food and a card game." At the mention of food Jules's stomach begins to rumble. "You're just like my brothers, always hungry!"

Jules laughs. "You're right about that; it does seem like I am always hungry. I would love to play a game of cards."

Smiling, Ella opens the basket and distributes the food.

A month after Richard's short visit, Theo hands Kass two letters. "These came for you today. I got some too, from Urlo and Hereward."

"Thanks," Kass mumbles as he eagerly opens the letter from Borus and reads it.

> *Kass,*
> *I'm glad you have time to continue to improving your archery skills.*
> *Perhaps with Richard, you should just cherish as much as he is willing to give. Isn't it better to be friends than to lose that completely?*
> *Kristoff and Geff are down here also. It has been nice to have some friends around. Blackwell is definitely keeping us on our toes and there is seldom a dull moment down here.*
> *Stay safe. See you when I see you.*
>
> *Yours,*
> *Borus*

Kass sighs. *Borus is probably right about Richard.* He folds up the letter and opens the next one.

> *Kass,*
> *Both Knight Commander Emberwood and Sir Alane send me progress reports on you. I just wanted to let you know that I am pleased by your decision to continue to further your archery skills and to*

learn falconry. Both seem to be undervalued by many knights, even though I have been in battles where the outcome is vastly different because of an individual with one or both of those skills.

Don't forget to nurture the friendships you are building with those around you. True friends are few and far between but are invaluable when you need them the most.

Yours,
The Wolf

Kass's eyes are still wide in surprise. *The Wolf wrote me a letter!* He looks over at Theo. "Anything good in your letters?"

Theo shrugs. "Just updates on how things are going. They're both assigned near Alderth Castle. I guess they've seen Roger recently too. He's even meaner now that he's a squire than he was as a page, if that's possible. I'm glad we're here and not anywhere near him."

Prince Richard, in his study at the Sapphire Coast Fort, is gazing over the map of the Etrian coastline and making notes for where he is going to send squads for the next attack. Wishing some of his friends were here with him, he decides to ask his father to see if they can assign any of them here to the fort. He smiles. *I guess being a prince does have some perks.* Richard takes a sip of water and is setting down his glass when he is startled by the blasts of the battle horns from the tower. The glass misses the table and shatters on the floor. The prince leaps to his feet as the doors to his study are thrown open.

Boom! Boom! Boom! The building starts to shudder. *Boom! Boom!*

Colonel Frankford, the officer in charge of the fort, runs over to the prince, breathless. "Wanonians…fireballs…" he gasps.

The prince grabs the pitcher of water and offers it to the man. The colonel takes a long drink. "There are more fireballs in the air. Many more. Your squad will be here momentarily, you must leave with them."

Richard shakes his head. "*No.* I will not abandon these men—" The prince is interrupted by a loud cracking sound. *Boom!* The outer wall of the study blows inward, spraying the prince and colonel with shards of rock and debris.

The colonel picks himself up and glances out the hole. "Run! Run!" he yells and grabs for the prince, pulling him as they run for the door. *Boom! Boom!* Two fireballs blast into the office just as they pull the doors shut behind them. Both men are thrown backward in the explosion.

Screams and yells echo through the fort. The study is on fire. With the doors falling off their hinges, it won't be contained for long. *Clank, clank, clank.* The steady tread of knights in plate armor can be heard coming toward them. The colonel wipes his hand across his face and is surprised when it comes back bloody. He looks around for the prince.

"Your Highness!" he calls in concern. The hallway is full of debris, dust, and smoke, making it difficult to make out any details.

Richard sits up, coughing. Hard hands roughly grab him and help him to his feet. "Your Highness, we must get you out of here," a familiar voice says as Richard is ushered out of the hallway and into the ballroom. The prince surveys the ballroom. He sees the smoke trying to work its way from the rooms lining the upper balcony.

"Can we defend ourselves?" he asks quietly, afraid he already knows the answer.

The knight lifts up his visor, revealing himself to be Sir Horton. Sir Horton shakes his head sadly. "No, it is too late for that. The towers are collapsing. We need to get you out now."

The prince looks at the knights around him, jaw set. He can still hear people screaming and yelling. In a calm, determined voice, the prince speaks. "We need to save anyone we can get to. I won't leave my people behind. I will not order you to stay—volunteers only—but I am going to stay until we can free them."

Sir Horton drops to one knee, the other knights in the squad follow suit. "For Etria!" Sir Horton yells.

"For Etria and Prince Richard!" the rest of the knights respond.

Prince Richard bows. Colonel Frankford slides into the room and hands the prince his breastplate, helmet, and sword. The prince quickly slips the armor on and then motions for Sir Horton to lead the way.

A few hours later Sir Horton and his squad lead a protesting prince to the waiting horses. Tears stream down the faces of many as they mount up and leave at a gallop, heading toward Port Riverdale.

Sir Alane, Kass, and their squad of knights are out on patrol near the Sapphire Coast Fort when Richard's squad comes racing down the road. Sir Alane signals for his squad to surround the prince and provide extra protection. He nods to Kass. Kass pulls out his bow and slows his horse to a trot and then reverses himself in the saddle so he's facing backward. He falls to the rear of the group, keeping his eyes peeled for any enemies following them back to the port. The road curves to the left. As Kass passes the curve, he sees movement on the oceanside. A man with a crossbow stands and aims, too slowly. Kass shoots two arrows into him before the man can get his footing to aim properly. The man tumbles back down the path. Kass slips his whistle into his mouth and blows twice, sending the signal to Sir Alane that there are enemies.

Two more crossbowmen come up the same path. Kass is farther away now. The men start running toward him before firing. The crossbow bolts go wide. One of Kass's arrows goes through a throat, the other through an eye.

Kass glances behind him to see if any of the squad is coming to help. Instead of the Etrian knights, he sees three enemy horsemen, who have somehow snuck between him and the squad. Cursing, Kass swings his legs back around so he's facing forward again. He grabs two more arrows and shoots, but they bounce off the enemy's armor. Slinging his bow over his back, Kass draws his sword and digs his heels into his horse. They burst into a gallop and charge the enemy horsemen. As Kass rides past, he sweeps up with his sword, slicing through the vulnerable armpit. He wheels his horse back for another pass. As he completes the turn, five knights rush past him and smash into the two remaining enemy horsemen.

Sir Alane nods grimly to Kass. "Good job. Hopefully that's the last of them. The prince and I agree that we need to just make full speed to get to the port. I sent one rider up ahead, so Knight Commander Emberwood knows we are coming with possible enemies behind. C'mon, let's go!" says Sir Alane, and then his horse leaps forward. Kass follows suit.

Knight Commander Emberwood meets them on the road up to the port. After some heated discussions between him, Prince Richard, and other officers, Emberwood clears his throat. "It sounds like it is time for me to propose to the rest of the council and the king that we should enter peace talks." Sir Alane and the prince murmur in agreement. Kass just looks between the three of them, uncertain why the details matter to anyone in their group.

"Ready, set, go!" shouts Greg. Borus and Kristoff square off in the training yard at Southwind Fort to practice swordfighting. Borus lets Kristoff lead. He hasn't had a chance to go against Kristoff since they were both pages and isn't sure what to expect. They start slowly, allowing themselves to warm up.

"Are you ready?" Borus asks.

Kristoff grins. "Bring it."

Borus grins back and they speed up. As the speed increases, they use more of the yard. For a while, it seems like Kristoff is of equal skill to Borus. Until Borus starts using combination moves. After about fifteen minutes, Greg, seeing how fast Kristoff is tiring, calls for a break.

"Wow, Borus," Kristoff says breathlessly, chest heaving.

"What?" Borus asks.

"I didn't think Geff was serious when he warned me against practicing with you. I can see why you're going for the full sword master title."

Borus shrugs nonchalantly. "Are you going to make a big deal out of it? Everyone seems to. I appreciate your willingness to practice with me. It's nice to be able to have different partners."

"No, I'm not. But, man, you are really, really good. When I heard rumors about what you did to save Geff before I got here, I didn't really believe them. Now I understand why Sir Gregory is OK with Geff being here because of you."

Borus blushes and looks away.

"You might not realize how good you actually are, Borus, but you are better than most seasoned knights. I am glad I don't qualify to go against you for your final sword master test in two years," Kristoff says sincerely.

Borus looks at Kristoff again. "I appreciate your vote of confidence in my abilities. I am not sure if I agree with you on how good I am, but I am glad you feel like I can adequately protect Geff."

A bell rings.

"Let's go get lunch while it's hot!" Borus grabs a towel and offers one to Kristoff. They both wipe off their faces and sheath their swords before heading to the mess hall.

Sir Alane, Kass, and the falcon master, Captain Veyron, are out in the practice field outside of Port Riverdale. Captain Veyron has a red-tailed hawk on his gloved fist.

"You are ready to try this, Kass. We wouldn't be using Mist if she weren't capable of helping you learn," Sir Alane says.

Captain Veyron nods. "With your superior skills in archery, this is a natural next step. She can help you scout, as well as possibly aid in an attack by attacking an enemy outright or dropping something for you to shoot. Don't worry—we will start out slow, and you have plenty of time to learn the more complex ways of using a hawk."

Kass frowns uncertainly and draws his bow.

Captain Veyron whispers to Mist, and she flies into the air, circles Kass, and then lands on the platform that's attached behind his saddle. "Remember, you need to be able to give Mist a command while you remain focused on your task," Captain Veyron reminds Kass.

Biting the inside of his cheek, Kass bumps his horse into a walk and murmurs. "*Volare*, Mist, *volare*." Mist launches herself into the air as Kass draws his bow back and shoots at the first target. He reaches back for another arrow and glances up. Mist is circling him overhead, waiting for the next command. She is trained in verbal and hand signals. Kass nudges his horse into a trot and gives Mist the hand signal to land. Mist lands heavily, causing Kass to tilt forward just as he's releasing the arrow. It falls into the grass. Kass sighs.

"Try that again at the trot!" shouts Captain Veyron.

Kass nudges his horse back into a trot. Sets the next arrow. "Volare, Mist." He commands the hawk. Kass braces himself better as Mist takes off and then shoots his arrow. He hits the target a little off center. He goes to the next target and the arrow lands dead center. Hand signaling for Mist to land, Kass sets the next arrow and shoots as Mist is landing. She still jostles him, but the arrow is already in the air.

Kass circles back at the trot to Captain Veyron and Sir Alane with Mist on the platform. "Better. However, I want you to return to the walk and get to where Mist is not jostling you before we work on the trot again. It is critical that she can take off and land without interfering in your shooting." Kass nods and slows his horse back to a walk and goes to the beginning of the target line.

4

SPRING 606

At the end of spring, the Wolf returns home to Wolfensberger Castle after almost two years away in the north. He rides up to the castle steps and dismounts, handing his horse off to one of the stable hands. Sighing, he heads up the steps and inside.

A nine-year-old Sabine Wolfensberger peers out the window in her room and sees the Wolf heading inside. She checks herself in the mirror before rushing downstairs. When she reaches the main hall, she exclaims, "Grandfather!" She runs over to hug the Wolf.

The Wolf hugs Sabine tightly. "Hello, my dearest. I missed you too." He pulls her away wanting to get a better look at his only granddaughter. She has red hair cascading down her back and bright green eyes, still petite. "Have I ever told you how much you look like Theaduuara?" he asks quietly.

Sabine shakes her head. "Who is Theaduuara?"

The Wolf gives her a look filled with sadness. "Let's go sit in the library, and I will tell you about Theaduuara."

Sabine takes his hand and leads the Wolf into the library. Once she has tucked him on the couch comfy with a blanket, she grabs another blanket and snuggles up next to him.

"Who is Theaduuara?" she asks quietly. Her father, Kenric, has told her about some of the family history, but he has never mentioned anyone by the name of Theaduuara.

Softly the Wolf speaks, "Thea was the love of my life, your grandmother. She is the granddaughter of King Richard I. When we were first introduced, we became friends instantly and could spend hours just talking to each other. She died in a riding accident while I was away doing my duty for Etria as a general."

The Wolf pauses, his eyes glistening. Sabine pats his hand gently, trying to offer comfort but not sure how. He places his hand over Sabine's and gives her a gentle squeeze. Sabine hugs him. "I didn't know about Thea. I'm so sorry…Wolfie," she whispers.

"You look exactly like her," he whispers back.

Jules and Ella are walking down the pathway toward the palace, with the reins of their ponies in their hands. "Master Brixx talked you into testing?" Ella says in surprise.

Jules shakes his head. "He didn't talk me into it. He did a full-on presentation about why it would be beneficial to me and those around me if I were to test. It was *sooooo* boring!"

"You didn't say yes to get him to be quiet, did you?" she says in concern.

Jules laughs. "No, I promise I did not say yes for that reason. I have been debating about doing the test, since I have been getting more training and I think it's time. It is not going to physically harm me or anyone I know if I now have an official title that says I am a real genuine mage."

"Is there a such thing as a fake mage?" Ella says, giggling.

"Probably…I know there are people that do tricks and try to call them magic, when really it's just different compounds reacting," he replies sagely.

"Hopefully we don't run into one of those," Ella murmurs. "Are we walking the whole way back or can we ride again? I think they've cooled out enough," she says. She puts her hand on her pony and it comes back dry, but dirty.

"Sure, why not, as long as we don't go too crazy," he says with a shrug. They stop walking and mount up.

"Is this too crazy?" Ella says with a smirk before kicking her pony into a gallop. Jules rolls his eyes and laughs before following the princess, galloping back toward the palace.

Sir Waldorf and Master Brixx are on the palace wall looking out into the field beyond. Jules, Lord Armand, and Master Efaris are in the field. Jules is sparring with Lord Armand using swords while maintaining a shield around both of them to block Master Efaris's attacks using air magic.

"He is ready to be tested as a journeyman mage," Master Brixx says, breaking the silence.

"Are you sure?" Sir Waldorf asks, gazing at the scene unfolding in the field.

"Yes, I am sure. Watch."

Together they lean farther over the wall. The shield around Jules and Lord Armand is a sparkling blue dome. Master Efaris sends a huge bolt of magic at the shield, just as Lord Armand begins a combination sequence. Jules parries Lord Armand perfectly and a lightning bolt flies out of the shield, meeting Master Efaris's magic and causing both to vanish. Jules begins his own combination against Lord Armand, as a small series of lightning bolts fly out of the shield toward Master Efaris.

Master Brixx turns toward Sir Waldorf. "Most certified journeyman mages cannot do complex spells while maintaining a shield *and* actively attacking someone. What Jules is doing below is the equivalent. Since he is still a page, I need you to sign off on the testing."

"Does Jules know you're asking?" Sir Waldorf asks, still not sure about the request.

Master Brixx smiles. "Yes, he knows."

"Very well, then. You can test him the day after he completes his third-year page tests."

Sir Gregory shrugs. "If you don't believe me, Colonel Rhys, then if Borus is willing, you can spar with him. Borus?"

Borus shrugs. "I'm fine with it, Sir Gregory. I will go grab my sword." Borus bows and leaves the office, heading for his room.

Sir Gregory looks at the colonel again. "We should head down to the training yard." The colonel nods and leads the way to the training yard.

Borus reaches the training yard and looks around. A crowd is forming at the perimeter. He walks toward Sir Gregory.

"You're still sure about this?" Sir Gregory asks again.

"Yes, I told you, I will go against Colonel Rhys. I wouldn't mind the practice."

Sir Gregory watches the fight unfold, shaking his head. Colonel Rhys's friends are cheering him on, sure the colonel is going to beat the wet-behind-the-ears second-year squire. Ten minutes later, the colonel has been disarmed twice. Borus is holding the colonel's sword.

"Do you yield?"

The colonel glares at Borus and quietly mutters, "I yield." Borus flips the colonel's sword over and offers it to him hilt-first. He salutes the colonel and then turns and walks back into the building, followed by Sir Gregory.

They head back into the office.

"Why do the infantry officers keep needing to test me?" Borus asks.

Sir Gregory walks behind Borus and drops into one of the big chairs. "Probably because they don't believe a mere squire is capable of being better than a seasoned officer. Others want to see for themselves that you are as good as the Wolf. Sword masters within the infantry are almost as rare as within the ranks of knights. Officers like Colonel Rhys are young enough they likely don't have any firsthand experience with a sword master. Which means they think you earning the junior title as a page is a joke and an empty title. You could always say no when someone wants to challenge you."

Borus unbuckles his sword belt and drops it next to the other big chair and sits down opposite Sir Gregory. "I just want them to know I'm not a joke, that I do actually know how to fight."

"I like your dedication, but there will always be doubters. Ask the Wolf if you don't believe me. He has dealt with his fair share over the years," Sir Gregory suggests.

"Here you are!" Prince Geff says, slipping into the office with Kristoff on his heels.

"Where'd you think we would be?" Borus mutters.

"I checked a few places first. It is almost lunchtime," the prince reminds him.

"I requested lunch be brought up here earlier. I had a suspicion you two would be joining us. A meal for four should be here shortly," Sir Gregory says with a grin. There's a knock on the door before it opens. Four serving men come in with platters of food and pitchers of drinks.

The four of them relocate to the table.

"Father sent me a letter. If the peace negotiations go through, Phaedra will be marrying the heir of Wanonia. I'll have to return for the wedding. He wants the whole family together." The prince makes a face. "I love my sister, but there are other places I'd much rather be. Besides, I'm sure they will insist Richard and I dance with all of the eligible ladies."

"At least you get to go home if the wedding does happen. Until the king says otherwise, my men, including Borus, Kristoff, and I, cannot join you when you return to Burmstone Palace," Sir Gregory reminds the prince.

"How long have you been here?" the prince asks.

"Almost two years," replies Borus.

At almost thirteen, Jules is the youngest mage attending this year's journeyman mage testing. He is also the first student in the history of the school who is also a page at Trinity to take the test. Onaxx does not have age restrictions for who is eligible to test, only skill restrictions. The journeyman mage test has two parts: a written exam and a skill test to demonstrate control and ability of their magic. The students must declare their intent to test and be approved, ensuring only those who are truly ready are tested.

"Welcome to the journeyman mage tests of the year 606. Let us begin." High Mage Ivy's speech is short and to the point. She moves off to the side and the first student to test steps into the marked space with his evaluators. In addition to the five students who will be testing today, all of the master and journeyman mages in residence at the school are also in attendance. Evaluations of each student will be conducted by two master mages.

"Julien Wolfensberger," an unfamiliar voice calls out. Jules walks over to the marked area and bows respectfully to the evaluators.

The mage closest to him is a tall, lanky man with chin-length, wavy black hair and brown eyes, wearing a purple robe with the black trim of a master mage. "I am Master Winslow," the purple-robed mage introduces himself. Noticing Jules's curious looks at the robe, Master Winslow smiles. "I have come from Lightbridge School of Magic in Stinyia. I am a metal and fire mage." Jules is intrigued that Master Winslow is from Stinyia. Although the country has been a long-time ally of Etria, he has met very few people from there.

The other mage, Master Efaris, clears his throat. "If the two of you are done, we do have a test to conduct." Master Winslow blushes and nods.

Master Efaris explains the first task. "Very well. Jules, your first task is to create six balls of ice. Once you have the six balls, you will do several things. First, rotate all six balls together in a circle. Second, split the balls into two groups and have them rotate in two circles. Third, while the two circles are rotating, create three balls of water and a third circle. Make sure that the first six balls you create are ice."

Jules takes a couple of steps away from the two evaluators and creates the six ice balls. The first task is easy. Master Brixx told him the tests are always different, but that they will test whether he has control over his magic for tasks that are considered journeyman-level. Finally, Jules reaches the third step. He has two circles, each of three balls of ice rotating clockwise. As he creates the three balls of water, Jules decides to show off a bit. Instead of having his third circle rotate clockwise like the other two, it moves counterclockwise.

When both Master Efaris and Master Winslow finish writing their notes from the first task, Master Winslow explains the second task. "Jules, you will now create a dome, or shield, over this circle of rocks. One of the journeyman water mages is graciously providing us with a block of ice. You will be protecting the block of ice with the shield and ensuring the temperature within your dome does not increase enough to melt it. I will be using fire to try to penetrate the shield." Master Winslow finishes his explanation, and Master Brixx takes a block of ice over to a ring of stones.

There are two large black rocks about ten feet away and on opposite sides of the ring of stones. Master Efaris leads Jules to one of the rocks and Master Winslow takes up a position at the other one.

High Mage Ivy claps her hands together once. "You may begin."

Concentrating on the circle of rocks, Jules forms a thick dome of ice over the top of the ice block, making sure there is ample room between the two. When the dome is complete, he stands in a relaxed position, waiting for Master Winslow to start.

A ring of fire forms around the edge of Jules's ice dome. The flames slowly gain height. When the flames are about six inches tall, Jules can feel his ice dome beginning to melt. He reaches down into his core of magic and sends power toward his shield to strengthen the ice before it disappears. As the dome returns to its original thickness, the flames shoot up higher, blocking the entire dome from view.

Jules once again draws on his magic, funneling it into the dome, but the dome continues to melt. The inside of the dome is also beginning to warm up and the ice block's once sharp edges are turning round. Biting his lip in concentration, Jules raises his hand and points at the dome. Blue magic streams from his fingers and into the dome. The air inside the dome around the ice block begins to cool again. As an extra measure, Jules doubles the thickness of his dome.

Master Winslow allows his ring of flame around the dome of ice to shrink until it is almost nothing. The test is for approval as a journeyman mage, meaning he cannot use the full extent of his master level magical ability to conduct the test. Only the rough equivalent of a journeyman mage. He watches Jules carefully, and the moment when Jules begins to relax Master Winslow turns the ring of fire into a piece of red-hot metal. Red-hot metal vines sprout from the band and climb up the dome. The longer the metal is in contact with the ice, the faster the ice begins to melt, but the metal also begins to cool, changing from bright orange-red to a dull black.

Caught off guard by Master Winslow's shift from fire magic to metal, Jules stands there with his mouth open, watching his dome melt. He shakes himself, forcing his mind back to the task at hand. Since the metal is cooling off as it touches the ice, Jules decides to create a miniature storm. A small, almost black cloud appears a few feet over the top of the dome and dumps rain. Steam rises off the cooling metal.

Creeaaaak.

The dome breaks in half as the weight of the metal becomes too much for it to handle. High Mage Ivy steps forward again before Jules can perform anymore magic. "This task is concluded. The students who have been evaluated will now have an hour-long break while the results are determined."

Jules nods and walks over to a bench and sits down. He looks at his hands and realizes they're shaking. Master Brixx walks over to him with a canteen out. "Here, drink some water. Then we can go get refreshments while we wait. You did very well."

"I did?" Jules asks uncertainly.

Master Brixx nods. "Absolutely! You should not worry so much." He watches as Jules takes a couple of sips of the water before leading the way to the refreshment table.

Precisely an hour later, High Mage Ivy takes her position in front of the gathered mages. She gives the group a rare smile. "It is my pleasure to announce that all five students have passed their tests and are now journeyman mages! Please come forward." The five students come forward and receive a handshake from the high mage and a new robe in the color of their element with white trim. "Take these robes and wear them proudly."

A cheer goes up through the crowd. The five new journeyman mages look at each other, smiling. Jules looks into the crowd and finds his parents and grins. *I did it!*

Three days later, Jules is walking in the royal garden. Ella is supposed to meet him here so they can say goodbye for the summer.

Jules walks slowly around the garden. He's starting to wonder if she forgot when he hears footsteps. He turns around, and his smile falls. Queen Vivienne and her guards are approaching, but Ella is nowhere in sight.

The queen stops in front of Jules. He bows deeply to her. "Your Majesty."

"Jules. I'm sorry, but the king decided to take Ella on a ride. She rarely gets time with her father because he is so busy. She asked me to bring you this...for your thirteenth birthday," the queen says quietly and offers Jules a small box. He hesitates; the queen smiles to encourage him, and Jules opens the box. Inside is a tiny but exquisitely detailed golden horse. He pulls it out and then sees the other one. "Your Majesty, they are beautiful, but...what are they?"

The queen chuckles. "They're cuff links. For when you are wearing a formal jacket." Jules looks at her quizzically. "Your mother or father can show you how to use them."

Jules bows. "Thank you, Your Majesty."

The queen reaches out and touches Jules gently on the shoulder. "You are most welcome. We hope you enjoy your summer." With that, the queen turns and departs.

Sadly, Jules puts the cuff links back into the box and replaces the lid, then walks back to the pages' wing, wishing he could have seen his best friend instead of receiving a gift.

Kass shoots the last arrow in his quiver before circling his horse back to his knight master.

Sir Alane smiles in approval. "Good. You are making nice progress. For the next round, I want you to try the targets from twenty yards at a canter."

Kass dismounts to retrieve his arrows. Once they've been returned to the quiver, he mounts his horse and takes out two arrows. With the reins loose around the horse's neck, he asks his horse to canter. The horse snorts and moves into his smooth canter. Kass shoots the first arrow, and it hits the edge of the target. At the canter, he doesn't have time to worry about what he did or didn't do. Kass must focus on the next target immediately after the first. He nocks the second arrow and shoots it before reaching back and pulling out two more. The second arrow also hits the opposite edge of the target. Third arrow in place, Kass changes his position slightly and looses. It gets within the inner ring but not at the center. The fourth and final arrow sails through the air and lands within the inner ring as well. Sighing, Kass heads back to Sir Alane, disappointed that he is not hitting the dead center of the target as he has become accustomed to.

"Don't get frustrated. You are hitting the target. There are many people who think they are good at archery, until you get them on a horse going any speed, let alone a canter, and then they fall to pieces. We have lots of time ahead of us for you to meet your goals with this skill," Sir Alane says reassuringly.

"Really? Because you're right, I am frustrated. It feels like I'm not making progress," Kass reluctantly admits.

"Did you already forget that you have been in a skirmish using this skill? You stepped up and used what you knew then. Now is not any different." Sir Alane walks over and grips Kass's leg. "Trust yourself and be patient. I'd like you to do one more round before we head back."

By the end of spring, a peace agreement between Etria and Wanonia is reached. For the first time in over one hundred years, the two countries will be united through marriage of their royal families. A formal wedding announcement and invitations have been sent throughout Etria and Wanonia. Lord Commander Urich Stone stands in front of his assembled soldiers and knights in Southwind Fort and reads from the announcement.

King Renard and Queen Vivienne of Etria are pleased to announce the marriage of Princess Phaedra of Etria to Crown Prince Kabili of Wanonia.

The lord commander summarizes the rest of the letter: "The wedding will take place in Etria at King Renard's Burmstone Palace. All citizens of Etria and Wanonia are welcome to attend. Those of you under my command who wish to attend, please find me sometime today so that I can review your request. Unlike those in the north, we are still facing a very real threat here in the south."

5

FALL 606

Roger is just concluding his training session with one of the infantry captains at Camp Tooth when he notices his knight master waiting for him. Now sixteen and entering his third year as a squire, Roger is hoping they'll finally get assigned somewhere else.

"You're in luck, squire. We have been released from our duties here for the next month. Of course, the expectation is we will use the time to attend the royal wedding," Sir Lars says, spitting.

Roger stares at his knight master. "If we're not going to the wedding, what are we doing?"

"I'm laying some plans. I can't tell you yet, but I know you'll like them, given our shared dislike of the Wolfensbergers," Lars says with a cruel smile.

In northern Etria at Alderth Castle, Urlo and Hereward, both now third-year squires, are out for a ride in a rare moment of downtime. Both squires are paying more attention to the conversation than their surroundings. "Did you get a letter from Borus too?" Urlo asks Hereward.

Hereward shakes his head. "No, but I did get one from Theo. It looks like none of us get to go to the wedding. But I can't decide if that's a good thing or bad thing. From what I've heard, they are B-O-R-I-N-G!" Urlo opens his mouth to reply when there is a noise, and his horse spooks. Unprepared for the sudden leap to the side, Urlo pops out of the saddle and lands in a big puddle with a *splat*!

Hereward sees Urlo's shock and laughs. Urlo sticks out his tongue and Hereward laughs harder, clutching at his stomach. *Snap!* Hereward's horse half rears as more twigs snap around them. Thrown off balance from laughing, Hereward slides off his horse's rump and lands in a heap next to Urlo in the puddle.

Urlo covers his mouth, laughing and pointing at Hereward's soaked torso, when he hears another branch cracking. Instantly on alert, they both get completely silent. Urlo draws a knife out of his belt and slowly gets up on one knee, trying to look around.

A knight materializes from behind the trees. Urlo takes a deep breath and sighs in relief as he recognizes his knight master, Sir Caradoc. Sir Caradoc smirks at the two squires. "You are both a complete mess."

Hereward looks mournfully at his filthy clothes and stands. Muddy water cascades off his hair and shoulders. Urlo runs his fingers through his hair before shaking his head like a dog, spraying Hereward with more water.

"What was that for?" Hereward says, giving Urlo a shove.

Sir Caradoc takes a step closer. "C'mon you two. Let's get going so you have time to get cleaned up before dinner. I don't think you'll be allowed in the dining hall if you show up like that," he says, poking them with a long stick as though touching them would make him dirty too.

Muttering about horrible friends, Hereward steps all the way out of the puddle and starts walking toward his horse.

Two days after the wedding announcement, Prince Geff is preparing to leave Southwind Fort to return to Burmstone Palace for his sister's wedding. Unfortunately, the lord commander did not grant his request for Borus and Kristoff to accompany him back.

"Don't grow too much," Geff says wryly.

Borus laughs. "I don't think I can make that a promise."

"I'll see you when I see you," Geff says. He and Borus grip each other's forearms tightly and then embrace.

"Be safe," Borus says quietly. Geff nods, then shakes hands with Sir Gregory. Lord Commander Urich Stone bows to the prince. Geff mounts his horse, and he departs with his escort of knights.

The lord commander clears his throat. Borus and Sir Gregory stop on the steps and turn back around. "We will have our own celebration for the wedding of Princess Phaedra. The men deserve a reason to celebrate."

Sir Gregory nods. "Wonderful idea, Lord Commander. Borus is at your disposal for anything you need for the celebration."

Borus groans. *Great, I get to be a party planner!*

At Stone House, in the city of Ironhaven, just a few minutes' ride from Burmstone Palace, Sabine twirls in front of the mirror in her new dress. The seamstress just finished the final alterations. It is a deep forest-green velvet with tiny pearls on the collar and sleeves.

Diana smiles. "I'm glad you like the dress, dear."

The royal wedding will be Sabine's and Jules's first formal event rubbing elbows with other nobles. Although Jules has been a page for three years, there have been no formal banquets that the family has attended during that time. While sad that her older two children will miss out, Diana knows they are needed at their posts more.

Diana goes to her dresser and pulls out a flat case. Sabine sees the case and walks over.

"What is that, Mama?" she asks excitedly.

Diana opens the case. Inside is a simple gold necklace with a large oval emerald. Sabine sucks in her breath. She's never seen anything so beautiful before.

"Your grandfather gave this to me on my wedding day. One day, when you're old enough, I will pass it down to you. However, for Princess Phaedra's wedding, your dress and shoes will be enough. After all, you are a nine-year-old girl, not an adult yet."

When the seamstress finishes with the women, she heads over to the music room where the men are hiding. She smiles. "You can't hide from me."

The Wolf rolls his eyes. "No, but I can go last, and Jules will go first." The Wolf pushes Jules toward the seamstress.

"Can I at least put away my book?" Jules says, waving it in the air. Smiling, the seamstress offers Jules his dress shirt. He sets the book down and takes the shirt. Jules is surprised by how it feels. "This is not the same shirt," he says in confusion..

The seamstress laughs. "No, it's not. The other one was for me to size you. This is the shirt you'll wear to the wedding and banquet."

Jules slips the shirt over his head. It fits perfectly. He reaches out his hands for the jacket. His jacket is black with silver buttons set with sapphires. The sapphires match the exact blue of his eyes.

"Diana must have had a hand in the design of that jacket," Kenric murmurs.

The seamstress beams at him. "Yes, she did." The seamstress tugs in a few spots, making sure the jacket sits perfectly on Jules's shoulders. "Wonderful, you didn't grow in the past two days!"

Jules laughs. "You're lucky. It's good the wedding is tomorrow, or I might grow."

Sabine keeps running her fingers over her dress, reveling in how soft the fabric is. Together with her family and other guests, she awaits the royal wedding. The Wolf is on her left and Jules is on her right, with their parents farther down the bench. Sabine watches in awe as King Renard escorts Princess Phaedra up the aisle to Crown Prince Kabili.

"She is so pretty," Sabine murmurs. The Wolf glances sharply at her, finger to his lips. Sabine gasps, not realizing she said that out loud. Gulping, she bites her lower lip and returns her attention to the king and princess.

When they are a few feet away from the prince, King Renard stops and gently kisses the princess on the cheeks before handing her to Prince Kabili. The king's steward begins the ceremony. Shifting her feet and fussing with her dress, Sabine finally understands why Jules didn't want to come. Weddings are boring. Not only are they boring, but you can't leave or find something else to do. You're trapped.

A hand touches Sabine's arm, and she jumps, startled. "What?" she yelps.

Jules laughs. "You fell asleep! It's time to go to the banquet now. I hope you won't do that at my wedding if I ever get married." Sabine blushes, embarrassed that she fell asleep at a royal wedding. Keeping her eyes down, she follows her family out of the hall.

Much to the Wolf's dismay, he is sitting at the head table directly across from King Renard. *So much for sneaking away*, he thinks. He looks around the table, but all of his friends are either not present or too far away to have a polite conversation. Armand catches his

63

eye from down the table and gives a small wave. The Wolf nods his head and continues identifying guests.

Several tables away, Jules finds his seat at the banquet hall. There is a rustle of fabric behind him and then the empty chair next to him moves. Jules looks up, and his mouth falls open in surprise. Sliding into the seat next to him is Ella. She is wearing a shimmering pale-pink dress. Her brown hair is piled on top of her head.

"Jules?" the princess says in surprise. As one, they glance up at the head table. The queen catches his eye and winks. It appears someone wants her daughter to have fun tonight instead of being bored at the head table. Jules bows to the queen, then smiles at Ella.

"Did you enjoy the ceremony?" Jules asks quietly.

Ella starts laughing and spits out the water she just sipped, spraying Jules. "Oh my gosh!" she says. Face heating up, she covers her mouth in embarrassment. Jules glances around the table and realizes no one saw.

He gives her a reassuring smile and lets his hand hover just above his wet shirt. A blue shimmering light emanates from his hand and when he pulls it away his shirt is dry. "See, good as new…the ceremony was that amazing huh?"

Ella shakes her head. "You got me through it. I was going back over our last card game in my mind."

"Hmm, I didn't think about the card game. I was going through the principles of water and air…probably just as boring to you as the wedding," he says quietly.

Ella shakes her head, "You're not boring, Jules. Besides, at least now we can enjoy the rest of the wedding festivities together." Jules smiles, realizing how lucky he is to have his best friend sitting next to him tonight.

Borus is just finishing putting up the decorations for Southwind Fort's royal wedding party when Sir Willet bumps hard into the chair Borus is standing on, causing him to fall onto the floor and rip the banner.

Borus pulls himself off the floor and looks around for Sir Willet, who is hastily walking away. Borus runs after him and grabs Sir Willet's arm. "What was that for?" he asks in an even tone.

Sir Willet yanks his arm out of Borus's grasp, glaring at him. "Everyone around here thinks you're so good at everything, but you're not. You're still a squire, with only a few years of battle experience. Your grandfather might be the Wolf, but you are most definitely *not* the Wolf, or a general. Stop acting like you know more than everyone else does before you get killed."

Borus opens and shuts his mouth, not sure what to say. With one last glare, Sir Willet stomps off. Taking a deep breath, Borus slowly walks over to the overturned chair and sets it back up, then looks at the ripped banner. *It's ruined. Instead of just talking to me, Sir Willet ruined something so that now no one can enjoy it.* He climbs back on the chair and very carefully removes the banner, trying not to destroy any of the other decorations.

As Borus surveys the room, the lord commander walks in and heads to Borus. "The men will appreciate your effort; I am sure of it."

Borus bows. "Thank you, sir."

The lord commander looks at the squire. "You are young, with minimal experience in the field. This celebration may not seem like much to you, but I have found over the years that small things, such as what we're doing tonight, can bring joy to an assignment that is often fraught with darkness. It is not always the enemy outside the walls that is the worst one, it is the enemy inside your head. One day, if you follow in your grandfather's footsteps and have your own men to command, you will understand. Until then, be grateful the only person you must worry about is yourself."

A knight calls out to the lord commander from the across the hall and he excuses himself, leaving Borus lost in his thoughts. *I'm not sure I am the only person I worry about, but I think I see his point. When you are a leader, the people you are leading depend on you.* He shakes his head. *There's no way anyone is going to put me in an official position of leadership as a squire. That would be crazy.*

Kass and Theo, along with other knights assigned to Port Riverdale and the surrounding areas, are helping with the efforts to rebuild what was lost during the war with Wanonia.

Kass is hammering a nail into a board of what is a soon-to-be-complete chicken house when Theo walks up behind him and tickles his sides. Not expecting the touch, Kass's grip on the hammer slips and he smashes his thumb. "Ouch!" he yells, dropping the hammer and jumping up and down, holding his thumb.

"Man, I am so sorry!" Theo hastily apologizes. Kass shudders and looks at his thumb, which is rapidly turning purple. "Is there anything around here I can use to help with the pain?" Kass asks shakily and starts one-handedly rummaging through the box of tools.

Theo pops up in his face again, this time holding one of the chickens. "I have a chicken, will that help?"

Kass shoves Theo out of the way. "Really? A chicken? How about a healer...or something."

Theo drops the chicken, which squawks in protest. "A healer, right...I will go find one. Be right back!" Theo sprints off in the direction of the larger group working on one of the village houses.

6

SUMMER 607

Roger is sitting in a chair in his room at Camp Tooth. There is a thick layer of dust on the chest of drawers in the corner, and random heaps of clothing dot the floor. Lars looks around the room, surprised his squire won't at least clean up after himself.

"If you don't hurry up, we're going to be late," growls Sir Lars, as he impatiently waits for his almost fourth-year squire to finish getting ready.

Roger stops pulling on his boots and looks up at Sir Lars. "I'm almost ready. What's the big deal if we're a few minutes late?"

Sir Lars glares at him. "I have told you before, the people we are working with require a delicate touch. The last thing we want to do is anger a mage that can barbecue us." Roger rolls his eyes but stays silent and finishes pulling on his boots.

Together they mount their horses and ride off into the forest for the meeting with the mage.

When they arrive, the mage, in a bloodred hooded robe, is waiting for them on a black horse.

"You're late," says a cold voice from under the hood.

Sir Lars bows from the saddle. "My apologies, Pyr. At your request, I have my squire, Roger, with me today."

Pyr nods. "The agreement with Blackwell is in place. It is only a matter of time before the fort is in flames."

Sir Lars is about to say something when the mage looks at Roger and shakes his head. "I am not ready to discuss the plans we have for the rest of Etria with your squire. He must prove himself able to keep a secret. Just know that the spies are in place to gather the information we need to continue moving forward."

With that, the mage turns his horse, walks off into the forest, and disappears.

Roger looks at Sir Lars. "I didn't realize the plan was so far-reaching."

Sir Lars laughs and kicks his horse into a canter without commenting.

A few days before Theo leaves Port Riverdale to return to Burmstone Palace, he is out with Kass in one of the training fields. There is a wide assortment of targets for different styles of fighting, although all require a high skill level. After months of watching Kass practice archery, Theo has taken up using a crossbow while on horseback.

"Can you believe how much we've improved since we started this?" Theo asks. "You can shoot up to twenty yards at a full gallop and can do some crazy things with Mist."

Kass laughs. "Yeah, and you can use a crossbow, which is a pain to reload, but you do it…and at a gallop, with accuracy to fifteen yards."

Theo grins. "About the reloading thing…what do you think about this idea I have…I want to talk to Huntsberg about how to reload quicker."

"That's a brilliant idea. You know Huntsberg made this?" Kass says, raising his yew bow in the air.

Theo nods. "Yes…hopefully he will talk to me. He has a reputation for being selective about whom he works with."

Kass shrugs. "I wouldn't worry about it. He probably already knows who you are and the exact specifications of your current crossbow." Theo gives Kass a quizzical look. "Huntsberg pays attention to any knights or men-at-arms that are of a high skill level as potential clients. That way when someone approaches him, he knows if they are clients he wants."

"Hmm…sounds strange to me, but I'll take your word for it," mutters Theo.

Glancing at Kass's quiver, Theo notices he's changed something. "You're using hawk feathers now as fletching?"

Kass shrugs. "The falcon master, Captain Veyron, gave me the suggestion. I like them better than the other feathers I've tried."

Theo smiles slyly. "Maybe instead of calling you Kass, I will call you Hawk."

Kass groans. "Why? I already have a nickname that's four letters…"

Theo just laughs and reloads his crossbow, before taking off for another round.

Kass pulls out some arrows and follows Theo, so they are almost running together stride for stride. Each time Theo shoots a bolt, Kass lets an arrow fly.

On the last one, Theo pulls his horse up short, hissing. "Ouch!" Theo shakes out his hand and a few drops of blood hit Kass in the face. "You grazed me!"

Kass rolls his eyes. "It's just a scratch, you'll survive. Maybe next time you should think twice before you give me a nickname… hawks do have talons."

Theo bursts out laughing. "Really, that's the best you've got? 'Hawks have talons'?"

Kass blushes. "I guess that is pretty lame, huh?"

"Yep…it is, Hawk!" Theo shouts and urges his horse into a gallop before Kass can grab him.

One summer morning that is hotter than usual, Sir Gregory sorts through the letters that came with the most recent supply caravan. Borus knocks on the door.

"Sir Gregory," he says, bowing.

Borus's knight master riffles through the stack of letters. "I have some letters for you from Kass, the Wolf, and Jules." Greg pauses and looks up, seeing Borus's expression. "What is it?"

"The scouts are reporting movement at the east side. It looks like Blackwell is preparing to attack tonight," Borus replies.

Sir Gregory puts the letter down and stands up. "Thank you, Borus. I want you to lead the green squad tonight. You'll be on the far-left flank. The only difference between what we practiced and your orders is that you will be in charge, not Sir Willet."

Borus waits to see if Sir Gregory is going to offer any more information or explanation. Since he doesn't, Borus decides to ask; after his confrontation with Sir Willet, he has been cautious when around the knight and is concerned about taking the squad from Sir Willet. "Why are you putting me in charge?"

Sir Gregory looks at Borus, not expecting the question. "You're ready to lead. The men know you and respect you."

Borus turns red at the compliment. "I just don't feel like I'm ready. I'm still just a boy playing with a stick," he whispers.

Raising his eyebrow at Borus's comment, Sir Gregory shakes his head. "You are definitely more than just a boy playing with a sharp stick. Do remember the first time you were allowed to go riding with your brothers alone? Your parents trusted you to be responsible. But they also knew that things don't always go as planned. Just like then, I trust you, Borus. I do not expect you to be perfect. You are ready for this next step."

Borus bows and departs to gather what gear he needs and prepare himself for the eminent battle.

Borus collects his armor and weapons, then heads down to where the green squad is assigned to meet. Sir Willet glares at him as he walks up.

"As you might have already learned, Sir Gregory has given me orders that I will be leading the green squad tonight," Borus says.

At this announcement, several other knights in the green squad grumble.

"You all know that when we are given orders, we follow them regardless of our opinions or feelings on the matter. I do not want to take over green squad; however, my orders say otherwise," he says firmly. The knights of the green squad are mostly men who believe Borus is getting special treatment because of his ties to the Wolf and that his weapon skills are abysmal. Even Sir Willet, who has been in combat with Borus, is unhappy tonight, because he is being replaced by a seventeen-year-old.

The sun is rapidly descending behind the trees as the green squad rides into position. Their task is to prevent Blackwell's men from sneaking around the far-left side of the fort. They have a view of the west watchtower, where the scout spotted the initial movement, as well as the edge of the east watchtower. However, the tree line curves closer to the east watchtower, creating some difficult-to-see areas.

Borus takes a deep breath and counts to ten. Either the knights follow his orders or when they return, he will report them as insubordinate. Borus pinches himself. *If I report them, everyone at the fort will know, and then I'll be in deep trouble.*

The trees to the left of Borus start rustling; he turns in the saddle toward the noise. Arrows whistle through the air from his right. He hastily pulls his shield up to protect himself. Stupid mistake. He hears the rustling again to his left; not to be fooled a second time, Borus ignores it.

Out of the corner of his eye, Borus sees a flame swirling toward him. He kicks his horse, and they shoot forward. The flame hits

71

the shield of the knight next to him, Sir Willet. Another flame comes sailing out of the forest. Glancing around him, Borus realizes they're waiting for his command. *Oops! I'm going to have to get used to leading and not having someone giving orders.*

"Charge!" Borus yells, and together the green squad put their shields, up, raise their swords, and gallop toward whatever is throwing the flames. Suddenly, another flame is coming straight toward him from the right. With no other option, he throws himself out of the saddle and rolls. Borus pops up to his feet as his horse runs back toward him in sheer terror as the flames consume it.

"Split!" he yells and dives out of the way, praying the other men see the flaming horse in time. Flames begin to crisscross through the trees. Several other knights jump off their horses and barely miss getting burned themselves. The men huddle around him in the shelter of a bush.

"We need to find the source of the flames and eliminate it now. They must be magic. Let's spread out and search. Be careful," Borus orders quietly. The men nod in agreement.

The squad splits up. The men with horses let them go and encourage them to run home. Quietly, using as much stealth as possible, they search. Borus wonders if it is a ghost throwing fire at them when he comes across a strange-looking post with symbols painted on it. He reaches out a finger to touch it, and as soon as he does, it glows red-hot and flames shoot out of the top. Borus jumps back just in time. He pulls his axe out of its loop on his belt and swings at the side of the post. The axe gets stuck. Careful to not let his skin touch the post, Borus shimmies the axe until he gets it loose. Then takes another swing. It seems like forever has passed when Borus finally slices the post in two. The two pieces turn black and then crumble into ashes.

"Really weird," Borus mutters to himself.

"What's weird?" asks Sir Willet coming up behind Borus.

Borus points where the post was. "That was a post. I believe it's what was shooting flames at us."

Sir Willet looks at Borus and then at the pile of ashes. "If you say so…" he says skeptically.

"We need to make sure we destroy all of these, if we find more. If no one has come across any actual people, this must have been put here as a diversion or backup plan if they weren't expecting any of the fort's defense to be positioned this far out. My brother is a mage. He's told me about spells that can be triggered from a distance. These must be the same sort of thing. It also means Blackwell has a fire mage."

Sir Willet whistles. This is the first time information on Blackwell indicates he has mages. A fire mage will make a significant difference in the lord commander's battle tactics.

"We need to tell Sir Gregory or Lord Commander Stone," Sir Willet announces.

Borus growls in annoyance. "I know *that*, but we must destroy the posts first, or we may not make it out of the forest alive to tell anyone."

An urgent message is sent to King Renard from Southwind Fort. The messenger arrives when the king is in his private training yard, sparring with Prince Geffrey. The king indicates the messenger should give the note to the prince, not to him. He wants to see how his son reacts to whatever the news is.

The prince opens the letter and reads it.

> King Renard,
> We just discovered that Ruschmann Blackwell has a fire mage. If a mage is available, please send one as soon as possible.
>
> Sincerely,
> Lord Commander Urich Stone

Geff is stunned by the news. "Blackwell has a fire mage!" he exclaims.

King Renard is silently thinking. *Usually, the best results in a magical battle are when mages of opposite elements fight. Which means Blackwell's spies must still be feeding him information.* King Renard doesn't have any water mages that are able to travel that far. *Unless...*

"Do you think Julien Wolfensberger would be willing to go to Southwind Fort to fight the fire mage?" blurts King Renard.

His son's face changes from stunned to angry. "How can you even say that? You would send a mere boy, who is almost fourteen and barely a squire, to fight a full-fledged mage? Your Majesty." Geff adds the title out of spite.

The king, eyes narrowing, takes a step back before saying his next words. "You would choose your friend over your country?" The king knows it's harsh, but war is not easy. "Julien has just completed his tests and is a squire. Whether or not you're aware, he has been training with various master mages from Onaxx Academy for the past four years as a page, and even for some time before that, and I recently learned is a certified journeyman mage."

"While that might be true, you also know that he wants to become a mage-knight. A path he has chosen, so he won't be used the same way his ancestor, the weather mage Trieste Rowanwood, was. Jules is terrified of being consumed by his magic because he is ordered to use it. What you are proposing goes against everything I believe in," Geff replies vehemently.

"I guess you just answered my question. You would choose a friend over our country. I'm glad you are not my heir. You do not have what is needed to make decisions that will save Etria, no matter the personal cost." As soon as the words are out of the king's mouth, he regrets them. Seeing the look on Geff's face, he knows he may not ever be able to take them back.

Geff bows stiffly to his father and runs out of the training yard.

Finally, the prince reaches his room. Breathing hard, he shuts the door and leans against it, angry tears threatening to spill over.

"How can he treat his subjects like they're not people?" Geff says to the empty room. "Maybe this is why we don't understand each other—because he doesn't take the time to get to know people, so when he has to make terrible choices, he doesn't have feelings about those people." Wiping at his eyes, he tries to master his anger and begins pacing.

Geff snaps his fingers in excitement as an idea comes to him. "I can go with Jules to Southwind, to make sure he stays safe…" Anger momentarily forgotten, Geff sits down at his desk to write a list of things he needs to do before he goes to Southwind Fort.

King Renard,
As you requested, I am including supplies and additional instructions that Julien Wolfensberger might find useful when he goes to Southwind Fort. Please make sure his knight master gives these to him when they get to the fort.

Sincerely,
Master Brixx

Master Brixx folds the letter and seals it before turning to the sack of supplies he is sending. He goes through the bag one last time.

There's a soft knock on the door before it opens. To his surprise, High Mage Ivy walks in. Brixx stands hastily and bows.

"High Mage Ivy. To what do I owe the pleasure?" he says gracefully.

The high mage arches an eyebrow at him. "I know you disagree with sending Jules down to Southwind Fort, but you cannot travel that far. Remember what happened last time?"

Brixx shudders involuntarily at that memory. "I know, I know. It's just risky for everyone to send such a young mage. A mage who hasn't even been attending Onaxx full time."

The high mage sighs tiredly. This is not the first time they have discussed Jules. "The very same young mage who tested and passed his journeyman test a year ago. A feat many don't manage until they are graduating from Onaxx. You know very well the potential within Jules. Why are you afraid to let him use it?" High Mage Ivy asks.

Sighing deeply, Brixx replies, "Because Jules doesn't want to go down that path. He has been very clear about it. I have told him if he changes his mind and wants to continue advanced training then we would be happy to go that route."

"You know he could replace me," she says quietly.

Brixx glances at her sharply. He was not prepared for the high mage to admit Jules could be as good or better than she is.

"The path he is on is one that no one else has been on," Brixx says. "I am following the lead the Wolf has set. Giving Jules access to the tools he needs to make his own decisions. *If* Jules were ever interested in pursuing the master or high mage titles, it would be my honor to mentor him. As much as I am enjoying our chat, I really do need to get this to the king." Brixx holds up the pack and the letter.

High Mage Ivy reaches for the door. "I will see you later, then." She walks out.

Brixx sets the pack back down and sits in the chair heavily. He has had suspicions of the depth of Jules's power before, but having High Mage Ivy confirm it was unexpected. Given the modesty of all three Wolfensberger brothers, Brixx is sure Jules has no idea of the potential he has, which to date is largely untapped. He rubs his face, stands, and grabs the pack to deliver it to the messenger.

There is a knock at the door. Jules opens it, expecting his father. He bows when he sees Sir Oweyn of Chateau du Clervin in Stinyia, his new knight master. "Can I help you, sir?"

The knight pushes the door open farther and steps inside, then shuts the door.

"Please sit." Sir Oweyn indicates Jules's chair.

Jules sits. He's only met Sir Oweyn a few times and doesn't yet know how to read him well. Jules stays silent, deciding to wait for the knight to speak.

Sir Oweyn clears his throat. "I just received new orders that we are to depart for Southwind Fort tonight."

Jules looks at him in shock. "Tonight?"

"I don't understand the haste either, but I have learned not to question orders such as these. We will be taking several extra horses with us, so we can take turns letting them rest. It is going to be a long couple of days. Pack only your necessities and weapons. Leave a list on your desk of what else you want sent and a wagon will bring the rest a few days behind us," Sir Oweyn says.

Jules looks at the knight, not sure what else to say. "I will start gathering my things and making the list."

Sir Oweyn nods. "Very good. I will see you in a few hours."

Kass is sitting at his desk at the port, holding a letter. There's a tap on the door.

"Can I come in?" Sir Alane calls.

"Come in!" yells Kass and grabs the letter again. He skims it and then looks at his knight master.

"Any interesting news?" Sir Alane asks.

Kass makes a face. "Depends on what you call interesting. This letter is from Prince Richard…I guess his parents are going to have some fancy parties so that he can find a wife."

Sir Alane perks up at the mention of fancy parties. Kass notices.

"You like fancy parties?" he asks in surprise.

The knight laughs. "Yes, as a matter of fact I do. I view them as a chance to let all the problems we face as knights go away for at least a few hours. To let go and just have fun."

"I guess I never thought of parties that way. But I suppose I haven't really been to any, either," Kass admits. "Richard also says that there was an argument between Prince Geff and the king and tension is still high."

Sir Alane shrugs. "I came in here to see if you'd like to go fishing? A couple of us are going out on one of the ships in about an hour."

Kass smiles. "Yes, I'd love to!"

"Great, then I will see you at the dock in an hour. Just make sure you bring a hat," Sir Alane says, and departs.

Borus, now in his fourth and final year as a squire, walks into Sir Gregory's study for their nightly meeting. After Borus's success leading the green squad when Blackwell's fire posts were discovered, Sir Gregory made Borus's position as a leader of the green squad permanent.

Tonight, Greg is sure the meeting will go differently. "I just received news concerning your brother." Anticipating Borus's next question, Greg continues, "As far as I know Kass is fine. The news is about Jules…he is on his way here with Sir Oweyn."

Borus is confused, and then it dawns on him, and his eyes get huge. "No!"

"Unfortunately, yes, he is coming, and it seems you have guessed why," Greg replies.

Borus paces. "Does he know?"

Greg shrugs. "I have no idea if Sir Oweyn even knows why they are coming here. I'm sure he is aware that Jules is a weather mage." He pauses. "Does anyone even know how much Jules can or can't do?"

Borus stops pacing and shakes his head. "Master Brixx might know, but Jules keeps it to himself. I made him a promise, Greg—a promise I won't break. You'll have to kill me first," Borus declares.

Sir Gregory lifts his eyebrow at Borus's words. He's never heard him speak like this. "What exactly is it that you promised?"

"To not let the king or anyone use him the way our ancestor, Trieste Rowanwood, was used."

Greg sucks in a sharp breath. He knew the story of Trieste Rowanwood but hadn't ever realized she was part of the Wolfensberger family.

"I understand and respect your promise to your brother, but I also have orders that have consequences if they are disobeyed. What if we explain the situation to Jules when he gets here and let him decide what he wants to do? Even if all he does is somehow finds and destroys those fire posts, that will be a huge help."

Reluctantly, Borus agrees.

Lord Commander Urich Stone meets Sir Oweyn and his squire as they ride in. He offers Sir Oweyn one of his rare smiles. Sir Oweyn smiles back. "Good to see you, brother!"

Jules looks at them both in surprise. *Brothers?*

"Lord Commandeer Urich Stone, may I present Julien Wolfensberger." Sir Oweyn glances over at Jules. "The lord commander and I are brothers by marriage. He married my older sister."

Jules bows following protocol, unsure what to make of this news.

"Are we just going to stand here, Uri, or are you going to at least give us some chairs?" Sir Oweyn asks playfully.

"C'mon, we can go to my office. Sir Gregory is waiting for us."

The lord commander leads the way to his huge office on the ground floor. Sir Gregory is waiting for them at the map and is fiddling with some of the extra pieces. He straightens hastily when they enter. "Lord Commander, Sir Oweyn," he says with a bow, then notices Jules. "Squire Julien," he adds.

"I feel things will go better if we discuss our orders before there is any interference," the lord commander says with a pointed look at Sir Gregory before continuing. "King Renard made the decision to send Julien Wolfensberger, journeyman mage and squire, to

Southwind Fort to aid in fighting against Ruschmann Blackwell's fire mage." He stops speaking, watching Jules.

Jules is struggling to hide his emotions. He barely knows Sir Oweyn and has never met the lord commander. He is afraid to respond and compromise his position with these two men. He looks over at Sir Gregory for help. Sir Gregory shakes his head. Jules is on his own.

Taking a deep breath, hoping his voice won't betray his feelings, Jules responds, "Can you explain what the fire mage has been doing and what your expectations are for me?"

Sir Gregory decides to reply before the lord commander can, hoping that Jules will be able to relax. "We have not yet come across the mage in the flesh. However, there are fire posts that have been set randomly throughout the forest that shoot fire out of them when you are within a certain proximity. So far, our only way of detecting these posts is by being close enough so they shoot fire. As you can imagine, that has been detrimental to those in range."

Jules considers. "I might be able to detect the posts without having to be close enough to set them off. I don't know if I am strong enough to destroy them. I'll know more once I am able to see one."

"What if the fire mage decides to attack us outright and not just with these posts? Will you defend us?" Lord Commander Urich Stone says, asking the question looming in the room.

Jules sighs. "Honestly, since my interest is becoming a mage-knight, not a mage, I have not been studying traditional battle magic. My focus has been primarily on how to fight with knight weapons using the magic as an enhancement. Whether I can be effective or not will largely depend on how the fire mage is attacking."

Sir Oweyn cuts in. "To be clear, he has been training exclusively with Lord Armand for all of his sword work." He looks meaningfully at his brother and Sir Gregory. The last student Lord Armand put that much work into is none other than Jules's brother Borus. "I had a discussion with Master Brixx, the mage overseeing Jules's training. Jules knows how to make spells that are tied to objects that can be activated by non-mages. I think typically they are shields or rain, but we might be able to experiment with tying them to a magical attack, such as a lightning bolt. The benefit of this type of spell is they can be done in advance, meaning we could have them as a backup plan, and it won't deplete his magic levels if we are in a situation where that is a concern. Master Brixx also sent a pack with supplies and additional instructions for Jules."

"I can see how the spells tied to objects will be very useful. At the very least, we can use them to buy us time. Any chance you can make thunderstorm stones?" the lord commander says hopefully.

Jules shakes his head. "No."

Sir Gregory looks at Jules, wondering if he's answering honestly or not, but decides it doesn't matter. He is already offering several things he can do, which will help tremendously.

"Jules, you can go. The three of us have some other things to discuss. Borus is in the training yard. Go down the two flights of stairs and through the door on your right. The training yard will be to your right," Lord Commander Urich says. Jules bows and departs, leaving the three men.

Urich Stone waits for Jules to leave. He walks over to the door and firmly shuts it, then returns to the table. "I want to be straightforward, Oweyn. Blackwell is getting bolder. The past couple of years we have had some remarkably close calls. Even though they ended on a positive note, I have lost many men. I almost lost the prince."

Oweyn's eyes get wide at that admission. It is seldom Uri shares details of his campaigns.

Uri continues, "Blackwell having a fire mage is a huge concern. As much as I am sure all of us dislike putting a wet-behind-the-ears squire in a position of such importance, he is the tool we are being given. Our success or failure here may very well ride on his shoulders alone."

"Uri, I am well aware, but you must understand that I have known Jules for three weeks. I did my research to learn if we are a good fit for each other, but our relationship is still in its infancy. Greg probably knows Jules better than I do," Oweyn replies.

Greg laughs at his last comment. "While I have known Jules for longer than three weeks, I am not sure I know him well enough to claim to be an expert. The first Wolfensberger brother I met is Kass, when he was sent here with the Wolf when he was nine."

Oweyn whistles in surprise. "Nine?"

Greg nods. "Yes, rather unusual, I know. The things I do know can be applied to all three brothers. They highly value honor and loyalty. They are modest about the skills they have but have all been personally trained at some point by the Wolf himself. Borus and Kass made several close friends among their year-mates. Jules shares those friends but does not have anyone he is very close to other than Kass, Borus, and..." Greg hesitates.

"And who?" Oweyn asks, curious.

"Princess Ellandre." Greg says quietly.

"He's friends with the princess?" Oweyn says shocked.

"I know it sounds strange, but the Wolfensberger brothers are very close to some of the royal family. Borus and Kass are like brothers to Prince Richard and Prince Geff. My point is that he is loyal to those he is close to. He will do anything that is in his power to protect those people. All of the Wolfensberger brothers are that way," Greg confirms.

Uri mutters, "So is the Wolf."

Greg laughs. "Then it shouldn't be a surprise his grandsons share that trait."

Uri clears his throat, trying to get them back on track. "We have now established that Jules is likely significantly more talented in all areas than we think."

Greg nods in agreement. "Yes, that's likely. However, he is still a fourteen-year-old boy with feelings. Ordering him to do something he is already telling us he doesn't want to do won't go well.

However, I strongly believe if the situation were to arise where Jules must cross the line he has set or watch his comrades die, he will cross the line."

Uri sighs. "Let's start simple. I want Jules to go out with the patrols and start seeing if he can locate some of those posts without being on top of them. Oweyn, for the time being I'd like you to accompany Jules every time he goes outside of the wall."

Oweyn nods and stands. He reaches over the table to shake hands with Uri and Greg. "I will see you both later. I would like to finish unpacking and find some food."

Once a week, Jules goes out with Sir Oweyn and two squads of knights and searches for more of the fire posts. So far, Jules has found and destroyed three of the posts. He has discovered that if he meditates and goes deep within his magic that the posts pulse. Jules is then able to put a marker of his own magic on them, so he can locate the post without having to meditate.

Today, Jules is working with Bo, his new horse, in the riding area within the fort. Sir Gregory agreed that if Jules was willing to make everything he needs to work on jumping, then he could store it and use it inside. Jules set up a small course of three jumps. They are all two feet high, but each is of a different style. As a squire, the possibility of Jules being faced with something to jump while on patrol is much higher than if he would come across something during page training. Because of this he is opting to train Bo over natural jumps.

Jules warms up Bo and then sets him toward the first jump. Counting in his head one, two, three, squeeze...Jules and Bo clear the first jump with plenty of room to spare. They continue over the next two easily. Jules repeats the jumps in the same order two more times before stopping. When he sets the jumps, his plan is to give himself an easy option and a more challenging one. To increase the difficulty without raising the height of the jumps, a rider can add tighter turns and less space between the jumps.

Nodding to himself, Jules urges Bo into a canter. They circle the outside of the jumps twice before cutting across the middle approaching the first jump. After the first jump, Jules makes a tight turn to the left. Bo fusses, dropping into a trot for a few strides before picking the canter back up. They come across the middle heading for the second jump, then a ninety degree turn to the right and over the third jump. Jules heads straight for the first jump again, wanting to practice the tight turn. After several more attempts, Bo is willing to make the turn without trotting. Jules praises him and drops his reins, allowing Bo to relax and walk around to cool down.

Sir Oweyn is at the rail, watching. Borus walks over to him. Sir Oweyn smiles at Borus. "If you want, I would be open to practicing sword work with you later. Jules is doing his training with Colonel Frankford this week."

Borus nods. "That would be great. I appreciate the offer."

Sir Oweyn shrugs. "We're here to defeat Blackwell. It is our duty to make sure our weapons skills are at their very best. How often are you able to practice without holding back? I know Sir Gregory works with you when he can, but he has a lot of other responsibilities as well. I'm not here in a leadership position, merely a knight with his squire."

Borus coughs, trying to hide is amusement at Sir Oweyn calling himself "merely a knight with his squire." The number of sword masters among the still-serving knights would make up two squads; the number of squires attempting to be a mage-knight...is one. He's the only sword master in the history of Etria to have a mage-knight as his squire.

Riding over, Jules dismounts and passes Bo off to one of the grooms before walking over to Sir Oweyn and Borus. "Are you going to practice together?" he asks eagerly.

Borus grins. "Yes, we are. You can watch if you want. You know, at some point you should practice with me, Jules. I'd be happy to let you practice while using your magic," Borus offers.

Jules nods. "I would like that." Very few people are willing to practice with him if he uses his magic.

7

FALL 607

Grinning, Sir Alane walks up to Kass in the practice yards on the first day of fall at Port Riverdale. "Guess what?"

"What?" Kass says, not sure why Sir Alane is so happy.

"You know the discussion we had a while back about fancy parties? Well, we get to go to one. Knight Commander Emberwood just gave us a month-long break."

"A real break?" asks Kass in surprise.

Sir Alane nods. "Yes, a real break. The Wolf is at Burmstone Palace too."

Two days later, Kass is unpacking his gear in a room at Burmstone Palace near Sir Alane's. To his surprise, most of his things that were left behind at the palace in the page's wing over two years ago are in a trunk in the new room. Kass opens the trunk, not quite sure what he'll find. On top are several sets of page training clothes. He pulls out the first shirt and pants and holds them up to himself, then laughs.

Sir Alane peers through the open door between their rooms. He sees the clothes Kass is holding up and laughs too. "I guess you won't be needing those anymore." The pants only come down to Kass's shins.

Grinning, Kass folds the clothing back up and sets it on the desk, then returns to the trunk to see what else is inside. There are some wooden practice weapons, a small knife, and a few knickknacks, but nothing of much interest. "I could probably just give this back to the page wing and let them redistribute the clothing."

Sir Alane nods in agreement. "I don't know if you've heard, but some of your friends are also in residence for the moment—Squire Theo, Squire Lewis…" Sir Alane trails off.

Kass is smiling. "Do you need me for the rest of the day?"

Sir Alane shakes his head. "No, you're free to go do what you want. I'll find you if something comes up."

Kass bows to his knight master, pulls on his boots, then dashes out the door in search of his friends. First, he checks the name-plates on the doors in the hallway his room is in. No luck. Kass is looking at the stairs as he's rounding the corner and bumps hard into someone. Muttering apologies, Kass looks up at the person.

Richard puts his hands out to steady them. He almost doesn't recognize Kass, now sixteen. Even though both remained in the Sapphire Coast area, their paths hadn't crossed in a long time. Kass takes two steps back and gives the precise formal bow due to the crown prince of Etria. "Prince Richard," he says stiffly.

The prince frowns. Even after such a long time without commu-nication, he was not expecting Kass to be so formal; he just thought they would go back to being friends like always.

"Squire Kassandros," the prince replies, also bowing. Voices are coming down the hallway the prince was heading toward. He sighs. "I must get going…see you around?" Prince Richard says with hope in his voice.

Kass hesitates. "I'll see you 'round." Kass quickly continues on his way.

When he his far enough away from where he ran into the prince, Kass stops and leans against the wall. He thought he had mastered his feelings when it came to the prince and their friendship. After seeing him again, Kass is not so sure. *I can't believe how much I miss my friend now that we're in the same place for once,* he thinks, missing their easy camaraderie.

Kass hears footsteps coming his way. Wiping his face, he pushes himself off the wall and straightens his shirt.

"Kass?" an almost-familiar voice comes down the hallway toward him. Then he hears running feet. Before Kass can respond he is swept up in a bear hug.

"Lewis?" he says incredulously.

Lewis laughs. "You do remember me! I was beginning to wonder if you'd forgotten when your letters stopped." Lewis finally releases Kass and takes a step back. They stand there appraising each other. Lewis is a head shorter than Kass. His auburn hair is cropped short.

"Where are you headed?" Lewis asks.

"To find you and Theo…have you seen Theo?" Kass asks.

Lewis shrugs, replying, "I haven't seen Theo today, but I know he's here. His knight master has been asked to step into a training position, and Theo is helping with that."

"Ah, so he is not on an official break. That's too bad. Sir Alane and I are on a month-long break before we head back to Port Riverdale…do you want to go for a ride? I'd prefer to not just stand in the hallway," says Kass. Lewis grins and leads the way to the stable.

It takes much longer to leave Burmstone Palace than Geff would have liked. Tension is still high between him and his father. Instead of facing the king, Geff decided to head back to Southwind Fort to aid in the effort to defeat Blackwell once and for all. Finally, he is on his way, making his way to the top of the southern mountain pass with his small but necessary protection detail. When they reach the top, they stop and turn around to take in the view.

"I wish it weren't such a trek to get a view like this!" says Sir Thomas in awe. The prince looks at the view and then at the other four men with him. None of these knights are part of his circle. They treat him as their prince, not as a friend. Geff longs for someone to confide in and hopes that Borus is up to the task when he reaches the fort.

Sir Thomas turns his horse toward the path heading through the rocks. "We should keep going so we can get to a lower elevation before dark."

The prince nods and motions for the group to continue with Thomas in the lead.

Hours later, as the sky is darkening, the five travelers are about halfway down the pass. They will reach the fort by dinner tomorrow.

At his mother's insistence, Kass is attending the banquet the royal family is hosting tonight. He is finishing buttoning his jacket when there's a soft knock on his door. He opens it to his friend Lewis. Lewis steps in and they proceed to inspect each other. Lewis is wearing a dark-brown jacket with matching pants and white shirt, and he combed his wavy auburn hair in one of the latest styles. Kass has on a deep blue jacket with gold buttons, black pants, and a white shirt. His face is dirt-free, and his blond hair hangs loose around his shoulders.

"Is Theo coming?" asks Kass.

Lewis shrugs. "I did tell him we're going, but he didn't seem sure if he would have conflicting orders. I guess we will find out when we get there." They both glance in the mirror one last time.

"Are you sure we have to leave our weapons behind?" Kass says wistfully, looking at his sword on the stand.

Lewis shakes his finger at Kass. "No weapons. Remember this is supposed to be a fun evening of socialization."

Kass shudders. "I can be social with you and our other friends…I don't need all of the hoo-ha," he says, waving his arms to indicate their formal clothes. Lewis shrugs and together they depart for the banquet.

Kass and Lewis enter the banquet hall and survey the room. It's not set up for a traditional banquet like Diana had said it would be. Instead, there are scattered tables, a dance floor, and corners with sofas and chairs. Servers are walking through the crowd carrying platters with small plates of food and drinks.

A chime sounds as they reach the center of the room. Lewis and Kass turn around as the large double doors open. The king's steward, Jakub, enters and steps to the side to begin the formal introductions.

"His Majesty, King Renard, and Her Majesty, Queen Vivienne, of Etria!" The king and queen enter the room and the crowd parts, allowing them to go to the small thrones at the back of the room.

"His Highness, Crown Prince Richard, and Her Highness, Princess Ellandre." The prince and princess walk in arm-in-arm and take places next to their parents. Murmurs begin to circulate with people wondering at Prince Geffrey's absence. Kass is about to turn to find a corner to hide in, assuming the steward is done, when Jakub begins speaking again.

"Duchess Sunette of Wanonia and her escort, Lord Benin." A tall, dark-skinned man with short pewter-gray hair and a mustache is gently leading the duchess. She is of petite stature, olive-skinned, with jet-black hair and soft brown eyes. Lord Benin and Duchess Sunette enter the room and find a spot near the royal family.

"Princess Isabela of Stinyia and her uncle, Duke Marcos." A tall, fair-skinned man with sandy brown hair to his shoulders and a full beard smiles as he enters the room with his niece at his side. The princess is the same height as her uncle with sandy brown hair a shade darker and green eyes.

The doors close and the steward retires to his post by the king. The crowd begins to break into small groups again and the chatter of people can be heard throughout the room.

Kass grabs Lewis's hand and pulls him to a spot with a couch and a chair in the corner. Lewis is protesting and trying to shake Kass's hand off when Kass takes the last few steps backward and he throws himself on the couch, grumbling.

"Hey!" A muffled shout comes from under Kass.

Kass jumps up, beet-red in embarrassment. *I just sat on someone!* He whirls to face the poor soul he sat on and Urlo is sitting there, grinning.

"Got ya!" Urlo says and bursts into laughter. Lewis starts to laugh too.

Kass rolls his eyes. "You did that on purpose?"

Urlo nods, eyes glinting.

Kass blows out his breath. "Will you at least share the couch? I'd rather not sit on you."

Urlo scoots sideways and pats the couch next to him. "Come, sit, and I'll tell you tales of far of lands full of mystery and wonder."

Kass cocks an eyebrow at Urlo and hesitantly sits on the far end of the couch, as far as he can get from Urlo as possible, not convinced his friend won't prank him again. Looking from Lewis to Urlo, Kass asks, "Can you remind me again why I agreed to this?"

Lewis sighs. "To make your mother happy. You know sometimes these things can be fun. It's just hard to have fun if we hide in a corner the whole time."

Lewis motions for one of the servers to come closer. This one has glasses of one of the king's special vintages. Lewis takes three, offering one to Kass and one to Urlo.

Kass takes it and sniffs. "Well, it smells better than some things I've been offered at the port."

Lewis laughs and almost spits out what's in his mouth. "If all you've tried is whatever swill the knights drink at the port, then you are definitely missing out. Take a sip, I promise you'll like it!"

Kass looks at the deep red liquid in the glass, shrugs, and takes a sip. His eyes open in surprise. *It is good!*

"See, I told you. You really should take my advice more often," Lewis says. Kass takes another sip and reluctantly nods in agreement.

Although Lewis and Urlo are not successful getting Kass to leave the corner, Lewis is able to retrieve some visitors. Urlo leaves to dance with one of the ladies. Theo is sitting on the couch talking to Kass when he hastily stands up. Kass jumps up too, not sure why they are standing, when he sees the thirteen-year-old Princess Ellandre entering their corner.

"Your Highness," Theo, Kass, and Lewis murmur and bow.

She steps over to Kass and takes his hand. "Kass, please just call me Ella."

He nods and drains his current glass of wine. "Is there anything I can do for you, Ella?" he asks, not sure why she sought him out.

She smiles sadly. "Have you heard from Jules? My father won't tell me anything. I was hoping you might know where he is. I wasn't able to say goodbye to him after his page tests, and I haven't gotten any letters either."

Kass sighs. "The king gave Jules and Sir Oweyn orders to go to Southwind Fort. I haven't gotten any news since then. I do know that Borus is down there. Prince Geff and Sir Thomas went that way last week. Maybe your brother will send you news?"

Ella nods. She turns slightly and makes a motion with her hand. "I need to go. Thank you for the information." The princess smiles at them and then leaves. As she departs, they get another surprise visitor. The crown prince walks over to the group. Once again Lewis, Theo, and Kass bow.

"Good evening, Squire Theo, Squire Lewis, and Squire Kass," Prince Richard says formally.

Theo gives Kass a quick look, seeing all the blood drain from his face. He elbows Lewis. "I just saw Sir Waldorf wanting to talk to us...we'll see you later, Kass!" Theo and Lewis bow again and then hastily depart, leaving Kass and Prince Richard alone.

"Why are you here, Richard?" Kass says quietly. "Do you still want to be friends? After no word from you for so long, I don't know what to think anymore."

The prince looks away. "I am sorry for that. My duties as crown prince have kept me busy. I know I am a terrible friend. But I do still want to be your friend...Kass, please..." The prince takes a deep breath and looks at his old friend, eyes pleading.

Kass glares at him. Struggling to rein in his anger at what has felt like abandonment from his best friend. "Friends don't ditch each other for an entire year."

Prince Richard sucks in a sharp breath, thinking, *This is harder than I thought it would be.* "I did not intend to ditch you. But... being a prince really sucks sometimes. Much like as a squire, you go where your knight master's orders say. I go where my father says. No matter how much time has passed I hope I can get my friend back. So much has happened the past few months, not having anyone I can trust and talk to has been terrible."

Kass sighs and looks around, debating his next words. "Yes, I am willing to try again to be friends. I understand that you are busy. It's not like I sit on my butt all day doing nothing either. But...Urlo, Hereward, Borus, even the Wolf have written me letters. It's not that difficult to just pick up a quill and write a quick note."

The prince nods, realizing Kass is right. He opens his mouth to say something when Lewis walks over. "From over there," he says waving his hand in the direction he came from, "it looked like you're done with the serious talk. So...who wants to play some dice?" He pulls out three dice from his pocket and shakes them.

Richard laughs. "I'm in if Kass is."

Kass shrugs. "Sure, why not."

A winter chill seeps into Southwind Fort, even though fall is not yet over. Geff is sitting in front of a hearth with a blanket around

his shoulders. Borus is sitting opposite on the floor with a mug of hot cider in his hands.

"Did Richard's letter say anything good?" Borus asks curiously.

Geff shrugs, pulling the blanket tighter around himself. "Only that he thinks he knows which lady he is going to marry. It sounds like he has been hiding out at Sapphire Coast Fort overseeing renovations and delaying the announcement of his choice. He also is asking me to forgive Father."

Borus's mouth forms an O, but no words come out.

Geff makes a face. "Yeah, I'm not ready to forgive him or return home. Unlike my father, I enjoy meeting people and making friends. Learning new skills. Things that he thinks are beneath us. I made these the other day..." The prince reaches into his pocket and pulls out a couple of arrowheads.

Borus whistles in appreciation and inspects them. "Arrowheads can be tough...these are pretty good."

Geff smiles. "Thanks. The blacksmith was surprised I was able to follow his instructions successfully. I guess a lot of the men around here think I'm like my father, who takes a very hands-off approach with his subjects."

"It's good you're taking the time to demonstrate you are different. You will earn their respect...you already know I would gladly serve under your command, right?" Borus says quietly.

Geff laughs. "I still think you will make a better general than me. But we're both young yet; only time will tell."

Kass is in the training yard at the port with Sir Alane. They are taking a quick break before resuming their session. Kass's back is turned toward his knight master, and he's talking to some of the other men also taking break.

Prince Richard walks over to Sir Alane. "Mind if I take over?" he asks.

"If that's what you want. I have some reports I need to take care of. I'm sure Kass will enjoy the change," replies Sir Alane.

The prince nods and pulls his sword out of its scabbard before unbuckling the scabbard and leaving it at the weapon rack. He then walks to the spot Kass and Sir Alane were using before the break.

Kass finishes his break and turns around, seeing Richard. Grinning, he walks to the center.

"Are you sure you want to do this?" he teases. Last time they sparred, Kass disarmed the prince three times.

"Yes, I'm sure."

They cross swords, count to three, and begin. Once they settle into a rhythm, Kass asks the question he's been dreading the answer to. "You're returning to Burmstone Palace, aren't you?"

Richard nods, trying not to disrupt their practice. "I got a letter from Mother."

Kass drops the subject after getting confirmation. He does pick up the pace some.

The prince disengages first. "Let's call it a draw," he says wiping the sweat off his face with his arm. Kass walks over to where his water and scabbard are and retrieves them. Together they walk back to the building where Kass's room is.

"When are you leaving?" Kass inquires.

"Tomorrow. My plan is just to stay here tonight. I was able to wrap everything up at the fort this morning before coming here. How about we both get cleaned up, and I'll join you for dinner at the mess hall?"

"Sounds good to me." Kass walks into his room and shuts the door as Richard heads down the hallway to the room Knight Commander Emberwood has assigned him for the night.

Queen Vivienne sighs tiredly. King Renard walks over and sits down beside her on the couch in his study.

"I'm happy we have come to an agreement that both of you can live with," Vivienne says softly. "Although many of the young women would make suitable wives, I think Duchess Sunette is the right fit for Richard. Having an additional tie to Wanonia will only strengthen our relationship."

Renard pats her hand. "I know. Now all we need to do is make the formal offer and plan a wedding. Considering it is a crown prince marrying, I know that takes time to prepare. What about this coming spring?"

Vivienne is a little surprised at how soon Renard wants it. "It's traditional to wait a year..." she reminds him.

Renard shakes his head. "I know, but Richard is almost twenty-two, and Geff is twenty-one. Neither is married...there are some days I feel like a clock is ticking, and we're running out of time."

"A clock? You're only forty-three. Your father lived until he was sixty, and your grandfather until he was seventy-five. Why are you worrying about this now?" Vivienne asks in confusion.

Renard shakes his head. He didn't know how to explain this feeling. He's had it for months, but he was afraid to mention it even to Vivienne.

Roger and his knight master are practicing sword work in the forest, wanting privacy from the rest of the people at Alderth Castle.

"I got word from Pyr. Blackwell is preparing his final push on Southwind Fort. Once you are a knight, we can use the castle in Sneg as our home base. The mage agrees to give us some of the crystals with portals so we can easily get close to Burmstone Palace if we need to keep a closer eye on things," Sir Lars explains as they work through their warmup drill.

Roger stays silent, thinking, *Hopefully Borus will die in the fight with Blackwell.* "Only a few more months, then I'm free," he says quietly, before throwing all of his energy into sparring with Sir Lars.

The fall weather that they're supposed to have for a couple more weeks gives way to a brutal winter-like storm, dumping over a foot of snow in the valley that is home to Southwind Fort.

Jules is dreaming about a battle horn when he is jostled awake.

"Hurry up. We need you!" Borus says, urgently shaking Jules.

Jules rubs his eyes, realizing the battle horn isn't a dream. He can hear one being blown in the distance. Sir Oweyn steps into Jules's room and then sees Borus.

"Jules, grab your staff. Borus, grab his sword. You're needed *now!*"

Sir Oweyn runs out of the room and down the hall. Jules slips out of bed, cursing as his bare feet hit the icy stone floor. He reaches for his heavy leather pants with fur lining, slipping them on, then a shirt, and a lightweight jacket, followed by his heavy winter coat and fur lined boots.

Borus hands Jules the staff, grabs the extra sword, and they run out of the room and down the stairs. There is no access to the fort's outer wall from inside the main building. They open the door with the closest access to the wall and are thrown back inside. Borus glances at Jules. Jules takes a breath and nods at Borus. This time when he opens the door, the wind doesn't throw them back inside. Jules has a magic shield protecting them from the wind and snow. Borus shuts the door and they make their way through the yard and up the stairs to the outer wall. Jules looks out at the scene unfolding before them and curses again. Borus looks at him in surprise and concern before turning his attention to what has Jules upset.

Three of the watchtowers are on fire. There are fireballs flying through the air setting the snow-covered sharpened spikes ablaze too.

Lord Commander Urich walks over to Jules. "I need you to get rid of the fires. We can't send anyone out there until the fires are gone. I have men ready to go after the mage, but they have to be able to get there."

Jules listens while gazing at the fires.

Borus shivers as another icy blast hits them and realizes that Jules dropped the shield. "What do you need me to do, brother?" Borus asks.

Jules shakes his head. "I just need quiet, and I need whoever is going out there to be ready. I don't know how long what I'm going to do will last."

Borus relays this to Sir Oweyn. Lord Commander Urich looks at Borus. "You are going to be more useful to me down there than up here. Go." Borus is about to protest. "This is an order, *squire!*" Lord Commander Urich says firmly.

Borus hangs his head and hurries back down the stairs to where the knights are preparing.

Jules shuts his eyes, takes a deep breath, and counts backward from ten. When he gets to zero, he opens his eyes. The watchtowers appear as the red and orange of the flames with red and black magic weaving through them. He is surprised he can see the thread of magical power leading back to the fire mage. If a mage is trying to hide, they will ensure that this thread is not visible. Jules expected the mage to want to hide. Jules reaches out and grabs the nearest person, Prince Geff, eyes not leaving the field. "The fire mage is just past the trees to the far left."

The prince turns and passes this information on to the lord commander.

With that task done, Jules, begins the spell that will suppress the fire on the watchtowers. Lucky for him with the winter storm raging, he can draw from its power. Slowly the fires on the watchtowers shrink and the towers become coated in a thick layer of ice.

Down below, waiting by the fort's gate, Sir Gregory gives the signal, and several hundred knights—including Sir Oweyn, Sir Kristoff, and Borus—stream out of the side gate and into the snow. At first, riding through the snow is a struggle for the horses. Suddenly, the horses' movements are less labored.

"Thank you, Jules," Borus whispers under his breath.

The knights reach the trees and melt into them. Ahead, Borus can see torches and what seems to be a large bonfire.

Sir Gregory signals, and all the knights dismount. The horses disappear into the darkening forest. The knights fan out in a half-circle around the people surrounding the mage. Borus can no longer see Greg or Sir Oweyn. Kristoff is to his left, and Sir Willet immediately to his right.

"Meow." A cat can be heard throughout the trees. *Strange; why is there a cat out here?* thinks Borus. As one, the knights leap forward, shields up, swords swinging at the unsuspecting men protecting the mage.

Borus heads for the mage, knowing she is going to be the key to this battle. The mage turns, hood falling, revealing it's a woman on fire. Borus takes another step and slips on the icy ground, falling forward. He catches himself and rolls, popping back up, but not soon enough. Sir Willet charges the mage; he raises his sword and is blasted by a column of fire. The knight's body disintegrates into a pile of ash. Borus gasps in shock.

The mage hears the gasp and sends the column of deadly fire in Borus's direction. Borus gets his shield up just in time. The shield is charged with Jules's magic. Borus can feel it heating up, but for now his brother's magic is working. Borus advances toward the mage, protecting himself with the shield as much as possible. A knight approaches the mage from behind while she is distracted by Borus. Borus steps sideways, trying to keep her focus on him. He takes a second step and his foot slides out from underneath him on another patch of ice. A growl escapes from Borus as he drops his sword and almost loses his shield, but he catches himself.

The mage laughs and screams shrilly, "You're mine now, little knight!" She takes a step toward Borus and sends a wall of fire too large for his shield to block. When it's inches away from him, the wave disappears. Borus shudders and looks at the mage and sees a sword jutting through her slumped body.

Suddenly the remaining fires go out, leaving the knights in almost complete darkness.

"*No!*" They hear a shout coming deeper from the forest and a crashing sound.

Greg pulls his sword from the mage and walks over to Borus, offering him a hand. "You are lucky I was here; otherwise, you would have ended up like Sir Willet did, dust." Borus takes the offered hand to stand, then sheathes his sword and inspects his shield. The shield is completely black. He offers it to Greg. As he grabs hold of it, the shield breaks into pieces and falls to the ground.

Borus whistles. "I guess now we know how close I was to being charred."

Greg shakes his head. "Too close. This mage was definitely well trained."

Jules listens to the retelling of the battle against the mage, his worry growing. "The powerful column of fire means it was a master fire mage trained in battle magic."

Sir Oweyn looks at Jules. "Can you explain why that's a problem?"

Jules nods. "I am a journeyman; so is my father. It's a level of experience where you know how to use your magic but have either not been taught or are not capable of the complex spells that a master mage can do. At the master mage level a mage can choose to specialize. One specialty is battle magic. In Etria, the high mage is the most powerful mage we have. Currently, High Mage Ivy, the head of Onaxx Academy, is the only one in Etria.

A mage like the one you went up against has been training for years. Theoretically I have also been training for years, but I am only a journeyman mage. My knowledge and skill level are very far beneath that of Blackwell's mage. They also now know that I am here too."

Lord Commander Urich asks the question he knows the others are wanting the answer to. "Since you are not a master battle mage, how can we use the skills you do have to help us?"

Jules tugs at his lip, considering. "I think the best option is if I can put spells into the crystals Master Brixx sent for me. The large fist-sized ones I can set at the watchtowers. They can be activated from the wall with a special word. Meaning you won't need me to be present for them to work." The lord commander raises his eyebrow. "I'm sure it sounds strange, but I have developed some spells with Master Brixx and Master Efaris that can be activated from a significant distance by a non-mage. The spells can create a defensive wall of ice, random lightning, or ice shards if an enemy crosses the threshold, a wall of fog, and so forth. I cannot tie multiple types of spells to the same crystals, but I can create several sets for the same locations with different functions. The largest concern is time. We don't know how much time we will have before the next attack. The more time I have, the more powerful and longer-lasting the spells I can put in items will be. I can also consult with Master Brixx using the magic mirror he gave me for this purpose. There might be additional spells that will be helpful that I'm not aware of."

Sighing, Lord Commander Urich responds. "For the moment we need as much help as we can get, assuming the next attack is coming in an hour or two."

"I will warn you I can put the distance spell together in two sets of stones in that amount of time. However, it will drain me completely to work that fast. I'll need a full twelve hours before I should use my magic again," says Jules.

Borus is about to protest the decision, but Jules silences him with a shake of his head. Borus takes a deep breath. "Very well, let's get started. When you're done, I'll make sure you can rest in your room without being disturbed."

Two hours later, an exhausted Jules, sitting in his room, peers into the magic mirror.

"It's good to see you, Jules. I just wish it were under better circumstances," says Master Brixx.

Jules sighs tiredly. "I know. The battle-trained master fire mages scare me," he reveals.

Maser Brixx debates if he should say his next words, afraid to push Jules too hard. Taking a deep breath, he decides to go for it.

"Jules, you are at least as strong as they are, even without formal training. You may not want to believe it, but it is true…if you want, you can even become a high mage."

Jaw dropping, Jules just stares at his instructor incredulously. It takes him a few minutes to gather himself to actually speak. "A high mage?" he whispers, eyes huge.

Master Brixx nods, wishing he could be there to talk to Jules in person, not through a mirror. "If you want to become one, yes. The choice is up to you; it always will be. My point is that yes, you are going against a master-level battle mage…but you are capable of doing so. You just have to believe in yourself, as the others around you already do. I know this is a lot to digest and you do need to rest to regain your strength. If you have the opportunity and decide you want to continue you your training, just contact me through the mirror, and I will find a way to continue your training from a distance."

Jules's eyes start to droop. He yawns and then blushes. "Thank you, Master Brixx. I will consider your words. For now, I need to go to sleep. Good night." Master Brixx nods and the mirrors go dark. Jules yawns again and then slides under the covers on his bed and falls asleep instantly.

Weeks pass without any movement from Blackwell's troops, allowing Jules the time he needs to finish putting all the spells in the crystals and start daily advanced training with Master Brixx.

To pass the time and keep them both on their toes, Borus and Jules practice together twice a week. At the lord commander's request, Jules is experimenting with integrating more battle magic into his sword work. Occasionally, Geff, Kristoff, Thomas, or some of the other officers will join in, making the battle two on one or two on two.

One morning when Jules is just leaving the training yard, Prince Geff jogs over to him.

"There you are!" the prince says breathlessly.

Jules frowns at the prince. "Do you need something, Your Highness?"

At the title, Geff rolls his eyes. "I thought I told you to just call me Geff." Jules shrugs and waits for the prince to speak again. "I need to apologize to you. Not for me, but for my father. By sending you here, he put you in a position that no fourteen-year-old should be asked to be in. You have been invaluable to us here, but I wanted you to know that it is not a position I would have put you in, if it was my choice."

Jules blushes and begins shuffling his feet around, "Ummm... thank you? Your...Geff," he says, quickly correcting himself.

Geff gives him a smile. "I know I have been friends with your brothers longer than I have known you, but I do value your friendship too, Jules. If there is anything you ever need, don't hesitate to ask."

"Geff?" Borus calls from the stairs into the fort. Geff turns at Borus's voice, then glances at Jules. "Sorry. I forgot I have a meeting with Sir Gregory. I'll see you later." Geff gives Jules's arm a quick squeeze before walking toward Borus on the steps.

Not too long after Geff talks to Jules, he finds himself sitting in the office of Sir Gregory with Borus and Kristoff.

"I asked the three of you here so we can discuss what is happening over the next few months. Borus, of course, must return to Burmstone for his knight test at the end of the spring. There is also the matter of Prince Richard's wedding."

Geff frowns. Borus pats his friend's hand. "You know Richard will never forgive you if you miss his wedding."

Geff sighs. "I know...I just don't think I'm ready to go back yet."

"Then it's good you won't need to return for at least another four months. Borus and I will be going back a few days before his test. You're welcome to come with us if you'd like," Greg explains.

Geff nods. "I would like that."

Kristoff clears his throat. "Do I get a choice where I go?"

"As a matter of fact, yes, you do," Greg says with a smile.

"Then I'd like to join you as well. I want to be there for Borus's test as well as for the wedding," Kristoff declares.

"Very good then. I will let the lord commander know."

On the very last day of fall in Port Riverdale, Kass is walking from the barracks toward the dining hall.

"Lewis!" Kass yells and runs toward his friend and fellow third-year squire. They hug, grinning. "I wasn't expecting to see you here!"

Lewis smiles. "I know, I was trying to surprise you. See, it worked—you're surprised!"

Kass laughs. "Yes, I am surprised. C'mon, lunch is about to be served." Kass leads the way to the dining hall.

Once they have made their food selections, they sit down. Kass grabs a piece of his roll and tears it in half. "Lewis, how long are you here for?"

Lewis replies with his mouth full. "Im grrr frrr feee."

Kass punches him lightly. "I can't understand you."

Lewis rolls his eyes and finishes chewing. "I'm here for at least five weeks. Possibly longer. Do you get to go to Burmstone for the wedding?"

Kass shrugs. "No idea yet. Sir Alane wants to go back, but that will depend on what Emberwood decides…Borus's knight test is coming up, too, but it hasn't been mentioned if I'm allowed to go for that, either. The Wolf thinks Borus is going to test for his full sword master title, too. I'd like to be there if that's true."

Lewis nods. If it were his brother and best friend, he would want to be there, too.

8

SPRING 608

Borus glances at the cards in his hand, then around the table. He still can't believe they're all together in one place. Kass and Lewis, seventeen and a few weeks from being fourth-year squires; Kristoff, a twenty-year-old knight; and Borus's other year-mates, Urlo, Hereward, and Theo, also eighteen or almost eighteen and soon to be knights.

Kristoff sees Borus looking around the table and grins. "It's been a while, hasn't it? Since we've all been in the same place." The others all nod.

Borus smiles back. "We did all choose this life."

Urlo quirks his eyebrow up. "Maybe you were given a choice… my parents told me this is what I was going to do, so I did it."

Kass smirks. "I guess your parents are lucky that you are good at it then, otherwise they'd be mourning your death by now."

Urlo sighs and drops his eyes back to his cards.

"Whose turn is it?" asks Hereward.

Theo rolls his eyes. "It's your turn."

Hereward's eyes open wide. "Oh! That's why no one is going…"
Borus and Kass laugh. Hereward sticks his tongue out at them.

After four days of travel, Sir Oweyn and Jules make it back to Ironhaven, the city Burmstone Palace is in. At the Y in the road where travelers can go either up to Burmstone Palace or into the city, they stop.

Sir Oweyn looks at Jules. "Go see your parents. They are staying at Stone House. If I don't see you before the wedding, then I hope you enjoy our short stay."

Jules gives his knight master a quick salute. "I'll see you in a few days." Smiling, he clucks to Bo, and they take off at a trot into Ironhaven.

Jules settles Bo in the small stable at Stone House before walking inside. He hears a gasp and something dropping.

"Jules!" his mother shrieks in excitement. "I wasn't expecting to see you today." Diana pulls him into a hug and then takes a step back, realizing he's now taller than her. "You're growing up," she says with a smile.

Jules shrugs. "That does happen," he says quietly.

Diana pulls him in for another hug. "Do I get to keep you until the wedding?"

Jules opens his mouth before shutting it, debating his next words. He really wants to find Ella, but knows he owes his mother some of his time, at least. "I can at least stay the night," he replies with a smile.

Diana's eyes twinkle in excitement. "Wonderful…there are some things I've been wanting to discuss with you, but it always seems that as soon as I have time, you're off on another assignment. Come on, let's get you some food and then we can talk." Diana grabs her son's hand and leads him into the kitchen.

Later, Jules, completely stuffed, is sitting in the parlor with his mother. "What did you want to talk about?" he asks, almost reluctantly.

Hearing his tone, Diana smiles gently at him. "I am not here to interrogate you. But as your mother, there are things we must discuss about your future. I know you are really close with Princess Ellandre. You are young enough still that you might not know if you love her or are just good friends. It is important that you remember we are minor nobility in Etria. What status we do have has been hard earned by your grandfather and other more distant relatives through their prowess on the battlefield. A princess, who is one of the direct heirs to Etria, may not be an option, should you wish to marry." Jules is about to say something, but Diana holds up her hand to silence him. "I am not saying you cannot ask, only that usually a princess marries a suitor who can offer something to the kingdom."

Jules takes a deep breath to steady his thoughts. "I think...I think I love her. The queen is aware we are friends and has been chaperoning when we are together. I am definitely not ready yet to ask for Ella's hand in marriage, but I think...I think the queen will help me if that is what Ella and I want."

Diana reaches for Jules's hand and squeezes it. "I am glad to know that you have at least been thinking about it, and what it means to be friends with a princess. I just don't want you to assume that if you decide to ask for Ella's hand that it will automatically be a yes. Your father and I will support your decision, but King Renard, as her father and ruler of Etria, has the final say."

"I know," whispers Jules. He closes his eyes for a moment. "I'm glad to be here, to have this time with you. It is a nice change from being at Southwind Fort."

The night before Prince Richard and Duchess Sunette's wedding is a banquet for guests that are close friends and family. With the Wolf as one of King Renard's advisors and the three Wolfensberger brothers close friends with the groom, it comes as no surprise they were given an invitation, much to the dismay of Kass and Borus.

As the evening winds down, various guests trickle out of the banquet hall. Two such guests, Jules and Ella, have snuck into the royal stable.

"You know we're going to get into trouble if we're caught," Jules whispers, glancing around nervously.

The princess shrugs. "Mother knows…maybe not that we're out right now, but she knows…"

"Ella, I'm not worried about your mother," Jules hisses.

Ella pulls Jules into the open stall next to them. "You talk too much," she murmurs and tentatively kisses him.

A door slams shut at the far end of the stable. They both jump and their foreheads bang together.

Jules winces. "Sorry."

"Ella?" They can hear the queen calling from outside the barn. Sighing, Ella brushes off a few bits of hay.

"Duty calls," she mutters, before giving Jules a quick kiss on the cheek and heading out of the barn to her mother alone.

In an extra room not too far from the banquet hall, Kass sits at a round table with Borus and Urlo. *Creeeeaaaaaakkk.* The door opens. Geff pokes his head around it and grins.

Eyes wide, Borus sees Geff first. "How on earth did you manage to sneak over here?"

"Trust me, I have lots of practice. Tomorrow, since it's the day of the wedding, I won't be allowed to escape. The queen made me promise." Geff rolls his eyes. "Mostly, I think she wants me to be on display as an eligible husband."

Kass shudders. "Have fun with that."

Geff covers his mouth to hide a smile. "Your mother hasn't gotten after you yet about a wife?"

Borus glances at Kass, taking in his stiff posture, and decides to reply to the prince. "Nope. Besides, I don't think we've had time to be around potential wives yet. We both spent the past eight years in places that don't have very many ladies."

Geff grins at Borus. "I can help you with that if you want tomorrow?"

Borus shrugs. "Sure, why not? Might as well have some fun before I get sent off somewhere. What do you think, Urlo? Want to hit the dance floor tomorrow?"

"Absolutely!" Urlo stands up and pulls Borus out of his chair, then tries to spin him.

Borus takes a few steps and then stumbles, laughing. "Oooh you've got some skills, that's for sure. Skills at helping people fall."

"Hey, it's not my fault *you* don't know how to spin properly," retorts Urlo.

"Maybe it's because the girls are the ones that spin, not the boys. Want me to spin you?" Borus says, grinning and taking a step toward Urlo.

Urlo throws his hands up. "I'll pass."

Geff rolls his eyes and looks at Kass. Kass smirks and shakes his head.

True to his word, during the wedding banquet and evening festivities, Geff introduces Borus and Urlo to many noblewomen that would be considered "suitable wives." Borus catches his mother's eye a couple of times as he's dancing with various noble ladies.

There is a pause in the music. Prince Richard decides to take a break from dancing for a bit and mingle with some of the guests. He looks around and sees his new wife, Sunette, talking to his father at the edge of the dance floor.

As the prince is walking toward an open chair, someone brushes hastily past him.

"Watch it," he grumbles.

"Sorry," mutters Kass, before turning around when he recognizes the voice as Richard's. Kass turns to gaze at the prince, a smile slowly forming. "Congratulations, Richard."

Taking a deep breath, Richard smiles back. "Thank you, Kass. It means a lot to me that you're here."

Just as Kass is about to say something else, the queen walks up.

"Can I have a dance?" the queen asks, smiling at her oldest son.

Richard nods. Kass bows to both of them and walks away. Richard offers his arm to his mother. They walk onto the dance floor.

Two days before the official start of summer, and a week before his eighteenth birthday, Borus rolls over and falls out of bed with a thud. Groaning, he stands up and stretches. Sir Gregory has given Borus this day to himself. News from the north also just arrived informing King Renard and those in residence at Burmstone Palace of King Bokur's death. His death means Prince Kabili, Princess Phaedra's, husband will soon be crowned king of Wanonia.

Borus looks out his window. The early dawn light is filtering through the trees. He sighs. So much for sleeping in. After months of patrolling and sleeping on the ground where rolling didn't involve falling, it comes as no surprise he ended up on the floor. Borus gets dressed in a worn but comfortable tunic, pants, and boots. He grabs his bow, quiver, and sword in the scabbard and heads out toward the training yards.

Borus arrives at the archery yard and waves to Theo. Unlike Borus, Theo did not end up at Southwind Fort for any of his time as a squire. Instead, Theo spent much of his time traveling along the coast and at Port Riverdale, lending support for smaller skirmishes with bandits and aiding in the rebuilding efforts after Sapphire Coast Fort was destroyed. Theo has his crossbow. He left his standard bow back in his room.

Theo raises his eyebrow as Borus strings his bow. "I can't believe you're going to practice archery!"

Borus chuckles. "I know it must seem strange to you, but I do actually know how to use this thing," Borus says. To prove his point, he nocks an arrow, takes aim, and looses, aiming for the target set at forty yards. The arrow lands with a thud in the center. Borus smirks and repeats the feat twice more.

"Wow, I didn't realize you could shoot, too!"

"I am not going to claim to be as good as Kass, but yes, I can shoot a target from a sizeable distance." Borus reaches to the back of his belt and pulls out something shiny and small. "Have you ever seen these before?" Borus asks offering the items to Theo.

"No…what is it?"

Borus keeps one back. He moves over to a target at ten yards, sets his feet, positions the object properly, and then throws it. It lands with a thud in the target.

"Is that some weird type of throwing knife?" Theo queries.

Borus nods. "Yes, it is. It's from Wanonia. Some of their assassins favor throwing knives like these. One of the men in Sir Gregory's squad spent almost ten years in Wanonia and taught me how to use them. I was able to talk the blacksmith at Southwind Fort into making me a set. You never know when they'll come in handy. I've had some small sheaths made so I can strap them to my arms and legs if I need to go somewhere and appear to be unarmed."

Borus puts the knives back in their sheaths and both soon-to-be-knights slip into a comfortable silence, broken only by the occasional thud of arrows and bolts hitting the targets. They both run out of bolts and arrows at the same time. As they're removing them from the targets, Roger walks up.

"Borus, Theo," Roger says with a sneer.

"Hello, Roger," Borus replies, keeping his voice neutral.

"How are things in the north?" Theo asks, chiming in.

Roger looks at Theo. "Normal."

"Okaaay…are you going to practice some?" Theo says. Theo glances at Borus and notices how he's shifted from his best friend into a warrior.

Roger removes his bow from his shoulder and strings it, glancing sideways at Borus. "I heard a rumor up north, about Prince Geffrey attacking his father for no reason. They say the prince broke the king's arm in his fit of rage."

Borus growls and launches himself at Roger. Theo isn't quick enough to grab Borus before he punches Roger in the face. *Crunch!* A sickening sound as Roger's nose breaks and sprays both Roger and Borus with blood.

Theo grabs Borus, pulling his arms behind him and whispering in his ear, "Leave it, Borus! You know he's lying about Geff." Borus struggles against Theo's arms.

Roger, holding a handkerchief to his nose, laughs maniacally.

"Go away, Roger, before I finish what Borus started," Theo hisses.

Roger laughing, grabs his bow and walks away.

The day next day Theo, Borus, Urlo, Hereward, Roger, and the other fourth-year squires successfully complete their knight tests. In the evening, the royal family holds the knighting ceremony, presided over by King Renard. Borus retires early, wanting extra time to prepare for his sword master test the following morning.

He has been given a private room to warm up. The test itself will be in one of the viewing galleries. Sir Gregory already warned him they expect many people in the audience. With the frequency of banquets and parties the royal family has been hosting there are a lot of nobles residing in Burmstone Palace and nearby within Ironhaven. Borus is the youngest knight in the known history of Etria to take the sword master test.

Early the next morning, Borus goes through his warmup drills, starting without his sword and then with the sword. Due to the elite nature of the sword master test, there are several phases. The first is where the contestant demonstrates high proficiency with a traditional-style sword. For the second phase, the contestant is allowed to either continue with the same sword or select a different weapon. The caveat is that the sword master the contestant is sparring against is also permitted to change weapons for the second phase. Borus won't know until he steps into the ring which sword master he will be going against. The only one he knows it for sure won't be is the Wolf.

Sir Gregory interrupts Borus's warmup. "It's time."

Borus nods.

"Remember, focus on your opponent and ignore everything else. I know you are ready," Sir Gregory reminds Borus as they walk down the hallway and enter the gallery.

Borus finally looks up at the crowd and gulps. There are over a hundred people! He closes his eyes and turns toward the ring, then opens them and walks inside and over to the weapon rack. He examines it to make sure everything is in order. Once he has confirmed it is, he takes his traditional-style sword off the rack and walks to the center.

Sir John Waldorf, the knight in charge of Trinity Page and Squire School, steps in front of the audience. "Ladies and gentlemen. Today we gather to witness Sir Borus Wolfensberger take the sword master test. The sword master conducting the test today is Lord Armand of Tarna."

Borus almost drops his sword when he hears Lord Armand's name. He was not expecting the man who started training him almost eight years ago in his first year as a page to go against him in the test. With Borus's assignment in the south, they haven't seen each other in almost four years.

Lord Armand smiles and walks over to face Borus. They shake hands.

"Good luck," Lord Armand says and bows. Borus bows and plasters a smile on his face, trying to hide his nerves.

"Ready? Start!" says Sir Waldorf, projecting his voice so everyone can hear him.

The details Sir Gregory gave Borus on how the sword master tests work were rather vague. The most important piece, though, is that it is not a drill. It is a test of Borus's skills. Although he does need to pace himself because of the two phases, he should not hold back. Unlike most of the sparring Borus does with his friends, his opponent would be as good as or better than he is.

Borus strikes first, going low. Armand blocks it easily, pivots, and strikes high. Borus parries and strikes low again. Armand twists his hand as he's parrying, causing Borus to almost drop his sword. Borus adjusts his grip on his sword and changes strategies. He rolls and pops up behind Armand. He starts the dragon, a combination move that Armand had taught him. Armand spins, blocking the strike. Armand takes several steps back, swaps his sword to his left hand, and charges at Borus. Borus slides to the side and brings his sword up, meeting Armand's. The swords become a blur as both men increase the speed.

A whistle blows. Borus jumps, startled, and Armand's sword slices across his arm. "Sorry," Armand says hastily.

Sir Waldorf walks over to them. "Phase one is over. You can have a five-minute break, then phase two will start. Remember, you are both allowed to change weapons for this phase if you choose to do so."

Armand walks over to his weapon rack and sets down his sword, then sits in a chair. Someone offers him a glass of water. He takes it gratefully. A couple of friends come over, wanting to talk, but Armand shakes his head. It took Borus a while to get comfortable going against his former instructor. Armand is not surprised at that. Borus has never had a competitive nature. While Armand has been anticipating Borus would request the sword master testing immediately after his knighting, Armand was not expecting how much better Borus has become. His skill is well beyond that from four years ago. Originally, Armand's plan has been to dual-wield swords for the second phase. Now, he's not sure about that choice. He looks at the weapons on the rack. Two traditional swords, a broadsword, a double-headed axe, and two short- handled axes. The whistle blows. Time is up. Armand grabs his broadsword and heads over to the center of the ring.

Borus meets Armand at the middle. His arm now sports a bandage. Borus slips his second sword into his other hand so they can once again shake hands.

"Are you OK?" Armand asks, eyeing Borus's arm.

Borus shrugs. "It's just a scratch. Don't worry about me."

Armand sighs. "I am sorry."

Sir Waldorf speaks so all can hear, "Phase two. Lord Armand has chosen a broadsword, and Sir Borus has chosen to dual-wield swords."

A collective gasp goes through the crowd. Most have no idea Sir Borus can dual-wield, let alone be skilled enough to do so during his sword master test.

Sir Waldorf glances at the Wolf. The Wolf shrugs. Sir Waldorf's gaze falls on Sir Gregory next, who smiles. Shaking his head, Sir Waldorf yells "Begin!" and then returns to his seat.

Fortunately for Borus, months ago at Southwind Fort, when he mentioned possibly dual-wielding for phase two, Sir Gregory had insisted they begin specialized training together. Even though Sir Gregory never officially tested for the sword master title, he is just as skilled as most of them. He is also familiar with what weapons the various sword masters favor. The specialized training forced Borus to be comfortable dual-wielding—and not just against anyone with a standard sword. Sir Gregory introduced Borus to dual-wielding against swords and axes of all shapes and sizes. Sometimes they would even practice two on one. Ultimately, Sir Gregory left the final decision up to Borus, but he suspected Borus would go ahead with the decision to dual-wield in phase two.

Borus swings both swords in a complex maneuver. He feints to the left, and then increases his speed before initiating his strike.

116

Armand leaps to the side, narrowly missing a slice to his face. Bringing the broadsword up, he tries to break Borus's momentum to regain the advantage. Both knights are spinning and jumping in a blur of steel. The audience has difficulty following everything. Armand finally gets his balance, and they seem evenly matched. Neither one gains ground without also giving some up.

Sweat is dripping down Armand's forehead. He changes his grip on the broadsword so he can wipe his face. Borus is waiting for this precise moment. He twists his left sword and does a backhand strike at the broadsword followed by a second strike with his right sword. With only a single hand gripping the broadsword, Armand is not able to stop it from popping out of his hand and clattering to the ground.

The whistle blows. Armand grins and grabs Borus in a hug. "Well done. Very well done!"

Borus stands there, still holding both swords, stunned. *I did it! I actually did it!* A cheer goes up from the crowd. Queen Vivienne, quickly followed by the rest of the royal family and the audience, stands and claps.

Borus turns toward the audience, blushing. *A standing ovation? Was the fight really that impressive?* His gaze settles on the Wolf. The Wolf offers a brief smile; his parents are standing behind the Wolf, beaming.

King Renard walks over to Borus. Borus bows deeply. "Your Majesty."

The king holds out his hand, and Sir Waldorf hands him a sword in a black scabbard. The king runs his hands over it, then bows and offers the sword to Borus. "Sir Borus, congratulations on being worthy of the title sword master. Take this sword and use it well."

Borus bows again and takes the sword. "Thank you for the opportunity, Your Majesty."

Many people walk up to Borus and offer him their congratulations. Finally, the one person he is waiting for walks up.

The Wolf smiles at Borus and hugs him, whispering, "Well done, Borus, very well done."

Borus smiles back. "I would not be here if it wasn't for you, Grandfather."

The Wolf shakes his head. "That's not true. You made your dream happen. You put in the effort and made it here today because of you." The Wolf gives Borus one last squeeze and then slips out of the crowd.

"Are you ready?" Lars asks one last time.

"Yes, I already told you." Roger's freshly healed nose is still red from the healer's magic. "Our plan is falling into place. I finalized the last pieces that required me to be here at the palace; now we can go north to Sneg, and wait."

Roger mounts his horse, takes one last glance at Burmstone Palace, and spits.

"Let's go," Lars says and clucks to his horse. The last thing he needs is for Roger to get into another fight and blow his carefully laid plans.

9

FALL 608

After Prince Richard's wedding to Duchess Sunette, King Renard begins to include the prince in more of the day-to-day affairs of Etria, including his council meetings. On the first day of fall, King Renard and Prince Richard are in a council meeting with several of the king's advisors, including Sir Waldorf, Knight Commander Emberwood, and the Wolf.

Emberwood speaks. "I think it would be wise to send Prince Geffrey to Wanonia. With King Kabili settling into his throne, we must reinforce our desire to continue with peace between our countries. It will also give the prince a chance to learn more about Wanonia and meet his nephew and niece."

King Renard is surprised by the suggestion to send Geff. "Why the prince? Why not the Wolf or yourself?"

"The Wolf or I will likely raise some questions to whether or not we are being truthful about our desire to stay at peace, being that we are both seasoned commanders with decades of experience. The prince is less likely to be perceived as a threat, and I am sure he would enjoy visiting his sister," Emberwood explains. The Wolf nods in agreement.

King Renard considers the idea. *Is this trip going to push Geff even further away? Or will it help mend our relationship?* "The prince cannot go alone. Who will go with him?" asks the king, wanting more information before deciding if the trip will happen or not.

Sir Waldorf responds. "I have a list of possibilities. Sir Kristoff was with the prince at Southwind Fort. I know he is friends with the prince, as are Sir Hereward and Sir Borus. I know Emberwood has a list of knights with more experience. I think it is importance that the prince has some friends with him so it doesn't feel like a punishment. You were blessed with four children, allowing us to use the younger ones to help strengthen our ties with our allies. One day, Prince Geffrey could be leading our allies into battle. If they can get a measure for who he is now, he will be an even greater asset to us in the future. However, we also must ensure he has adequate protection without making us unwelcome. I think a squad to stay in Wanonia with the prince and a squad acting as escort only that will return to Etria would be prudent."

Emberwood nods. "I was thinking around the same number of people, and I do have a list of additional knights." He passes his list over to the king.

Taking his time to review the list, the king is also able to consider the idea in more depth. Allowing Geff to become well known by the Wanonians is a good, sound strategy with many benefits for Etria.

"I like the idea for this trip and the list of squad members for the protection detail," King Renard says, passing the list back. "I trust you will get this in motion? I'd like them to depart in three days. Adjourned." The king stands, gathers his paperwork, and heads out of the room toward his private quarters.

Three days later, Prince Geffrey, Sir Borus, Sir Kristoff, Sir Hereward, Sir Horton, Sir Adrian, and Sir Thomas—along with three other knights Borus has never met before but who seem to know the prince, and a squad of knights led by Sir Caradoc—head down the road. The council decided the group will travel most of the way with everyone wearing plain leather armor. When they get within a day's ride of the city of Sonkou, where King Kabili's Tsagaan Palace is, they have been instructed to raise the prince's standard.

"Are you ready for this?" Borus asks Geff.

The prince shrugs. "I guess…I really do miss seeing my sister. It just feels like Father is trying to parade me around when it's convenient for him. I suppose at least he can't continue to hound me about finding a wife if I'm not in the same country."

The group is riding with two knights in front and behind as scouts and everyone else in a loose group. Behind Geff and Borus, Kristoff laughs. Geff turns around just in time to see Kristoff almost topple out of the saddle. Hereward grabs his arm and hauls him back into the saddle, rolling his eyes.

"I didn't think it was that funny!" Kristoff straightens himself out.

"You don't? Hey, Geff! Did you know that every single one of us going with you is currently unwed and not betrothed?"

The prince shakes his head.

Borus smirks. "Are you sure your parents didn't send your sister a secret message about finding all ten of us wives?"

The prince reaches over and punches Borus lightly in the shoulder. "Yes, because Phaedra would never agree to something like that. I am sure, though, that she will help us set up training sessions to learn new styles of fighting, possibly even try new weapons, and meet other people our age that are part of the Wanonian cavalry."

For Kass's first three years as a squire, he and Sir Alane have been assigned to Port Riverdale. Today, Sir Alane receives orders to report to Sapphire Coast Fort. This will be the first time Kass has set foot in the fort since 601, when Borus and Kass saved Prince Richard and Prince Geffrey from an attack that started the war with Wanonia.

The villages along the Sapphire Coast between Port Riverdale and the fort have long been targets favored by pirates. With the treaty between Etria and Wanonia, the pirate raids have increased in number, but the quality of pirates has declined. Lately, it seems as though any privately owned boat or ship can be borrowed for a price. Unfortunately for the owners of the boats, the men who wish to be pirates know even less about sailing and end up crashing into the shoreline before they can raid any of the coast towns.

The fort serves as a watchtower for Port Riverdale and provides support to the coastal villages between the fort and port. Kass's status as a fourth-year squire means he gets sent out on patrols every three days. Sometimes Sir Alane is with Kass; others, Kass is assigned to another officer or knight.

"Kass, I want you to accompany a squad to check on Eagle Bluff. One of those pirate ships seems to be heading there. A show of force seems to be the key to discouraging them this year." Sir Alane shows Kass the map and points to where Eagle Bluff is. Many of the small villages are difficult to distinguish from one another and half of them are set on the cliffs above the ocean. Kass bows and heads out to talk to Captain Cyril, one of the squad leaders. With the war against Wanonia over for several years, squads stationed at the fort are a mix of knights and light cavalry. Captain Cyril's squad is solely light cavalry.

Kass knocks on the door to the barracks housing Captain Cyril's squad. "Captain?" calls Kass as he steps inside the door. He hears some bumping and a big thud before a muffled "Give me a minute!" comes from the back. Kass stands staring at a knot in the wood on the floor until he hears footsteps. The captain walks up with a book and a disorderly handful of papers.

"What can I help you with, squire?" the captain says and drops the papers and book on the desk in a heap.

"I was asked to bring you orders. I am supposed to go with your squad to Eagle Bluff as a show of force to scare off some pirates. We are to leave within the hour." Kass glances around the barracks again and hears some more bumping and shuffling of papers around in the back. "I will meet you and your men in the yard in an hour." Kass bows and leaves quickly. He's not sure if the captain is just reorganizing old files or something else. Kass crosses the yard and goes back into the fort to collect his gear and Mist from his room.

Once in his room, Kass puts on his chain mail, selects a helmet, and gathers his yew bow and two full quivers of arrows. He ties the leather shoulder and wrist guards on over the top of his mail. Both were designed to allow Mist or any other hawk he's working with to land on him. With one more look around the room to make sure he hasn't forgotten anything important, he departs and heads out to the stable. His black-and-white horse and the rest of the squad's horses are saddled and tied to the hitching posts. Kass walks over to his horse and ties his bow and quivers to the saddle and sets Mist on the small platform attached to the back of his saddle.

As Kass is untying his horse from the post, Captain Cyril and his squad file out of the barracks and begin untying their horses. Everyone mounts, and Kass falls in next to Captain Cyril with the squad following behind them in a double column. The captain looks at Mist curiously. "What do you do with the hawk?"

"Mist? I've been working with her on scouting. We have a signal she gives if there are people ahead that don't belong to our group. She also will attack on command, and I can give her things to drop."

"Things to drop?" the captain echoes.

Kass reaches into the pouch behind him and pulls out a rock and a small pouch. "Like these." Kass offers the two items to Cyril.

Cyril takes them and sniffs the pouch, then sneezes. "What's in there?"

"Explosives. Mist will drop them, and I'll shoot a fire arrow, and it'll explode on the target."

Cyril looks at him skeptically and hands back the rock and pouch. "You'd need to be able to shoot with incredible accuracy. I'll believe it when I see it." Kass shrugs and puts away the rock and pouch. Most people don't believe in his archery skills until they see him in action.

When they're a few minutes out from Eagle Bluff, Cyril sends two of his men to dismount and scout ahead. Kass gives Mist small piece of meat; she swallows it, then jumps into the air and flies away.

The rest of the squad waits for the two scouts. Almost an hour later, they still haven't returned. Kass clears his throat. "Captain, shouldn't we…"

The captain raises his hand, silencing Kass. "I know how to do my job. We wait." Kass opens his mouth to protest. "If you don't like my orders, then you are welcome to do your own thing, squire," Cyril says with a sneer. "Just remember, if something happens, you will be on your own."

Kass sighs, debating. Finally reaching a decision, Kass checks his gear. "I will go ahead on my own."

The captain shrugs. "You'll see. There's nothing to be worried about."

Kass scans the sky looking for Mist before clucking to his horse and heading down the road. When he's sure he's out of sight of the squad, Kass halts his horse and strings his bow, pulling several arrows out. He drops his reins, using only his legs to guide his horse.

There's a loud screeching sound from the sky as Mist drops into a dive a short way ahead of Kass. Her signal that people who don't belong are ahead. Cursing, Kass squeezes his horse, and they leap into a gallop. Mist pulls out of her dive and circles Kass before flying ahead of him to lead the way. Kass gallops down the road until they reach the path heading toward Eagle Bluff. Without missing a stride or slowing, the horse turns onto the path and keeps going. Kass can see smoke up ahead. Urging his horse to go even faster, Kass almost misses the dead men on the side of the path. The horse slides to a stop and Kass jumps off, bow ready as he creeps over to the light cavalry scouts. A quick inspection shows that they were attacked from behind. Possibly with throwing knives.

Knowing there's nothing he can do for them now, Kass climbs back onto his horse and keeps heading toward the village.

There's a whirring sound and then a dark streak as Mist hits something with her talons. Kass murmurs thanks to her and decides it's time to get off the horse. He's making himself too easy of a target.

Kass slings one of his quivers over his back, pockets some of the explosive pouches and stones, and slowly creeps around the first home at the edge of the village. Smoke is pouring out of several of the houses, filling the road running down the middle with gray clouds. Kass sees a dark shape running toward him and quickly nocks an arrow and shoots. He whistles for Mist and tosses one of the small rocks in the air; she catches it in her talons and disappears out of sight.

Thud, thud.

Kass jumps as two Wanonian-style throwing knives hit the fence post next to him. *Not just people playing pirate*, he thinks. Kass nocks another arrow and rounds a corner. Another dark shape comes running toward him. Without hesitation, Kass releases the arrow. The person it hits lets out a scream. Pounding footsteps rush into the road in the center of the village.

Knives start flying through the air.

"*Ahhhhh!*" a woman screams from the middle of the village.

Kass feels a whisper of feathers overhead and gets an idea. He lets out whistle, and Mist appears out of the smoke and lands on his fist. He gives her a small treat. "Good girl," Kass says taking a moment to stroke her feathers. He takes one of the explosive pouches out of his pocket and shows it to her. Mist lifts one of her talons. Kass delicately offers the pouch to the raised talon, careful to not slice his fingers on it. Kass offers Mist a second pouch, allowing the hawk to decide how she wants to carry it. Mist takes the second one in her beak and pushes off from his arm.

Now for the tricky part. Kass pulls out two fire arrows from the quiver and creeps around the house he's hiding behind, closer to the center of the village. Watching the air above the road, Kass waits for Mist to drop the first pouch. She does—from much higher than Kass was expecting. He does a quick calculation, lights the arrow, waits a moment, and then shoots. The arrow and the pouch disappear in the billowing smoke.

Boom!

Kass feels something weird on his cheek. He reaches up with the hand holding the extra arrow and touches his face. His fingers come away sticky. "What the..."

Another knife sails through the air toward his face. Kass brings up the bow just in time and blocks the throwing knife, causing it to fall to the ground.

Scanning the sky again, Kass sees Mist drop the second pouch. Another knife flies toward his face, Kass tucks and rolls. His arm stings. "Mist!" he mutters and quickly lights the second fire arrow and shoots it toward the middle again, hoping he didn't screw things up. Kass rolls to the side; another knife thuds into the wall he was in front of moments before.

Boom! Boom! Boom!

The ground shakes as the middle of the village goes up in flames and debris sails through the air. *Thud, thud.* Sharp pieces of wood and metal pepper the buildings. Kass looks around for Mist. Hoping she was out of range before the explosion.

A slight breeze picks up off the ocean and helps blow away the lingering smoke. Kass scans the sky again for Mist and finally sees her circling above. Cautiously Kass edges toward the middle of the village. Bodies are strewn everywhere. Some of them are clearly the villagers, others are the pirates. After confirming all the pirates are dead, Kass goes from home to home searching for more people. His search is futile. There are no living villagers left.

Kass whistles for Mist. She glides gracefully to a fence post. Kass tosses her a whole mouse. Mist jumps to catch it in her beak and swallows the mouse before preening. Kass offers his fist, and Mist hops onto it. With one last look around him, Kass heads to find his horse. Luckily his horse comes trotting down the road toward them. Snagging the reins, Kass swings himself into the saddle, and they go back the way they came to find Captain Cyril and the rest of the squad.

As Kass reaches the main road, he pulls up sharply, eyeing the mix of hoofprints on the road. He gives Mist the hand signal to scout and then tosses her into the air. Kass once again draws his bow and pulls out some arrows, worried about what he is going to find ahead. He lets his horse continue at a slow walk down the road, wanting to give Mist time to complete her task.

A few minutes later, Mist returns. She lands on her platform and raises her wings to hide her head. "Are you sure?" Kass whispers. Mist repeats the motion. Kass strokes her feathers sadly.

A few hours later, Kass is back within Sapphire Coast Fort. Shoulders drooping, he slowly walks into the main building with Mist perched on his shoulder, his bow and quivers in his hand.

Sir Alane sees Kass coming and rushes over, smiling.

"Easy, right?" Sir Alane says.

Kass just looks at him blankly. Sir Alane's smile falls.

"They're all dead," Kass whispers, voice breaking.

Sir Alane looks at Kass in surprise. "Do I need to send men back out there?"

Kass shakes his head. "No, Mist and I took care of all of the pirates. We were too late to rescue the villagers, and…Captain Cyril…" Kass lets the words hang.

Sir Alane gets a distant look in his eyes. "I know I probably should have sent a different squad. However, all the information I had indicated it was just another group of wannabe pirates."

Kass sighs. "I am sad for the villagers and for the captain's ignorance. But I am learning that more often than not the soldiers and knights we are with do the bare minimum. Captain Cyril is an example, but there have been others."

Sir Alane nods. "You're right. The best we can do is stay true to ourselves. If others want to help, then they help. If not, then we pray that we're wrong and things don't go sideways. I am glad that your work with Mist is paying off. Falconry can be a very useful tool for those with the patience." Sir Alane grips Kass's arm, then notices some of the small slices along his face and arms. "You should have a healer look you over."

Kass nods reluctantly and departs for the healer.

Roger, now eighteen and a knight, is scowling in the middle of the ruined village of Eagle Bluff. Sir Lars is next to him.

"This should have worked," Roger says, barely able to control his anger.

"And yet, once again we have underestimated the Wolfensbergers. However, this one is all on you, Roger," Sir Lars reminds his former squire.

Roger glares at him. "It was a good plan…"

Sir Lars shakes his head. "With no contingencies in place. It is a worthy distraction for King Renard though. To keep him on his toes. Now you have seen firsthand why I still don't feel you're ready to fully plan an attack without my assistance."

Roger turns red and walks away.

Sir Lars follows him at a slower pace. "Not all plans, even the most well-laid ones, go as we hope. You must learn from your mistakes and do better next time."

"But you just said I can't plan another attack without your involvement," says Roger, confused.

Sir Lars sighs. "I meant in the immediate future. I am sure down the road, when it is clear you have learned your lesson, there will be ample opportunities for you to devise your own plans."

Roger takes a deep breath before replying, "I look forward to when the next opportunity arises."

Sir Lars removes a black stone from the pouch at his waist and brings it up to his lips. As the stone touches his lips, it disappears, and a shimmering portal opens a few feet away. As one, both men step through the portal.

Master Brixx is standing in one of the Onaxx Academy classrooms giving a lecture on magical creatures.

"Now that you understand what dragons are, we will learn about elementals. Elementals are ancient beings that were created thousands of years ago. They are a pure source of that element and extremely powerful."

One of the students, a fifth-year novice air mage, speaks out. "More powerful than a high mage?"

Master Brixx chuckles at the question. "Yes, far more powerful than a high mage. Just like with mages, there can be differences in strength among elementals. Although the weakest one that you'll read about in any of the books we have is two times stronger than a high mage, some are ten times stronger. The difficulty with elementals is that it can be almost impossible to identify them. Many can take on different shapes, such as a dragon, animal, or human. Unless they are performing great magic, in which case you are likely dead…"

The same student speaks again. "Then how does anyone even know they exist?"

"Because…" Master Brixx pauses. "Occasionally they will meddle in our affairs. Fire elementals are known to be tricksters. We have accounts of survivors from their dealings with fire elementals, including the elemental named…"

Beep! Beep! Beep! The magic portal alarm goes off, echoing throughout the classroom.

The class groans, recognizing the sound and that it means Master Brixx must leave to investigate the newest portal.

"I'm sorry, everyone. We will finish this discussion on elementals tomorrow, I promise!" Master Brixx gathers his things and rushes out the door.

On a brisk fall day, Jules is out on patrol with Sir Oweyn and two squads of knights when he hears a tinkling.

"Whoa," he says, slowing Bo down. When Bo halts, Jules reaches back into his pack and pulls out a pouch with one of the magic mirrors.

He touches the mirror, and it reveals Sir Gregory. "Jules, Blackwell is coming. You don't have enough time to reach the fort. Find somewhere to hunker down and then you can skirt around, and we'll open the rear gate."

Sir Oweyn turns his horse around and walks over to Jules. "What's going on?"

Jules puts the mirror back in his bag. "Blackwell is moving fast. We don't have time to get back without ending up trapped."

"Did you check to see if he has a mage?" Sir Oweyn inquires.

Jules shuts his eyes dropping deep into his magic and spreading out his awareness. He jumps and falls out of the saddle. "Ouch!"

Sir Oweyn jerks his reins in surprise. "What happened?"

"They know we're here...I'm here," whispers Jules from the ground, rubbing his forehead.

"Who?" asks Sir Oweyn, not sure what just happened to Jules.

"The mages," Jules says shortly and stands up, taking a deep breath.

"Mages...plural?" Sir Oweyn questions.

"Yes, two fire mages. I could see the two distinct threads of magic," Jules confirms.

Sir Oweyn looks at the two squads. "Can you look again and see if they are coming this way?"

Jules slowly shakes his head. "No. If I do that, whatever trap they set the first time will do the same thing again. They did something, so if I look for them, I get…in simple terms, attacked."

Sir Oweyn is still trying to decide what they should do when a fireball lands in the middle of the squad. Luckily, it doesn't hit anyone. But they are out of time and without a plan. There is a mass of axmen surrounding the mages running toward the knights. Jules quickly mounts Bo, wanting the added height the horse gives him. Fireballs come cascading toward the knights. Jules throws up a shimmering shield over the whole squad. At first, the fireballs roll off the shield and fizzle out. Three rounds later, they are starting to drop through the shield and into the squad.

"We're going to have to attack them. Try to eliminate the mages. Swords ready!" Sir Oweyn shouts.

Jules debates his best course of action. *This is why we practice,* he grimly reminds himself, before he drops Bo's reins and puts his staff in his left hand and sword in the right, relying on his legs only to guide his horse.

"One, two, charge!" shouts Sir Oweyn. Twenty knights and one mage-squire charge straight for the mages and the axmen defending them.

One of the fire mages puts up wall of fire. Jules douses it in a cascade of water. He spots one of the mages and sends a massive bolt of lightning through his sword straight for the mage. The mage absorbs the bolt. Jules curses at his stupidity. *Of course, lightning is much less effective with a fire mage.* Next, he tries a giant icicle. It melts in a puff of steam.

Two of the knights and their horses are burned to ash. Jules pulls Bo back and circles around, trying to give himself a chance to think before wasting the energy on another unsuccessful attack. *A wave? Maybe. A wave followed by an ice wall?* Jules holds both the sword and the staff so they are horizontal. He takes a deep breath and counts to three.

131

While, Jules is preparing his spell, Sir Oweyn and the remaining knights are struggling against the axmen. Sir Oweyn realizes his mistake. They began their attack without knowing how many men are with the mages; instead of creating a plan, they went in unprepared. Sir Gregory's warning mentioned Blackwell. It dawns on Sir Oweyn that Blackwell is here, leading these men. Suddenly, the fire mages stop their attack, and a volley of hundreds of arrows comes sailing through the air. Sir Oweyn tries to pull his shield up but isn't quick enough. Two arrows make it through his chain mail. One in his thigh, the other in his right arm. He almost drops his sword as pain shoots through his arm. Hastily, Sir Oweyn tosses his shield and puts his sword in his left hand.

Several other knights are hit by the arrows too. One sways in his saddle before sliding off.

"Jules, whatever it is you're doing, hurry!" Sir Oweyn hisses, praying his squire can hear him and is able to do something.

A cool breeze caresses Sir Oweyn's cheek. "What!" he shouts in surprise before returning his attention to the battle. Water bubbles up out of the ground, shaping itself into a wave. As the wave grows, it gains momentum. The giant wave slams into Blackwell's men, pushing them out of the way. The wind howls. The wave continues to crush Blackwell's men as it speeds through the axmen. Snow starts to fall, and the ground freezes. The wave changes direction and shifts and hardens.

Sir Oweyn sways in the saddle, shivering and feeling faint from blood loss, and grabs his horse, trying to keep himself upright.

Jules continues to channel water magic through the sword to maintain the wave. Using the staff, he channels cold air and ice, causing snow to fall and freeze. Men that were soaking wet moments ago are now freezing and turning into ice statues.

Suddenly, there's a battle horn. The fire mages are struggling to keep themselves from freezing and have stopped all attacks. Jules ceases channeling the water and launches icicles at the mages while trying to turn them into ice statues too. The battle horn sounds again.

More arrows fly through the air. A different horn sounds this time. Jules has no idea who or what else is coming their way. He prays it is Etrians from the fort and not reinforcements for Blackwell.

Bo jumps sideways as a horse runs right into them. Jules's concentration on his magic is broken. He looks around in confusion and brings his staff up just in time to block a huge double axe swinging at his neck. Jules eyes open wide as he realizes this must be Ruschmann Blackwell. The massive dark-skinned man who wields the double axe like it's a child's toy. His armor is an odd mix of leather, metal, and animal skins. Bo's battle training kicks in and without a cue from Jules he rears, striking at Blackwell with his hooves. Hands vibrating from Blackwell's blows, Jules shudders and drops his staff. The axe comes down again, and Jules hastily brings up his sword, blocking it.

As though sensing Jules is tiring, Blackwell speeds up and laughs cruelly. Jules meets the axe with his sword, blocking each strike, but he is not able to get in any strikes of his own. Sweat trickles down his arm, loosening his grip on his sword. Blackwell changes tactics and swings wide. Unable to block from this angle, Jules feels Blackwell's axe strike his back, getting stuck on the chain mail. Jules groans in pain as Blackwell yanks the axe out hard. As Jules sways dangerously in the saddle, Bo spins, throwing his head into Blackwell. Blackwell is thrown off balance on his horse.

Jules grabs onto Bo's mane, struggling to keep himself upright. Pain shoots through his back where the axe connected. *Stay awake, stay awake*, Jules thinks as waves of pain roll through his whole body. He squeezes his eyes shut and takes a deep breath, murmuring to Bo, "Good boy, good boy."

Bo reaches back with his nose and nuzzles Jules's foot. When Jules opens his eyes, he sees Blackwell coming again. Jules gets his sword up just in time and is finally able to parry. Sparks fly. Blackwell thrusts hard against the locked weapons. Jules's sword slips as he shudders in pain and Bo backs up, taking Jules out of range. Growling, Blackwell spurs his horse forward and throws his axe in a last-ditch attempt to take Jules out. The axe spins through the air and out behind Jules. Jules reaches up with his left hand, touching the side of his face, and it comes back bloody.

"Uh-oh," he whispers and blacks out, sliding off Bo and onto the ground in a heap.

Lord Commander Urich Stone leads two thousand knights into the battle. He can see where the fight between the mages was and the fallen bodies around them. He is certain Blackwell is here. He just isn't sure where.

The knights sweep into the axmen. The axmen, with no place to go, fight for their lives.

The lord commander sees in the distance a big red horse without a rider being circled by a huge dark-skinned man wielding a double axe. "With me!" he yells and kicks his horse into a dead run.

Blackwell is on the ground focused on the red horse. The lord commander comes up behind him and jumps off his horse and on top of Blackwell. Surprised, Blackwell stumbles but quickly corrects himself. Whirling his double axe in complex movements, he attacks the lord commander.

"End this!" shouts Urich.

"Never!" screams Blackwell as he charges. Urich Stone's sword passes through Blackwell's neck as Blackwell's double axe cuts him in two. Both fall dead instantly.

Sir Oweyn watches in horror as his brother and Blackwell deal the final blows to each other. "No!" he shouts, stumbling his way over there. Silence falls over the battlefield as men on both sides realize their leaders are now dead. Sir Oweyn falls on his knees at the side of Urich Stone. He reaches out to touch him, hoping maybe he's still alive and it was a mistake. The body is still with no pulse. Silent sobs wrack Sir Oweyn's body as he mourns the loss of his brother and dear friend. Minutes tick by and Oweyn realizes he doesn't know where his squire is. Looking up, he sees Bo, lathered in sweat and streaks of blood, standing over something about ten feet away.

Using his sword as a staff, Sir Oweyn pulls himself up, wincing as pain shoots through his leg and arm from the arrow wounds. He slowly makes his way over to Bo. "Shhhh, shhh. You're all right, Bo," he says softly, offering his hand for the horse to sniff. Bo turns toward what he has been standing over, ears pinned back, teeth snapping in warning. His ears flick forward as he recognizes Sir Oweyn. The horse nuzzles the thing he's guarding and then looks at Sir Oweyn. He does this a couple of times before Sir Oweyn gets the message and walks closer.

"Jules?" he says, assuming Bo would not protect anyone else like this.

"Mmmmm," Jules mumbles.

"You're alive!" Sir Oweyn drops to the ground and hugs Jules tightly, relieved he will not have to inform the Wolf of his grandson's demise.

"Please let go. That hurts," Jules says, waking up more. Sir Oweyn loosens his grip but continues to hug his squire.

The king is in a meeting with his advisors when the door bursts open. The king's guards leap forward, swords drawn, ready to attack the intruder.

A filthy messenger, holding out a scroll in a shaking hand, stumbles through the door, gasping for air. "Your Majesty," he stammers. "An urgent message from Southwind Fort." The messenger collapses in a heap and one of the knights rushes forward to take the scroll, quickly offering it to the king.

King Renard opens the scroll and reads it out loud.

King Renard,
It is with deep sorrow I write to inform you that Lord Commander Urich Stone died. His death is the death all knights wish for. In service to our king and country.

135

On a positive note, Ruschmann Blackwell was killed by the lord commander and his mages destroyed. The war in the south is now at an end.
I await your orders on how to proceed.

Sincerely,
Sir Gregory

The king finishes and sets down the scroll on the table heavily. "I am glad the war is over. We have lost so many good men," the king says sadly.

The Wolf bows his head in acknowledgement, wondering if he had been there if the lord commander would still be alive. "At least it was an honorable death." The other men in the room murmur in agreement.

Knight Commander Emberwood folds his hands before speaking in a wavering voice. "We should make arrangements for the remaining soldiers and knights at Southwind Fort to come home. I don't think it would be wise to completely remove our presence down there, but we can significantly reduce our numbers over the next few months."

King Renard clears his throat and nods. "Good suggestion. I will let you take charge on sorting out those details, Emberwood." The king has another piece of paper in his hand and he fumbles with it, debating, if now is an appropriate time to broach the subject. "There is another matter I need to discuss with you before we adjourn. I have recently received communication from Empress Angélique of Les Tropiques Eternels."

There is a collective gasp from the table.

"Yes, I was in shock too when I got the letter. The empress wants to discuss establishing a trade agreement between our two countries," the king explains.

The knight commander is the first to speak. "I don't see why there is any problem with establishing trade with them. Considering Les Tropiques Eternels has such different weather and landscape, I imagine it could be quite profitable for both countries." The others nod in agreement, even the Wolf.

"Wonderful. I will reach out to her and see about initiating trade with them," the king concludes.

Two weeks have passed since Lord Commander Urich Stone and Ruschmann Blackwell died at Southwind Fort.

Sir Gregory walks down the steps heading toward the stable but stops when he hears a commotion coming from the training yard. He turns and heads that way to find out what is going on. A pathway clears for him so he can get up to the railing. The scene before him is not what he was expecting. Jules, sporting a bandage over his left ear, is in the middle of the yard, sparring with one of the infantry captains.

Sir Gregory steps over the railing and into the space. "Jules, what are you doing?" he says in his commander voice.

Jules turns in surprise. "Uh…"

"Does Sir Oweyn know you're out here?" Sir Gregory inquires.

Jules looks at him guiltily.

"That's what I thought. Sir Oweyn is following the healer's orders, and you decided they are optional." Sir Gregory turns toward the spectators. "I'm sure you all have places to be. Go now, or I will find things for you to do that you will not enjoy." The men who were watching the fight scatter.

Jules tries to follow the men heading back to the barracks. Sir Gregory reaches out and grabs Jules's arm. "Not so fast. You have orders from the healer to rest for another week. While I'm glad your back and ear are feeling much better, I need you to be completely healed. Meaning, all bandages must be gone and no healer orders to rest or take it easy."

Jules hangs his head. The past few days the pain from losing his ear has drastically improved, making it difficult for him to rest.

"I finally have traced the source of the portals. I'm sure you both recall that I agreed several years ago to continue looking into how Wanonia was getting spies into Etria and that it was through magical portals," Brixx announces in his meeting with High Mage Ivy and Master Efaris.

"Where do they go?" Efaris questions.

"They go different places, but the most important part is it is only one mage. Some of the portals the mage is making directly, while others are made through crystals with the spell imbued in them. I have found a couple of the crystals. In my tests, they disintegrated, so I can't show them to you. My biggest concern is that these portals are still being made, even though the first one we are aware of was back in 601. People or objects are continuing to be moved into or out of Etria.

"The portals the mage is making directly are coming from the far northwest, possibly as far north as Sneg. The ones with the crystals are originating from Wanonia and the south in La Jungle Noire. I have a record of a portal originating from the La Jungle Noire, as recently as a few weeks ago," Brixx finishes.

"Have you been able to identify who or what is coming through?" Ivy asks.

Brixx shakes his head. "No. Which is the most frustrating and worrisome part. We know people are coming through, but what if something else comes through? There are other magical beings that exist in this world and many are evil—demons, dragons, elementals, fairies...the list goes on."

Efaris's face pales at the mention of non-human creatures that might be coming through.

Brixx continues. "We are once again stuck in a weird position. Without any way of tracking when and where the portals will open or what is coming through, we don't have much to give to the king. Other than a warning. It sounds pretty foolish for us to go to him and say, 'King Renard, we know there are more portals being opened. At unknown times and places, allowing for unknown people or objects to pass through.'"

Ivy interrupts, "As king, he must always be on the alert for unexpected attacks. I want us to wait. If we can identify a location of a portal immediately after it opens, then we can alert him then." Efaris nods in agreement.

Brixx sighs.

"I understand your point. I just wish I could come up with more concrete information. None of us likes to know something could be coming without a way of defending ourselves."

Sir Lars, Sir Roger, and the mage, Pyr, meet on a snowy hillside somewhere in the north. The three men stand there regarding each other in silence.

Finally, impatient to begin, Roger breaks the silence. "Are we ready for the next step?" he asks Pyr.

The mage nods. "Of course. I would have informed you if I was not going to be ready on time."

"There is no more room for error. This must work," Sir Lars reminds Pyr.

Pyr shrugs. "I am aware of the stakes. I do not need a reminder."

"Ruschmann—" Sir Lars starts to say.

Holding up his hand, Pyr silences Sir Lars. "Ruschmann Blackwell made his own choices that led to his death. Our agreement was to supply him with fire mages, which I did. You did not ask me to guarantee his success, nor did you pay me enough to do so."

Sir Lars shuffles his feet. Pyr is right. They did not pay for a guaranteed outcome in the south. The next step, though, *is* guaranteed. Sir Lars pulls a clinking pouch out of his cloak and offers it to the mage. Pyr takes it.

"The next time I see you, the deed will be done." Pyr snaps his fingers and disappears in a puff of smoke.

King Renard is out for a walk through the gardens for a change of scenery when Master Brixx finds him. "Pardon the intrusion, Your Majesty, but I have some information the council at Onaxx Academy feels is important to share with you."

The king nods and indicates they should sit down on the bench. Once both are seated, the king says, "Please share your information."

Master Brixx nods and begins. "Over the past eight years, I have been studying magical portals that have been the method of travel for spies, and who knows what else, through Etria. In the past few weeks, I have made significant headway in determining where the portals are originating from. I can also determine when one is being opened as it's being opened. However, I do not yet have a way of predicting their opening or identifying what is coming through the portal unless there happens to be a witness."

The king is alarmed. "Why did it take so long to tell me the portals are continuing to be used? Did the council not think it is relevant for me to know that we are still being spied on?"

Master Brixx takes a deep breath and lets it out before replying. "The council has been concerned with identifying where the portals are being created and by whom. To answer your questions, it seems to be a single mage responsible. However, the mage has put some of the portals in crystals that can be activated without him or her being there."

"So what you're saying is, there are potentially numerous individuals out in the world that are capable of creating portals into my country, without my knowledge, to do who knows what?" asks the king incredulously.

Master Brixx nervously fiddles with his robe. "Yes, that is correct."

The king stands and begins pacing. "I need to inform my advisors…this very well could change some of our plans…" The king's voice trails off as he is lost in thoughts.

Master Brixx waits a few minutes, but when the king does not say anything else, the water mage bows and leaves.

10

SUMMER 609

It is the morning of the first day of summer at Burmstone Palace.
"See, the knight test wasn't bad, was it?" asks Sir Alane
immediately after Sir Waldorf announces Kass, Lewis, and their
other year-mates have successfully passed their knight tests.

Kass makes a face. "It's not that I felt like I didn't know how to
do things…it's just the order we did them in was rather awkward."

Kass is about to add something else, but Lewis walks up and
slings his arm over Kass's shoulders. "Are you ready to make a break
for it before someone gets the bright idea of sending us off on an
assignment?"

Kass laughs. "I am going home for a couple of weeks.
Remember…Sir Waldorf told us we can have a short break before
he sends out our new assignments. Besides, Blackwell is dead. I
imagine the king needs time to figure out where he wants us to be,
not just send us willy-nilly."

Lewis chuckles. "You have a good point. Can we trade families?
I like yours…"

Kass gives Lewis a playful shove. "Sorry man, after the things you've told me about your family, I definitely want to keep mine. I'm sure you'll survive a week. How about this, if it's really so bad, you can spend your second week at Wolfensberger Castle, but you must promise to go home and try it. People change, you never know how it'll be after so many years gone."

Hours later, Kass takes a deep breath in the stable, untacking his horse from a ride, when Sir Alane walks in.

"Kass, I need you to come with me when you're done."

Kass looks at his former knight master with curiosity but finishes putting away his saddle. When he's done, he looks at Sir Alane. "Is something wrong?"

Sir Alane shakes his head. "No, nothing's wrong. C'mon."

They walk down the pathway and around the palace grounds. They finally stop in front of the mews. Sir Alane smiles and opens the door. Kass obediently enters the mews and firmly shuts the door.

The royal falcon master, a short brown-skinned man with tightly curled black hair and leather arm guards over his green shirt, waves at them from the back of the building. He approaches them with a hawk on his arm.

"Kass, this is Master Wahib," Sir Alane says. Kass bows.

"This is Skye. She is a red-tailed hawk," Master Wahib says in a soft voice. He then offers Skye to Kass. Kass steps back, uncertain of taking her without a glove or armor for protection. Skye flies over to Kass and lands on his shoulder. Master Wahib chuckles. "She likes you already."

Kass looks from Master Wahib to Sir Alane in confusion.

"Skye is my gift to you, Kass. Over the past four years I have watched you dedicate yourself to your training and using your skills to protect others. I know how much working with Mist has meant to you. Master Wahib was able to help me find a younger hawk and has been training her the past six months so that she will be ready for you."

Kass just stands, mouth hanging open in shock, staring at Sir Alane. He finally realizes his mouth is open and closes it. "Skye is mine?"

Sir Alane nods. "Yes, she is yours."

Kass jumps as Skye runs her beak through his hair. He takes a deep breath, trying to settle himself, and then reaches up to stroke her feathers. "Thank you, Sir Alane," Kass says quietly with a slight bow.

Sir Alane smiles. "It is my pleasure, Kass."

Late in the afternoon, Kass decides to see what Skye knows how to do. He chooses a leisurely ride through the royal forest with Skye perching on his shoulder. He attempted to get her to ride on the platform at the back of his saddle but was unsuccessful. Skye prefers his shoulder. He reaches up to her and gently strokes her feathers. *A hawk of his own!*

Kass grins, and gives a shrill whistle. Skye launches herself into the air and his horse takes off at a gallop down the path.

Prince Richard and his wife, Duchess Sunette, take a slow stroll through the royal gardens. Knights are posted at all the entrances and Sir Kristoff trails the couple at a discreet distance.

Every evening for the past four weeks after dinner, Richard and Sunette take a walk somewhere on the palace grounds. Queen Vivienne encourages the walks as time for them to get to know one another before they welcome their first child into the world. The royal healer who will be delivering the baby encourages the walks to help Sunette's body prepare for labor.

Richard was reluctant at first, but the more walks they have gone on, the closer he has gotten to Sunette. Usually, the walk starts in companionable silence, and then as they relax and let the worries of the day slide away, they talk. Topics range from childhood adventures, legends of their people, and future dreams to everything in between.

Tonight, their pace is slower than usual. Richard lets Sunette set the pace, since she is the one with the burden of bearing the child. Suddenly, Sunette stops and gasps. Sir Kristoff rushes over.

Sunette grips Richard's hand tight. "Sunette, what's wrong?" Richard asks, concern lining his face.

Sunette shakes her head. He guides her over to a bench so she can sit. Sunette sits and takes a deep breath, trying to remember what the healer had told her. Slowly she regulates her breathing and can regain control. "I don't know if I'm in labor or the baby is just kicking me, but that was intense," Sunette says.

Richard nods. "Yes, it looked intense. Do you want to go back inside now or keep walking?"

Sunette considers her answer for a moment. "I think it would be better to go back inside. We can take our time getting back to the chambers and then have the healer meet us there," Sunette says. Richard smiles at her and stands up, then offers her his arm.

"I think that is a wonderful plan," Richard says.

The prince motions for Sir Kristoff. "Please send word to the healer that the duchess wants to see her in her chambers."

Sir Kristoff bows and walks over to one of the knights at the back entrance. Since they are heading back inside, losing one knight would not be a safety risk.

Geff, having just returned from Wanonia, punches his brother in the arm. Their mother has given him the task of providing Richard with something to do while Sunette is in labor, when it became clear having him in the room was not helpful.

"Are you going to pay attention?" Geff asks, wondering if practicing hand-to-hand combat is the best choice for a distraction.

Richard takes a deep breath and sets his feet and hands in a proper stance. "I'm sorry, and yes, I am going to pay attention," Richard says sheepishly.

Geff starts again. They had agreed to start with a drill for warmup and then shift into a freestyle practice. Weapons are not permitted, but the hand-to-hand techniques can be any style they are comfortable with. Over the years, both princes have learned a variety of hand-to-hand styles in their travels.

When the princes are eating a picnic lunch next to the training ring, their youngest sister, Ella, comes into the yard, smiling.

"You have a daughter!" she says excitedly and gives Richard a big hug.

Richard looks at her in shock. "A...a...daughter?" he says, his face ashen.

"Yes, silly. Sunette just had a baby girl," Ella replies with an eye roll. "C'mon, Sunette is asking for you," Ella says and tugs on Richard's hand. He finally grasps what she's saying and jumps up and gives her a hug again.

"Let's go!" He takes off at a brisk walk, leaving Ella and Geff to follow behind him.

The Wolf enters King Renard's study and shuts the door behind himself. Smudges of dirt mar his face and clothing.

The king grimaces as he takes in the Wolf's appearance. "You could have bathed first."

The Wolf growls, "If it wasn't urgent, then you should not have written the note that way."

"If I had written it as not urgent, then you would have taken forever to show up," retorts the king. The Wolf looks away, knowing the king is right.

"Anyhow...you are here because I am in the process of finalizing the details of the trip to Les Tropiques Eternels. Given the situation with the portals, I decided it is critical to keep our diplomatic intentions secret for now. Which means I need to send individuals who can be discreet and are capable of handling anything that will come their way," the king explains in an even voice.

The Wolf looks at him with his one eye, still not understanding why the final stages of the trip require his direct involvement.

King Renard sighs. "Let me be plain…I want your grandsons to go on the diplomatic mission."

The Wolf gasps and sputters, "Why on earth would you want them?"

Rubbing a hand over his face, the king slumps into his chair. "Because they are discreet and capable of handling themselves. People who will notice if you're missing and take note are much less likely to care if Borus, Kass, and Jules are not around."

Growling, the Wolf replies, "They have no experience with diplomacy and are just as likely to say the wrong thing to the empress as the right thing. I implore you, send someone who knows how to be diplomatic. My grandsons might just make you look like a fool."

King Renard narrows his eyes at that. "I am no *fool*, Burchard. I do know that with the uncertainty around the portals I cannot afford to send people who cannot defend themselves. Given Jules's status as a third-year squire, I will allow Sir Oweyn to accompany them. Is that satisfactory?"

The Wolf releases a breath he didn't know he was holding. "Oweyn is a sword master and is well traveled. At least he knows how to handle himself around foreign royalty. If you are certain that my grandsons must go on this trip, then yes, I will agree if Oweyn is going. Will you not at least consider postponing until we can eliminate whoever is creating the portals?"

Taking a deep breath and slowly letting it out, the king sits up straighter. "My fear with delay is that Empress Angélique will extend her offer to someone else. Etria will gain much by establishing trade with Les Tropiques Eternels first."

The Wolf for once says nothing, knowing all of the king's points are valid. He looks at the king, waiting to see if he has anything else to add.

"I am sending Kass down to Southwind Fort to retrieve Jules; Borus just returned a couple of days ago. This is going to happen as soon as we can get everyone together and on their way."

The Wolf nods and bows. "I will go talk to Borus and see about making arrangements."

A squad of knights trot at a brisk pace toward Southwind Fort. When they are within reach of the archers on the wall, one of the scouts on a bright red horse veers off to the right. In the field between the fort and the forest are a series of small walls made up of logs with sharpened ends meant to deter enemy forces.

The scout spurs his bright red horse into a full gallop, heading straight for one of the defensive walls. Just as it looks as though the scout is going to run his horse right into the wall, the horse launches itself over the top. The scout and horse turn in a big circle and jump the same wall one more time, before heading back into the other group of knights and trotting through the Southwind Fort gate.

There is applause as the squad rides back into the fort. On the stairs next to Sir Oweyn is a knight, with a red-tailed hawk perched on his shoulder; he's the one leading the applause. The knight on the red horse jumps down and passes his reins off, and then, recognizing the knight on the stairs, runs over and grabs him in a hug.

"Kass!"

"Hello, little brother," replies Kass, returning the hug to Jules.

"What are you doing here?" Jules asks, wondering if there was some impending attack they don't know about.

"I have orders from the Wolf that you must come home. Borus is returning from Wanonia and should be back by the time we have arrived," explains Kass.

Jules has so many questions, but his brother silences him with a look. While he does have news, it cannot be shared among the other knights.

Kass requests a private dinner for him and Jules in his rooms. After eating, with a tankard of ale in his hand, Kass looks at Jules. "Greg says you are completely healed now and have been back to your regular duties for a month."

Jules shrugs. "What of it?"

"King Renard has given us an assignment. The three of us, plus Sir Oweyn, will take a ship and act as emissaries between Etria and the empress of Les Tropiques Eternels. We will go to their capital city, Pont des Baleines, which is on the coast," explains Kass.

Jules looks at him in shock. "Les Tropiques Eternels? Their borders have been closed for almost two hundred years!"

"I know, but King Renard wishes us to establish a trade agreement with the empress," replies Kass.

"But we're not diplomats…" says Jules.

Kass laughs. "No, we're not, and we don't really have any business involving ourselves in diplomacy. However, you will also do well to remember that as knights we often get sent places that don't make sense to us. It is our duty to follow orders to the best of our abilities. It will be just the four of us. Sir Oweyn is coming since you are just sixteen and entering your third year as a squire and need 'supervision.'"

Jules grimaces. "I do not need supervision."

Kass chuckles. "I am aware of that, as is the Wolf. It is my belief that he wants someone who has more experience than the three of us alone to be on this trip. Sir Oweyn is not only from Stinyia, he also has traveled extensively, both to the south and east of Etria. His experience in different countries should prove useful. Now, back to what I was saying. There is a merchant ship that has been requisitioned for our transportation. Since we are trying to not alarm our neighbors, the plan is to announce who we are only when we are within sight of Les Tropiques Eternels."

"Richard is going to be annoyed that we're not at the celebration for the new princess…" Jules says quietly, thinking of someone else who will be disappointed…Ella.

Kass glances at him, reading his brother's mind. "You cannot tell her, Jules. She will be told something once we have departed on the merchant ship, but she cannot know that we will not be at the celebration feast," warns Kass. "There are possibly still spies in the court. The mage that is creating the portals allowing enemies to travel across Etria and beyond under our noses is still at large. The mages at Onaxx are working on tracking the portals. However, there are still followers of Blackwell around, and it would be in their best interest if we don't establish ties to the empress. No word of this assignment to anyone! Promise!"

Jules looks away in frustration. Queen Vivienne has promised Jules and Ella that once Jules is a knight, they will be able to become betrothed. Jules is worried that without him being present, King Renard will marry off the princess, despite Queen Vivienne's reassurances.

Kass tries to console his brother. "You know Ella will wait for you."

"It is not Ella I'm worried about. It is King Renard. He seems to be more concerned with continuing the royal line than acknowledging that his children have feelings about the matter too," replies Jules. Kass looks at Jules sharply; usually his little brother keeps his opinions about the king to himself. *How well do I know Jules anymore? Maybe this trip will be a good chance for us to all reconnect.*

A week later, Kass, Jules, and Sir Oweyn are heading down the road to go north. Kass isn't sure how long they will have at Burmstone Palace until they depart for Les Tropiques Eternels. There is concern that if they delay the trip too long, they could hit the bad summer storms that ravage the northern seas.

The Wolf and Borus ride down the road from Burmstone Palace to meet Kass, Jules, and Sir Oweyn. One of the king's messengers sent word to the Wolf that they were close. At the Wolf's suggestion, King Renard has altered the plan again. Now the Wolfensberger boys will not go to the palace at all but will stay at a small farm outside of the town surrounding the palace.

The five of them meet up around the bend in the road. The three brothers hug and then look to their grandfather for direction.

"Follow me," says the Wolf. He leads them off the road onto a well-used dirt path through the trees. After a while, they enter a small clearing with a cabin and a fenced area for the horses.

Once they've settled the horses, they go inside and sit down at the table. The Wolf looks at each of his grandsons in turn.

"You cannot go into Burmstone Palace or Ironhaven. It is too risky with the celebration preparations underway and the guests arriving," the Wolf says. Jules lifts his eyebrows in surprise. The Wolf shakes his head. "It is better that everyone thinks you three are on regular assignments somewhere in Etria. Not even Kenric and Diana can know."

Jules bows his head in acceptance.

"When do we leave?" asks Borus.

"Tomorrow after dinner. Until then you will stay here to rest and prepare. No magic, Jules. No one can know you're here," the Wolf says. "New gear is here for you. It is plain and unmarked. You can keep your weapons and your horses, but everything else will be replaced. I will make sure what you leave is stored in a secure location," continues the Wolf. The Wolf unrolls a map on the table. "This is for you. King Renard had it made. It shows the route you will take to get to where the merchant ship is. Once you get to Les Tropiques Eternels, you will act as diplomats. The hope is to get a face-to-face meeting with the empress and to determine what she wants. King Renard is hoping for a trade agreement of some sort."

Borus takes the map and examines it, then passes it to Kass. The route takes them through the forest and back roads, away from any towns where they would be recognized.

"It looks like it will take us about two days going this way…if we went the most direct route, it would only be one," Kass points out.

The Wolf shakes his head. "The direct route is not an option. The merchant knows when to expect you." He looks around the cabin, then stands up. "I must get back, or I will be missed. There is food here to last you until you leave tomorrow evening. You'll leave once it gets dark and ride until the following evening, then camp. I know it'll be a long day, but there are too many eyes in this area for you to leave at daylight." With one more glance at his grandsons and Sir Oweyn, the Wolf walks out and quietly shuts the door.

The three brothers sit in silence, looking at each other while Sir Oweyn walks around the cabin.

They are just under two years away from all three being knights, as impossible as it seemed all those years ago. They are still unmistakably brothers, although their appearances have changed. Borus now keeps his blond hair cropped short like their father. Kass still has his shoulder-length blond hair in a braid with feathers woven into it. Jules has waist-length blond hair currently tied back with a leather thong, revealing heavy scarring where his left ear used to be. Jules is also wearing a large blue stone in an intricate metal setting on a chain around his neck. Usually, the stone is under his shirt, but right now its glinting in the candlelight.

"Do you think the Wolf is telling us everything?" asks Jules quietly.

Borus glances at Kass before answering. "He is telling us everything that is safe to tell us," replies Borus.

"If they are worried about spies, then I would assume we must consider that we could be apprehended at any point. Grandfather would not have allowed us to be assigned to this if he did not feel like we are the best option," adds Kass.

"Or if the king strong-armed him into it," says Borus in a barely audible whisper, before speaking louder. "I am still not sure I would consider us the 'best option,'" he growls. "There are plenty of other more seasoned knights than us…I have just over a year, you have three months, and Jules is still a squire."

Jules shrugs. "I am sure that your experience has also taught you that not all of our assignments are logical. Besides…what's the worst that could happen?"

11

FALL 609

Day 1 of the Trip to Les Tropiques Eternels

Until we get at least a couple of hours down the road, we should maintain silence. Talking will only put our intent for our departure to be a secret at risk," Sir Oweyn reminds the brothers.

"I already wrapped our horses' hooves," Jules murmurs quietly.

"Very good. Kass, you're going to put the hood on Skye, right?" Sir Oweyn confirms.

Kass nods.

Borus takes one last sweeping look around the inside of the cabin. "Let's go."

Together they walk out of the cabin and Borus quietly shuts the door.

Kass puts Skye's hood on and settles her on her platform before mounting. Jules and Borus do one more check of their bags before following suit. The four of them ride, single file, down the path that will lead them around the outside of the town.

  **Day 3**

Dawn is breaking as Borus, Kass, Jules, and Sir Oweyn leave their horses in a small pen at a well-used campsite a twenty-minute walk from the trail to the beach. Kass removes the hood from Skye, and she takes off to stretch her wings. The four men carefully walk down the rocky trail onto the beach and the small dock with the merchant ship. The captain of the ship walks over to the rail and waves.

"Let's go before we miss the tide!" he shouts.

Borus, Kass, Jules, and Sir Oweyn walk up the plank onto the ship. The captain goes to his station and the anchors are quickly pulled up.

After stowing their stuff below in the two cabins assigned to them, Jules and Sir Oweyn head back onto the deck. Jules leans over the rail, the breeze blowing his hair into his face. He reaches back to fix his thong when it snaps. His long blond hair flutters around his face, making it difficult to see. Sir Oweyn laughs and digs into his pocket, pulling out a leather thong and offering it to Jules.

"What do you make of this trip?" Jules asks his knight master.

Sir Oweyn considers the question for a few minutes before answering. "I think if we are successful in establishing diplomatic ties with Les Tropiques Eternels that it will be the beginning of a prosperous trade relationship for both countries. Trade not only in supplies, but also in knowledge and skills. Our long-standing alliance with Stinyia provides many opportunities. I am confident this will too. Perhaps even more so, because Les Tropiques Eternels is so much different from Etria."

Jules looks at Sir Oweyn with interest. "How are they different? I know bits and pieces, but mostly my knowledge is of their magic."

Sir Oweyn smiles. "For one, the head of the country is always an empress. However, the heir to the empress does not have to be a blood relative. It can be any girl or woman of her choosing, even if there is a blood relative as an option. The empress is also not required to ever marry. Women and men are given equal opportunities to train and become warriors."

Jules nods. "I know that technically Etria has no rules against women training to become knights, but it seems like there are many who are opposed to it." Jules pauses. "Did you know that Les Tropiques Eternels has seers? Always a woman...sometimes they possess additional magical powers, sometimes not. But they have the gift of prophecy."

Sir Oweyn shakes his head. "No, I did not realize they have seers. I wonder if that is what led them to reach out to us now? A prophecy?"

Jules laughs. "Maybe, but it seems odd to me to drop everything and follow the instructions of a prophecy. Perhaps I can ask more about the seers and their type of magic while we are visiting."

 **Day 5**

Jules is standing at the rail of the ship with the wind swirling around him. The ocean is steel gray, with the occasional whitecap. They have had good weather so far. The trip is supposed to take about five days, which means one more full day at sea, and then they should begin to see land again. On the seventh morning of their journey, they will arrive at their destination. No one knows for sure how precise the travel time estimate is since no known Etrian ships have gone to Les Tropiques Eternels in over two hundred years. The captain has set a course based on two-hundred-year-old maps, which over the past forty-eight hours have proved surprisingly accurate.

It is about midday when the sky begins to darken to pewter. The sailors cluster around the captain, having a loud discussion, and finally the captain breaks free and walks over to Jules.

"It is rumored you are a weather mage..." The captain waves his hand indicating the rapidly darkening sky. "Can you fix that?" he asks.

Jules looks at the sky, considering, then back at the captain. "It would not be wise for me to interfere with the storm."

The captain is surprised and angry. "The storm could add several days to our trip. King Renard told me how urgent this is. You must get rid of the storm!"

Jules opens his mouth to speak as Borus steps over next to him, bristling. "I will say it again, I am not going to interfere with this storm. The consequences of doing so would be way worse than spending a few extra days at sea," Jules says firmly.

Borus stares at the captain with his hand on his sword, hoping the man will back down instead of pressing Jules further. The captain looks at the almost-black sky and shakes his head, then walks away.

"Thanks, I think," says Jules.

"I guess there is a lot more to weather magic than most people know, huh?" asks Borus.

Jules nods. "Much more. But I will say this—the captain is right to be worried about the storm. It is going to be really bad. If I must, I can try to shield us from some of it, but if I try to send it somewhere else, it will likely come back double the size since we are in the ocean, not on land."

The dark black clouds completely block the sun, making the ship and the ocean as dark as midnight without a moon. The water gets still for a long minute and then the wind picks up. Huge waves form in the ocean, causing the ship to rock. The sailors are still trying to get all the sails and rigging up and safe. A huge *boom* causes the whole ship to shudder and streaks of lightning flash from the clouds to the water. *Boom! Boom!* More thunder; the lightning is getting closer. The sailors manage to get all the sails and rigging stowed before the rain starts. A lightning bolt flashes less than a ship's length from them and the rain starts pouring. In moments, everyone on the deck is soaking wet.

Jules is still standing at the railing with Sir Oweyn beside him. Borus and Kass retreat into their cabin.

"Are you sure you want to be out here?" Jules asks Sir Oweyn without taking his eyes off of the water.

The knight shrugs. "I've been on ships in bad storms before."

Jules refrains from speaking out loud, afraid doing so will certainly lead to their doom, but thinks, *Not a storm like this. This is a once-in-a-lifetime storm.*

The captain is at the wheel, fighting against the pull of the wind that is trying to turn the ship. Other than the lightning flashes, it is nearly impossible to see. Suddenly, there is a flash of lighting directly above them. *Boom! Cr...ack.* A horrible sound comes from above Jules. He glances up and darts to the other side of the ship as the top part of the main mast breaks off and lands where he'd been moments before. Jules glances back but doesn't see Sir Oweyn. Overwhelming concern for his knight master defies logic, and Jules is about to go back and look for Sir Oweyn. There's another flash of lightning and sickening cracking sound. The mermaid carved onto the front of the ship falls into the water.

The ship shudders. "Sir Oweyn!" Jules shouts. "Sir Oweyn!" No response. Jules decides to look for the knight. He creates a shield to protect himself from the worst of the wind and slowly works his way to the fallen main mast. Unfortunately, Sir Oweyn is not there. "Sir Oweyn!" Jules shouts again. Trying futilely to see through the darkness into the raging ocean.

The wind whips, the rain pounds like daggers. *Boom! Boom!* The thunder sounds across the ocean. The ship starts to roll. The captain loses his grip on the wheel and is thrown into the railing. The ship bucks wildly in the wind and waves. Instead of going over the giant waves bow-first, the ship spins so they're now broadside. A wave more than double the length of the ship crashes over them.

The ship rolls, and Jules and several sailors are thrown overboard. Borus and Kass slam against the walls of their cabin as the ship completes the roll. Another wave batters the ship. Borus and Kass grab onto the walls as the ship rolls again. When it seems to be righted and hasn't started rocking again, Borus tries to open the door. It won't open.

Borus slams all his weight against the door, it still won't budge. "Help me, Kass!"

Together they break the door down. Water rushes into the cabin. Borus struggles up the couple of steps and stops. Kass runs into him, throwing Borus forward, and Borus falls into the water.

"Borus!" yells Kass, looking for something at the top of the stairs he can throw to his brother.

Borus hits the icy water in surprise, breath forcefully expelled from his lungs. He starts to sink and then comes to his senses and kicks to the surface, fighting the drag of the water on his clothing. Looking around for anything that might help him, he hears his name and looks up at Kass. "Rope?" Borus shouts, hoping his brother can hear him over the roar of the wind.

Kass peers down worriedly at Borus before desperately searching for something nearby he can throw to Borus. Kass jumps down the stairs to see if there is anything he can use in the cabin. He stumbles on the last the step and slams into the wall as another wave rocks the ship. Water floods in even faster, lapping at his knees. Kass finally finds a rope. He decides to grab their weapons and settles Skye on his shoulder, worried that they won't get another chance to recover them. As Kass is taking his last step up the stairs, the part of the ship he is on is flung into the air, and he is launched out into the ocean.

 **Day 6**

The storm is gone, and the ocean is calm again. Debris from the merchant ship is spread out far and wide across the Oxbonear Ocean.

 **Day 8**

Something soft and wet touches Jules's face. He opens his eyes slowly, worried about what the soft and wet thing is. Large golden

159

eyes stare back into his, and the touching stops. Jules blinks, trying to make sense of what he's seeing. He rolls to the side and sits up, praying whatever the creature is, it doesn't decide to attack him while he's trying to get his bearings.

In a better position to see the creature, Jules is surprised. It's a horse. Or at least it looks like some sort of horse, although he's never seen one with golden eyes before. He quietly stands up and offers a hand to the horse for it to sniff. The horse obliges him and sniffs the hand, then begins licking Jules, first the hand and then his arm. Jules chuckles and reaches out to stroke the horse's neck. It is a chocolate-brown color with a thick blond mane and tail, dark feathering on its legs, and golden eyes. Jules continues his inspection of the horse while it watches him with interest. A quick check confirms it is a stallion. Jules pets the horse awhile longer and then decides he really needs to figure out where he is.

Jules surveys the area. He's on a beach with white sand. The ocean is turquoise blue. In the distance, he can see a pod of dolphins. Behind him, the sand continues into trees. The trees are much different than anything he's ever seen before. To his left, the beach continues as far as he can see; to the right it turns a corner, and beyond is ocean. There are a few pieces of wood scattered on the beach, but no other people. Taking a deep breath, he inhales the salty air with a hint of something else he can't identify yet and the familiar smell of horse.

Next, Jules examines himself. His leather vest has some tears in it; his shirt sleeves are both shredded and bloody. There is a long gash from his wrist to his elbow that is red and puffy, but not actively bleeding. His sword is missing, but his blue stone is still on its chain around his neck. He runs his hand over his face and finds more blood, lots of sand, and a good-sized lump on his head. His pants have some holes in them, and his boots are missing altogether. Overall, it could be worse, except Jules also has no idea where he is or where his brothers are. He thinks there might be someone else he's missing too, but he can't remember who.

Borus groans and thrashes around in the water. His eyes open, and he loses his grip on the piece of wood and sinks. Realizing the water is shallow enough that he can stand, Borus stands, coughing. Suddenly memories of the events of the past few days rush back: the storm and getting thrown into the water, Kass trying to help him and getting tossed off the ship, and Borus losing consciousness. He looks around quickly, searching for Kass, Jules, and Sir Oweyn. He can't see any of them. Directly ahead of him is what appears to be a small sandbar. It is roughly the size of the merchant ship they had been on, with a few seashells scattered across the white sand. Beyond the sandbar, he sees what might be another island.

Borus pushes the piece of wood out of his way and wades slowly out of the water onto the sandbar. In the middle of the sandbar, he can clearly see his surroundings. Borus's guess was correct; there is a large landmass in front of him with trees and possibly a mountain in the far distance. The only problem is he will have to swim from his sandbar to the landmass. The clear turquoise waters get quite dark between his sandbar and the other beach.

Not sure what to do, Borus sits down on the sand to evaluate himself and come up with a plan. His once-green shirt is now gray, his pants are in tatters. The knife he wears strapped to his ankle and hidden by his boots is still there, along with his boots. The sword was left behind in the cabin on the ship. Using his knife, he cuts off the pieces of his pants so that they are not as ragged and are just above his thighs. He is surprised that he doesn't have any cuts, although his arms and legs have various bruises from being battered by the pieces of the ship.

A wave of exhaustion suddenly hits Borus. He decides to take a nap before swimming to the other beach. He stretches out on the sand, and using the scraps of pants as a pillow, closes his eyes and promptly falls asleep.

Kass rolls over and then jumps up in surprise when he feels sand. "What the…?" he squeaks before he realizes he's speaking out loud. Kass assumes a fighting stance and looks around cautiously. He's on a small strip of sand in a rocky cove. Rising above him is a large black mountain. To the right is a strange-looking forest that the sand disappears into, and to the left, the rocks drop off into the ocean. A few feet away, Skye is sitting on a rock, preening.

Kass takes a step to the left and trips on something. Looking down he realizes he somehow kept ahold of the weapons. His sword is strapped to his hip, but his bow, quiver, and Borus's sword in its scabbard are on the ground. Everything is coated in sand, but he has them. He reaches to pick them up and winces at a sharp pain in his side. Glancing down, he notices there is blood seeping out of his shirt just above his left hip. Gingerly, he lifts the shirt. He has a large gash about the size of his hand that is bleeding. Sighing, he undoes his sword belt and removes his shirt. He rips a piece of the bottom of his shirt off to use as a bandage and presses that over the wound, then rolls the shirt so it's like a rope and ties it as tight as he can bear to hold the fabric in place over the wound. Grunting, he grabs his sword belt and puts it back on, puts Borus's belt on as well, and then swings his bow and quiver over his shoulder before setting off into the trees. Skye follows, flitting from tree to tree.

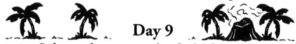 **Day 9**

Once again, Jules wakes up to the feel of something wet and soft on his face. This time though, he knows it is the horse and opens his eyes smiling. The chocolate-colored stallion nibbles on him a little bit more, then moves out of the way, allowing Jules to get up.

The sun is just coming up, and the sky and ocean are turning hues of pale pink and purple. Jules looks at the stallion, considering what he can do next. He still has no idea where he is or if his brothers are alive, let alone on the island with him. Jules gasps suddenly, remembering. "Oweyn," he whispers, falling to his knees. The image of the mast breaking and his knight master disappearing flash through his mind.

Standing up and wiping his face with his sleeve, Jules clears his throat.

"Sir Horse."

The stallion looks at him expectantly.

"Sir Horse, my name is Jules, and if it is your pleasure, I would like to ride you." Jules stops, not sure what else to say. The stallion spends a couple of minutes gazing at Jules, then lies down and eyes him expectantly. Jules looks at the stallion in shock. *The stallion understood me?* Jules takes a deep breath and then walks closer to the stallion. Taking a handful of coarse mane in his left hand, he swings his right leg over the stallion and grabs more mane with his right hand, hoping that he isn't going to get thrown—or worse. The stallion flicks his ears and then ever so carefully stands up and glances back at Jules.

Jules bumps his legs against the stallion, but nothing happens. He tries again; the stallion swishes his tail in annoyance. "Hmm," Jules says to himself. "Walk?" he says, not sure that voice commands alone would do anything. The stallion flicks his ears again and starts walking down the beach, staying close to the tree line.

The height of the stallion is a blessing, giving Jules a better view of the area around him. Although they are still on the beach, Jules can see there are other islands and possibly some sandbars in the ocean. He's hoping that he'll come across a landmark of some sort that will indicate where he is.

Kass stretches, immediately regretting the decision as it pulls his wound. His perch in the large tree does not give him the view he was hoping for. All he can see is more trees and the mountain, but it does make for a good place to sleep. He is following the base of the mountain hoping he'll come across people or his brothers. Climbing the mountain might be his best bet, but he is concerned that strenuous exertion will reopen his wound and be disastrous.

Kass cautiously climbs down the tree. He takes his sword and marks the tree trunk with a large X and a small K, hoping if either of his brothers pass through here, they will know he was here. Once the tree has been marked, Kass continues his path through the forest with Skye once again following from tree to tree.

Borus's eyes flutter open. The sun is just visible on the horizon. Swearing, Borus stands up. He'd slept through the night! The sandbar is almost completely submerged in water because of the high tide. Checking to make sure his hunting knife is secure, Borus wades back out into the ocean. When the water is deep enough, he swims toward the beach ahead of him.

Several times during his swim, he must convince himself to keep going. The distance from the sandbar to the beach is much greater than he thought. By the time his feet once again have sand beneath them, the sun is blazing overhead. Exhausted, Borus finally makes it onto the beach and over to the trees where there is some amount of shade. There is a good-sized rock in the shade that he sits on.

Borus thinks he shut his eyes for a few moments, but when he opens them, the sun has begun to set. His stomach rumbles. Borus looks around. He thought there had been some fish in the ocean, but he wasn't sure. Without the proper tools, he isn't sure how successful his attempts will be. A little way down near the trees, he notices a circle of rocks. He stands up, running toward them. Sure enough, there is evidence of a recent fire in the ring of rocks, and the sand has been quite stirred up. Whoever it belonged to couldn't be too far away—at least he is hoping that is the case. He follows the tracks and as the sand gets more compacted, he stops, puzzled. They're hoofprints. Whoever made the fire also has a horse. This realization meant two things, neither very promising. It would be impossible for the person to be one of his brothers—none of their horses were on the ship—and riding on a horse, an individual can travel much farther in one day than a person on foot.

Borus decides to follow the hoofprints for as long as he has light, hoping maybe he'll get lucky and find who they belong to.

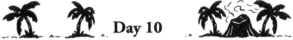 **Day 10**

Borus follows the hoofprints much longer than he expected due to the abundance of moonlight once it got dark. He finally is too tired and has to stop for the night. An urge to keep going keeps him from sleeping for more than a few hours though. Wishing he could have slept longer, Borus presses on, following the hoofprints.

As the sun is coming up over the ocean, he spots a mostly fresh pile of horse poop. Jules would know more about these things, but Borus estimates that the poop is from no more than an hour or so prior. Excitement bubbles up in Borus; he is now within a reach of the mysterious horse. *Maybe I'll catch up!*

With the sun in his eyes, Jules sits up and stretches. He'd continued following the beach for the rest of the day yesterday. Every time he tries to direct the stallion onto a path into the forest, he plants his feet and refuses. Jules is surprised the beach continues for as far as it does. He is not aware there are any islands this big in the Oxbonear Ocean.

Jules gathers up his things and settles himself on the stallion. Having slept much longer than he wanted, he is ready to continue his exploration of the island.

"I'm ready to go. Let's walk," he says. The stallion is lying down, and he twists his neck to look at Jules and sneezes on him. Jules groans and wipes off the slime from his face and arms. He bumps the stallion again, urging him to stand. The stallion instead rolls, and Jules slides off the other side. Before Jules's leg gets pinned and hurt, the stallion stands up. Jules glares at him. "OK, you don't think we should leave yet...too bad you can't explain why. Or can you?" The stallion looks at Jules and yawns, then lies back down and shuts his eyes to nap. Jules dusts himself off and stands up. He made a fire the night before so his stones for the fire ring are still there. He decides if he can't leave, then he'll see about making his breakfast.

Borus sniffs the air. He can smell a fire. Mouth watering—he hasn't eaten in almost three days—Borus unstraps his knife from his ankle and holds it in his right hand. As he slows his pace, he listens for any other telling sounds. A horse nickers. The fire sizzles. Borus slides into the trees so that he can approach with more cover at his back.

Jules rotates the two fish over the fire. They're just about done. He's about to sit down when the stallion bumps him hard and shakes his head then stares into the trees. Jules glances in the direction the stallion is looking and sees a slight quiver of the trees and a shadow. He crouches down and grabs for his sword before realizing he doesn't have a sword. The shadow shifts and then darts toward him. As it darts, the shadow changes to the shape of a man with a hunting knife. Jules throws up a shield of magic; a moment later he drops it as recognition hits him.

"Borus!" he exclaims.

"Jules!" Borus says in shock. Borus drops the knife and pulls him into a hug. "You have a horse?" Borus asks.

Jules opens his mouth to reply, then changes his mind and turns back to the fish. He hastily pulls them off the fire and props the stick against the rock so they can cool a bit. "I guess it's good I caught two fish, eh?"

Jules offers Borus a canteen of water before sitting down. Borus gulps the water greedily, then sits next to Jules.

"Being a mage has its perks," murmurs Borus.

"Yes, it does at times," replies Jules. Jules gently touches the fish, determining they are cool enough to eat. He snaps the branch in half and offers one half to Borus, keeping the other for himself.

"Thanks," Borus mumbles through a mouthful of fish. Jules is too busy eating to reply.

When they both finish eating, they sit in silence for a few minutes. "How did you end up with a horse?" asks Borus.

Jules shrugs. "Sir Horse found me and has been allowing me to ride him. This stallion is not like most horses. He's smart and understands sentences, not just single-word commands."

"That sounds rather peculiar, but perhaps it is normal for horses that come from wherever we are. Have you been able to figure out where we are?" asks Borus.

Jules shakes his head. "No. I have tried reaching out to one of the king's communication mirrors, but I am out of range. I haven't come across anything that can indicate where we are either."

"I don't recall a group of islands on the map we were given. Do you have any idea how far a storm like that could have pushed us off course?" Borus says.

Jules considers the question. "There are too many factors that are unknown for me to guess at how far we are from where the storm began. However, with the intensity of that storm, it would not come as a surprise if we were quite a way off the charted course. Which means the chances of any search party finding us are slim."

"The only way someone would be out searching for us is if there are any survivors. Given the nature of our task, I doubt King Renard is going to be concerned if he doesn't hear from us for a few weeks. The Wolf mentioned not having any set expectations for when we would return. Which means we are on our own, in an unknown place," says Borus quietly. He looks around, searching for more words but unable to come up with any. At least he has found Jules. Together they will find Kass and Sir Oweyn and figure out how to get home.

Day 15

Kass is growing weaker each day. His wound is festering. He stumbles along the path and doesn't see a log in time and trips. Skye drops from the air above, screaming. Kass hits his head on the log and blacks out. The hawk lands, nuzzling Kass, running her beak through his hair, trying to get him to wake up, to no avail.

There is a soft swishing sound, and Kass feels as though he's back on the ship, swaying in the ocean. He opens his eyes; the trees above him are moving. Disoriented, he tries to roll over but can't because he's bound. Kass struggles and then a wave of pain washes over him and he blacks out again.

Kass hears a woman's voice. "E moe mālie ke kanaka ma'i. E ho'ōla 'o Keeaola i ke kāne ma kauhale." He can't make any sense of what she is saying. It is not in any language he's heard before. He slowly opens his eyes, expecting to see the trees moving again, and is surprised to see that he is in some sort of a tent. A short woman with long, dark-gray hair in a braid, dark-brown eyes, and olive-colored skin is gazing at him from a stool, at what appears to be her workbench.

Kass tries to shift his position to see his surroundings better, but his wrists and ankles are still bound. The woman walks over to him with a bowl and spreads a brown sticky substance onto his wound. Kass gasps as sharp pain stabs at his side. Slowly it ebbs away into a numbing coolness. The woman sings softly to herself as she is dressing his wound. Once all the contents of the bowl have been used, she puts it on the workbench and grabs some yellow cloth. She makes a motion with her hands and two women that Kass did not notice come forward and untie his bonds around his wrists. They lift Kass up while the woman wraps his torso in the yellow cloth. When she is done, they lay him back down and re-tie the bonds.

168

The woman moves around the tent and then comes back over to Kass. "'O Keeaola ko'u inoa," she says with her hand on her chest and repeats, "'O Keeaola ko'u inoa."

Kass thinks she is trying to tell him her name, so he responds. "My name is Kass." Keeaola smiles and puts her hand on Kass's chest.

"Kass," she says and then puts her hand on her chest. "Keeaola." Kass nods, understanding.

Keeaola fills a cup with a colorless liquid and carries it over to Kass. She helps him sit up slightly and holds it while he drinks. The broth has some strange flavors in it but does not taste bad. He's about to ask Keeaola question when his eyes start to droop. *A sleeping draught!* Kass sighs and falls into a deep, healing sleep.

"Hiamoe, Kass," Keeaola says softly, then sets down the cups and walks out of the tent.

Keeaola goes across the village to the largest tent and enters. When inside, she kneels, and with her palms on her thighs bows to the woman inside. She keeps her head down, waiting to be acknowledged by her priestess.

The High Priestess Iukikina of Lua Pele'ele is a tall white-haired woman with dark brown skin of an undiscernible age. She stands and steps off the dais to approach Keeaola. The high priestess circles around Keeaola slowly and speaks in their language. "I was informed by Kekipi that you found a wounded man and brought him here without seeking permission. We have strict rules about strangers being allowed in our village. Rules that your grandmother helped write. Explain!"

Keeaola lifts her head but does not rise, preferring the submissive position for this discussion. "I came across the man when I was out gathering herbs to replenish my stores for winter. He had fallen and passed out, giving me the opportunity to examine him before deciding. His wound is killing him, but with proper care he can still heal. He has strangely made weapons, the likes of which we have not seen for many years. My grandmother told me a prophecy when I was a very small girl and although I could not recall the whole thing at the time, I remember enough to know that I could not ignore this man with strange weapons." Keeaola finishes her explanation and watches the high priestess.

The high priestess walks away from Keeaola quickly and over to a shelf filled with scrolls. She selects one and carefully unrolls it, then reads aloud in a clear voice that carries to Keeaola:

> *In a darker storm than ever seen*
> *Will arise the golden-haired man*
> *With a sword of steel and a bow of yew.*
> *Refuse to help the golden-haired man*
> *And the Mouth will devour the diamond.*

Keeaola sucks in a breath at the mention of the Mouth and the diamond. The first time she'd heard this prophecy the whole thing had sounded like nonsense. Now it makes more sense. Eleven days past, the sky turned black and Lua Pele'ele awakened for the first time in over one hundred years. Keeaola shivers. She looks to the high priestess, waiting for her decision.

High Priestess Iukikina re-rolls the scroll without examining the rest of its contents. She is satisfied that Keeaola has acted out of what she believes to be best interests of the village, not out of malice. "When this golden-haired man is well enough to walk, bring him here."

Keeaola bows and stands. When she's halfway out of the door, the high priestess speaks again. "He is still a prisoner, Keeaola. Do not forget."

Keeaola bows and hastily leaves before the priestess can complicate anything else.

12

DAY UNKNOWN

Of the Trip to Les Tropiques Eternels

Borus and Jules have lost track of the number of days they have been exploring the island and searching for Kass and Sir Oweyn. They have been slowly getting closer to the massive black mountain on the one side of the island. Occasionally, Borus thinks he can see smoke coming out of the top of the mountain, but then it disappears. Most of the time they alternate riding the stallion, giving each other the opportunity to rest their weary feet. They had agreed Borus would take the sword so that they each had a weapon, instead of Jules having two.

"When we find Kass we will make our way to the beach and then construct a raft or small boat and sail home," says Borus.

Jules sighs. They had been going over Borus's plan for the past few days, but Jules isn't sure it will be that simple. "Yes, we have agreed to your plan already. Except we don't know where we are… so how do we know where to sail to?" asks Jules.

Borus shrugs. "Maybe by the time we find Kass we will know where we are." Then he changes the subject. "Why don't you tell me about Ella?" Borus asks.

Jules blushes.

Borus smirks. "Ah, I see."

Jules swings at him and misses. Borus laughs, jumping back out of the way.

Jules grumbles, "Mother and the queen know, and they both approve. Your opinion of the matter is not important."

"You do realize that if King Renard allows the two of you to get married that he will be your father-in-law?" asks Borus.

"You do realize that if he allows it, I will outrank you?" Jules fires back and smirks at Borus's shocked expression. "To answer your question about the king as my father-in-law, yes, that is a topic Mother and I have discussed in depth. Have you ever been in love, Borus?" Jules asks him seriously.

Borus shakes his head. "I have not been in love, at least not that I know."

Jules looks at him. "You would know if you had...the idea of not ever seeing Ella again makes me not want to keep living. We need to find Kass and Sir Oweyn and get off this island," says Jules firmly.

Borus looks around. They're both walking side by side with the horse a few paces behind them. The trees around them have slowly been changing as they get closer to the mountain. Borus signals for them to halt; he's spotted something. He walks over to a tree and sees a faint large X with a small K next to it and dark-brown smears.

"Jules!" Borus exclaims. Jules rushes over to him. "Look at the tree!" Borus urges.

Jules examines the tree and the marking. "That looks like something Kass would do, especially with the 'K.' We must be finally going the right direction to find him," Jules says quietly. He looks at the brown smears and brushes one very lightly with his index finger. The smear glows, then disappears. "Borus, that is blood—Kass's blood," Jules says, worried.

"We need to find him before we're too late," agrees Borus.

There is a rustling in the bushes. The stallion lets out a piercing whinny as a javelin is thrown into the tree the X is on, narrowly missing Jules. Jules throws a ball of ice in the direction the javelin came from. More javelins whistle through the air. Borus deflects several with his sword, the others Jules blocks with a shield of ice.

"Can you see them?" Borus whispers to Jules. Jules shakes his head. He still couldn't see the people attacking them. "Can you make them visible?" Borus asks. He wasn't sure what Jules could and couldn't do with his magic. They also have no idea if the enemies are using magic or are just talented at blending in with their surroundings.

Jules closes his eyes for a moment to gather his magic and calm himself. As he opens them, dense fog begins to rise from the ground around them. As the fog envelops the area around them, the javelins stop coming. A light misty rain starts to fall. With a flick of his fingers, Jules changes the rain to hail.

Borus keeps his eyes away from Jules. As tempting as it may be to watch his brother work, he can't afford to lose focus. Although Borus can see the dense fog and mist forming, followed by the hail, he cannot feel any of it. It is as though Jules has placed them in some sort of bubble.

As the hail falls, Borus sees shapes in the trees beyond them. With a target in mind, Borus quietly creeps to the side of the closest attacker. He is surprised to see it is a brown-skinned woman, but he doesn't hesitate. He swings the flat of his blade down, hitting her collarbone hard. The woman screams in pain and collapses into the leaves.

Borus's element of surprise is lost with the scream. Another brown-skinned woman runs toward him with her javelin poised to run him through. He steps to the side and sweeps down on the javelin with his sword. The woman parries and then spins, using the javelin more as a staff than a spear. Borus shifts and strikes using the dragon combination. The javelin flies out of her hands and his sword slices through her right arm. She glares at him and backs up.

Snap! Borus spins and switches his sword to his left hand, raising it in time to block the next javelin from going through his thigh.

He continues to engage this second woman but is wary that the one he injured will come back up behind him.

Jules watches Borus head off, assuming he can finally see someone to attack. Hearing the woman scream, Jules lets go of the fog and the hail. Without his magical hold, the fog disappears quickly. He scans the area immediately in front of him and sees two warrior women armed with curved sabers talking quietly. Jules throws a blast of water at them. The water knocks the sabers well out of reach. They stare at him open-mouthed, then turn and run back into the forest.

Jules is confused by their reaction; he looks at Borus. There is an ever-so-slight whisper by his ear before he is grabbed by the throat in a choke hold. Jules's training kicks in. Although hand-to-hand combat is not his favorite skill, he is proficient in breaking holds like these without having to rely on magic. Jules twists and then goes into a roll, throwing his assailant on the ground. Surprised, his attacker lets go and springs up. Jules takes up a fighting stance.

Borus comes up behind Jules with one of the women at sword-point walking ahead of him. The woman Jules is facing is surprised.

"Pehea hiki oe e ia oe iho loaa'i ka pio?" she says, directing the question at Borus's captive.

Borus looks at Jules quizzically. He's never heard anything like this language before.

The woman at swordpoint fires back angrily, "No ke aha i make 'ole ai ka mea ho'okalakupua?"

Jules's eyes get huge. He recognizes the language they're speaking but can't believe he's hearing it. He clears his throat. Everyone stares at him. "'O 'oukou ka po'e o ka lua pele 'ele'ele?" Jules asks in the same language.

Borus almost drops his sword hearing Jules speak the same way. He edges it back up so it's at the woman's throat again. Hoping his brother will explain to him sooner than later what was going on.

The woman at swordpoint is just as surprised as Borus is that Jules speaks her language. She replies slowly, "'Ae, 'o mākou ka po'e o ka lua pele 'ele'ele."

"Borus, you are not going to believe this...but these are the people of the Black Volcano," says Jules excitedly. Borus just stares at Jules. He has no idea what the Black Volcano is. "Oh, sorry... we're on the Lost Isles," Jules apologizes.

"The Lost Isles?" asks Borus in disbelief.

"Yes...some of the very old spells I learned are in their language. I also learned some of their history and was given the traditional warning of not trying to find the Lost Isles," explains Jules.

Borus is still confused but realizes it doesn't matter. They now know where they are. Which means they can get home. "Can you ask them if they have seen Kass?" asks Borus.

Jules nods then speaks. "Ke 'imi nei mākou i ko'u kaikaina 'o Kass, ua 'ike 'oe iā ia?"

The woman who has been speaking replies, "'Ae, Kass. E hahai mai ia'u a e lawe mākou oe ia ia."

"They will take us to him," Jules translates.

Borus drops his sword point and bows to the woman in front of him. Jules motions to the one he'd been fighting and together the two women lead the way. Borus is afraid to say too much, in case the strange women can understand more than they are letting on. He hopes Jules knows what he is doing. Otherwise, they might be walking into a trap.

Kass thinks he has been in Keeaola's tent for several weeks but isn't certain. His wound is almost completely healed. The high priestess agreed to allow him to no longer be bound, but he cannot leave Keeaola's tent without an escort. After trying to leave a few times without an escort, Kass has given up. Instead, he focuses on doing stretches and exercises to regain his lost strength. Keeaola watches him with disapproval but does not interfere.

This morning she brings Kass breakfast. Usually, she will eat with him and tell him about what is going within the village in her language. Today is different. She hastily gives him the bowl and then leaves the tent. Kass eats and then begins his stretches. He has learned that these people do not tolerate insubordination. If he wants to know what is going on, he will have to wait until they are ready to share.

The two women leave Borus and Jules just within the circle of tents. They wait warily. It took the four of them a whole day to get to the village from where they originally fought. Jules is just about to speak to Borus when a woman with long white hair and in a black dress decorated with shells and bits of stone walks toward them. She moves with a cloak of authority about her. The women that brought Jules and Borus to the village follow at a distance.

The high priestess stops a few feet away from Jules and Borus. "Owau no ka High Kahuna Wahine oʻeleʻele lua pele," she says in a voice filled with authority.

Jules quietly translates for Borus. "She says she is the high priestess of the Black Volcano."

He opens his mouth to respond when the priestess raises her hand to quiet him. "You do not need to translate. I can speak your tongue as well as you speak mine."

Jules and Borus stare at her in surprise.

Jules, remembering his manners, jabs Borus with his elbow and bows. Borus hesitates for a moment, then bows, following Jules and bowing the exact amount as his brother.

"I have been told that you are looking for your brother, Kass?" she asks them.

Borus nods. "Yes, we are looking for Kass. Is he here?"

Considering her next words very carefully, the high priestess replies, "There is a man here that calls himself Kass. He has blond hair like yours. Perhaps he is your brother. My healer found him

176

several weeks ago, wounded, and brought him to the village. His wound is healed. I will have him brought out and you can determine if he is your lost brother. Then we will talk more." The high priestess turns and walks away.

Jules and Borus gaze at each other uncertainly. "Hopefully, the Kass she mentioned is our Kass, and we can be on our way," says Borus.

Jules shakes his head. "I doubt it will be that simple. No one known to Etria has returned from this island in over three hundred years. The ones that have returned never made it to the island. These women of Lua Pele'ele are not going to be willing to let us go that easily. We must tread carefully to ensure all three of us leave here in one piece," replies Jules.

Keeaola returns to the tent and beckons for Kass. Puzzled, Kass looks at her and then follows Keealoa out into the center of the village. At the edge of the circle of tents, he sees his brothers. Ignoring Keeaola's warning glance, Kass ducks around her and runs for Borus and Jules. "Borus! Jules!" he yells.

High Priestess Iukikina is standing in front of her tent. Having anticipated something would happen, she sends a signal, and the two women that had been guarding Kass's door jump in front of him, blocking his path to his brothers. Kass dodges to the left and rolls.

Borus and Jules hear Kass yell their names and surge toward him but are suddenly blocked by a wall of dark-skinned warrior women. Jules glances at Borus. They have no idea how many people they will have to fight if they attack to get through to Kass. The high priestess said they will talk again. Jules still believes they might yet walk out of here unharmed.

Kass sprints toward Borus and Jules, but the line of warrior women splits in half and pivots. Kass slides to a stop in a cloud of dust.

"Let me through!" he shouts at the women.

"E wehe i ke ala," orders Jules in their language. The warrior women do not budge. "The high priestess must have given them orders to only obey her."

Borus looks at Kass, thrilled to see him but still worried. "Are you OK?"

Kass shrugs. "My wound is healed, and I have not starved, but they will not let me go."

The high priestess finally heads back over to the three brothers. Her warriors have moved behind Borus, Kass, and Jules, preventing them from leaving. "Come with me. We will eat in my tent and then discuss what happens next."

The Wolfensberger brothers follow her into the tent. A table has been set up with platters of different types of food. Plates are at each of the chairs. "You may fill your plate with as much as you'd like, then please, sit."

The high priestess sits down in an intricately carved chair at the head of the table and sips from a silver cup. Watching the way these three boys interact with each other—seeing them together—there is no doubt they are brothers and trained warriors; it just seems odd that they are so young. It has been many years since any skilled warriors had survived the storm protecting the island.

After her argument with Keeaola about the prophecy, the high priestess has studied the scrolls written around the same time with more intensity. She has gone back and read the entire prophecy, not just the piece Keeaola had referenced.

In a darker storm than ever seen

Will arise the golden-haired man
With a sword of steel and a bow of yew
Refuse to help the golden-haired man

And the Mouth will devour the diamond

Saving the golden-haired man
Three warriors will rise
One will know the language
One will fight with swords

The diamond can be found
Three warriors will seek
The horse will guide
The Mouth will fight

A second scroll has a more obscure reference:

Golden warriors three
Rise from the sea
Lightning Steel Wood
Open eyes

A third scroll focuses on timing:

The Waha must be slain by the full moon after
The golden-haired men are found
Or Waha will rule the island forever

The high priestess muses over the words of the prophecies... lightning, steel, and wood. She assumes the steel is the mainland-style swords that Borus and Kass have with them. The wood could reference a staff or a bow. Kass arrived with a yew bow. But the lightning reference is the one she is not sure about. The women who brought Borus and Jules from the forest were talking about mysterious fog and pellets of ice falling from the sky. Which, although strange, does not have anything to do with lightning. The horse reference is a surprise as well. There are whispers of horses on the island, but no one has been able to confirm seeing one in over a hundred years. Long ago her people had an agreement with the horses, but she does not know what it was or how it was broken.

Borus, Kass, and Jules have finished eating and are looking at the high priestess expectantly. She blinks and returns her attention to the men in front of her. "There is a prophecy that speaks of your coming to Lua Pele'ele—the 'three golden warriors.' However, there is one part of it that I do not understand. Perhaps one of you does. It refers to lightning, steel, and wood."

Jules sucks in a breath. Borus and Kass both look at him sharply. Jules hesitates before speaking. "What does the prophecy say?"

The high priestess obliges them and recites the prophecy. As she recites it, she is focused on Jules's face, since he clearly understood the lightning, steel, and wood reference. When she gets to the part about the horse, she sees more recognition on his face. So, he has already come across the horse that will guide.

Her decision is made. "As the High Priestess of Lua Pele'ele, I beseech you to help my people and rescue the diamond from the Mouth."

Borus is the first to speak. "What is the diamond and the Mouth?" He is sure it is not an actual diamond or the mouth of a creature, but he wants to know what they're agreeing to before they get themselves into something they can't get out of.

The high priestess looks at him, surprised. "Oh, I suppose you are not familiar with those terms. The Mouth, Waha, is a sorcerer who lives at the top of Lua Pele'ele and likes to take on the shape of a dragon. The diamond is the daughter of our last king and the empress of Les Tropiques Eternels. She was stolen by the Mouth when she was a baby." She pauses, allowing them to digest the information.

Jules blurts the first words that come to mind. "You know the empress of Les Tropiques Eternels?"

The high priestess smiles. "Yes, of course I know her—or I knew Empress Angélique Manaudou. Is she still the empress?"

Jules nods.

The high priestess continues, "Since the sorcerer stole the baby from us, the stones that allow the empress to travel here have stopped working."

Jules would love to know more about the stones allowing for travel off the island but doesn't believe that information is relevant to the matter at hand.

Kass, after listening to everything, decides to speak. "High Priestess, it is your wish that my brothers and I defeat the sorcerer and rescue the princess. What will we get in return?"

"The three of you will be allowed to leave the island. Which is what you want, to go home, is it not?" she responds. Her mood has shifted, and Kass eyes her warily.

"Yes, we want to go home," Kass confirms.

"Good, then we are agreed on the terms. The three of you will have two days to rest and then you will be given a map to find the sorcerer. If you defeat the sorcerer and return here with the princess, then you will be free to go. If you survive but do not defeat the sorcerer, then you will stay here with us as slaves for the rest of your lives." The high priestess finishes her speech and stands, choosing to omit the part of the prophecy that if Waha isn't defeated within the next full moon he will take over the island—a fate far worse than slavery for all.

"You will be given a tent to share with your weapons returned to you. Tomorrow, Keona and Lehua will show you around the village. Farewell, golden-haired warriors." With that the priestess disappears into the shadows of the tent.

Kass, Jules, and Borus all stand and leave the high priestess's tent. Keeaola leads them to their new tent. Kass notices that there are no guards near their tent. Borus opens the flap and urges them to follow him when he sees, as promised, their weapons have been returned.

The three brothers are finally alone. Borus looks at Jules. "Can you…?" he asks and waggles his fingers at the tent.

Jules rolls his eyes. "Yes, I can, and I already put a sound shield on the tent. We can speak freely, and they won't be able to overhear what we're saying."

Borus sighs in relief. The discussion he knows is coming is not one he wants the high priestess to overhear.

Borus begins, "This has been a very strange day. As the oldest, I want to highlight what I think are the most important points, and then the two of you can contribute your own thoughts." Jules rolls his eyes before he and Kass nod in agreement. "The empress of Les Tropiques Eternels is Empress Angélique Manaudou. Her daughter is being held captive by a sorcerer. We started this journey for a diplomatic meeting with the empress and somehow, we end up here making an agreement to rescue her daughter? I know we don't believe in prophecies, but this whole situation is weird. I also don't like that instead of being asked to help we have been given an ultimatum. We don't know these people or their customs. We should not trust the high priestess," Borus finishes.

Jules chimes in, "You're right, we should not trust the high priestess." He drops his voice to barely a whisper. "I also don't think Sir Oweyn made it. We have not found any sign of him on the island or in the village. During the storm when the main mast broke, it fell on him." A single tear works its way down Jules's face. He wipes it away before continuing. "I feel like the high priestess is omitting valuable information for us to be successful in defeating the sorcerer. In her prophecy, the reference to me is obscure, which confused the high priestess, but there is no one else it could be…'lightning.' Steel, wood, and lightning."

Kass looks at Jules and laughs. "Does that mean I'm wood and Borus is steel?" Jules nods confirmation, then Kass continues, "The weapons are something I am concerned with. We have two swords and my yew bow. Ideally, all three of us have swords. A bow is not very helpful in close combat, and I don't want to leave you weaponless, Jules."

Jules closes his eyes, takes a deep breath, and opens them. Preparing himself for his next words, words he had never planned on saying to anyone. "I don't need a weapon, Kass. Over the past nine years, since the year after my magic was discovered when I was seven, Master Brixx has tried to convince me to change my mind about becoming a knight and instead to become a mage. I refused, of course." Jules pauses and takes a breath to steady his nerves. "I think both of you know that in my third year as a page, I passed the journeyman mage test. The mage council at Onaxx sent me a letter just before Kass came to Southwind Fort. I was awarded, without formal testing, my master mage title."

Borus and Kass are staring at him open-mouthed.

"You're a master mage?" Kass asks in surprise.

Jules replies quietly, "Yes, I am a master mage…and almost a knight. Possibly the first ever in the history of Etria." Jules pulls out the chain around his neck with its blue stone. "This stone amplifies my power if I need it. Theoretically, a staff is more suitable, since it can hold a larger stone, but it's a lot bulkier to carry around, especially when I already have a sword and crossbow."

Borus coughs and then takes a sip of water, not completely sure he understands what his brother is saying. "Jules, you are agreeing to let Kass and me have the swords, and you will be defending yourself without a weapon?"

Jules nods. "Like I said, I am a master mage; I do not need a sword or knife." He pauses again, trying to decide what he can show them that will be useful on this quest. " Give me your hands," Jules says and reaches out both of his. Borus and Kass each give Jules a hand. "This might feel strange, but it will not hurt."

Jules's hands underneath theirs begin to glow blue. Borus and Kass feel this strange tingly sensation going up and down their arms. The blue glow disappears, and the sensation goes away.

"If I have to use magic on you or send it through you, that is what it will feel like. You will also be able to see the slight blue color. It is possible there will be times when we engage Waha or anything else that shielding you or channeling some sort of magic through your weapon will be the best choice. I don't want either of you to react negatively to what I'm doing if it changes how you're feeling."

Borus rubs his hand and arm. "That felt very strange. I'm glad you showed us now instead of surprising us during a fight."

Kass nods in agreement. "I think it would be best if we rest now. We only have two days before we depart on this quest." Kass sets his sword and bow down by one of the beds. He strips down to just his underclothes and then climbs under the blanket and falls asleep immediately. Borus is about to make a comment to Jules on how fast Kass fell asleep when he realizes Jules is also asleep. Shaking his head, Borus climbs into his bed and closes his eyes.

13

SUMMER 609

In a castle built into a mountain in Sneg, two men conspire. Roger, now nineteen and in his second year as a knight, looks at his former knight master. "I just met with Pyr, and everything is ready."

Sir Lars nods. "Good work. They will never know what's coming until it is too late."

There is a rustling of silk in the corridor. Empress Angélique Manaudou of Les Tropiques Eternels hurries toward the throne room where a messenger is waiting. Her second-in-command, Lady Odette, hands the empress the letter as soon as she enters.

"You should sit down first," Lady Odette recommends when the empress opens the letter. She looks at Lady Odette sharply and then sits in her throne before opening the letter.

Your Majesty Empress Angélique Manaudou,

It is with deepest concern that I send this message. Over three weeks have passed since the ship departed. Debris from the wreck has been washing up onto my coast for the past two weeks. Have any of the men aboard reached you? Please send word immediately if they have.

Sincerely,
King Renard of Etria

The letter is written in the script of the high priestess in the palace. The empress looks at Lady Odette in surprise. "How did they send this?" she asks.

"Magic," responds Lady Odette. Not being versed in magic herself, Lady Odette had not asked for details on how the message was obtained.

"Now we have confirmation that something happened to the ship, not that King Renard went back on his agreement," murmurs the empress with relief in her voice. With no sign of the ship, the past week Angélique has wondered if now is not the right time to establish ties to Etria again.

Lady Odette watches the empress, unsure of how to reply.

"I need to speak to High Priestess Thérèse. You will go ahead of me and let her know I am coming. This needs to be a private conversation in her library," says Empress Angélique.

Lady Odette curtsies and leaves the throne room.

Twenty minutes later, Empress Angélique orders her guards to stand outside of the library and enters, then shuts the door firmly behind her. High Priestess Thérèse approaches the empress, and they bow to each other.

"How exactly did you receive that message from King Renard?" the empress asks, getting straight to the point, surprising the high priestess.

186

"They did a magic casting. It appeared in the mirror by my desk. It was King Renard, not his mage, who delivered the message," explains High Priestess Thérèse.

"Bold…but it doesn't matter. What does matter is that the ship was wrecked. I need to see the scroll that was made with the words of the seer after the stones closed between us and Lua Pele'ele," demands the empress.

Again, the high priestess is surprised. *What do the stones closing have to do with the ship wrecking?* wonders Thérèse. She has only recently come into her position after the death of her predecessor, about two months ago, the night of the bad storm. The death had been unexpected, and her training was not complete when Thérèse was thrust into a role she didn't want. Instead of commenting, worried that it will just annoy the empress, Thérèse moves over to the shelves, looking for the scroll in question. With some difficulty, she finds it and offers it to the empress.

Empress Angélique takes the scroll and unrolls it, then begins to read out loud.

The stones are closed and the diamond lost
Three golden warriors will travel on a hidden ship
In a darker storm than ever seen
A giant wave will destroy the ship
If the three golden warriors are true
They will be in Lua Pele'ele

If help is given freely in Lua Pele'ele
Three warriors will rise

One will know the language
One will fight with swords
One will fight with a bow
One will accept his true fate

The horse king will guide
The diamond will be saved
What was lost will be returned

Beware
Honor the sacrifice
Forgive the unforgiven
Or the highest price will be taken

When she is done reading the scroll, the empress looks over at the high priestess. The high priestess is young, younger than the empress's daughter is. Although magically talented, the empress is worried this scroll is more than Thérèse can handle. The empress sighs and decides that she will give Thérèse a chance to prove herself.

"What do you think the scroll means?" the empress asks.

Startled by the question, Thérèse takes a moment to consider her words before replying. "The stones are the ones you used years ago to get to Lua Pele'ele?" she asks, looking for confirmation. The empress nods. Thérèse continues, "Then the diamond must be a reference to your daughter. After the message from King Renard, the next part appears to refer to the Wolfensberger brothers being lost at sea." The empress nods in encouragement, pleasantly surprised Thérèse has made the same connections she has so far. "If we are to take this scroll as truth, then they are now in Lua Pele'ele and not lost. It seems, however, that their success is dependent upon whether Lua Pele'ele's high priestess decides to help them. If they are indeed the golden warriors being described in the scroll. Do you know if they are?" asks Thérèse.

The empress shrugs. There are rumors about the Wolfensberger brothers and their talents, but without having met them, she could not confirm or deny.

Thérèse considers the end. "The warning is somewhat peculiar... whose sacrifice? Forgive what?" She looks over at the empress and realizes the empress has turned ashen. "My lady, what's wrong?" Thérèse asks, stepping quickly to the empress's side.

Empress Angélique shakes her head, refusing to explain herself. "I need to go. Thank you for your help, Thérèse. If I need anything else, I'll send for you." She opens the door and hurries into the corridor, not waiting for her guards.

Empress Angélique practically runs the whole way to her private garden sanctuary, filled with lush tropical plants and a waterfall. She sinks to her knees in front of a small stone with a horse etched on it, crushing some of the jasmine that has grown around the stone, filling the air with its delicate scent.

"Are you still alive?" she whispers, tears streaming down her face. "Are you both still alive?"

Kristoff kicks his horse into a gallop when he recognizes his friend Lewis on the road heading toward Burmstone Palace. Lewis grins when he sees Kristoff, glad to see a familiar face. "Hey! Have you seen Kass at all? I was supposed to hang out with him at Wolfensberger Castle after I saw my family, but he was a no-show. His parents said he got orders to go somewhere."

Kristoff scratches his chin with his finger in contemplation. "Kass got orders? That's news to me...but I'm not his nanny, so...?" he says, throwing his arms in the air and causing his horse to jump.

"Have you seen Borus?" Lewis asks hopefully.

Kristoff shakes his head. "Nope. But...the Wolf has been around and definitely seems grumpier than usual, but I'm not claiming to be an expert on the general...want to get some dinner?"

Lewis nods and they turn the horses toward Ironhaven and ride in a companionable silence to the Bad Dog Inn.

Beep, beep, beep. Master Brixx opens his eyes. *Beep, beep, beep.* Flinging the covers off, he jumps out of bed, jarred out of his midday nap. Throwing open his door, Brixx takes off at a run down the hallway. When he reaches High Mage Ivy's chambers, he bursts through the door, gasping for breath.

"A portal just opened. It's close, too close," he says.

High Mage Ivy looks at him in alarm. "Are you sure?"

He nods vigorously. "Yes! Within Ironhaven or possibly the palace itself."

"We must warn the king!" the High Mage declares and gathers her things for a trip to the palace.

King Renard and the Wolf stand at the top of the highest tower in Burmstone Palace. The king's guards have been posted at the bottom of the steps, out of earshot.

"Well?" demands the Wolf. King Renard has been staring out at the forest for several minutes without speaking.

Coming back to himself, King Renard looks at the Wolf, then begins to speak. "The high priestess of Les Tropiques Eternels responded to my message and said the Wolfensberger brothers are not there. However, it seems to me as though she is holding something back. They did not request I send replacements to continue the trade discussion, so I am uncertain of where we stand with the empress."

The Wolf grips the tower's stone wall until his scarred knuckles turn white. Taking a deep breath, he carefully responds, reminding himself he's speaking to his king, not a subordinate. "Can we assume that they are alive? I can't imagine the empress would not tell us if she can confirm they are dead."

The king glances sharply at the Wolf. "Even if they are not dead, we don't know where they are, or if they can come back. Without more information, we must proceed as though they are not returning." The Wolf turns, starting toward the stairs, but King Renard grabs his arm roughly. "You cannot go after them. If we are able to find out where they are, I will consider the request, but I can't afford to lose you too."

The Wolf pulls his arm out of the king's grip and leaves, afraid if he replies what the consequences of his words will be. The guards salute the Wolf as he leaves and stand quietly at their post.

King Renard sighs and moves back over to the wall, gazing out over the trees. He fervently hopes that the three Wolfensberger brothers are alive somewhere. His decision to send them against the Wolf's recommendation and now their disappearance has strained their relationship to the point that it might break.

Lost in thought, the king doesn't see or hear the arrow until it hits him. He falls sideways onto the floor, black arrow protruding from his chest, the blood spreading across his shirt. The king's guard are still following his orders to maintain their post at the bottom of the stairs.

The queen takes her time returning to the palace, wanting to settle her own thoughts after going for a ride. Two hours later, she walks into the private chambers she shares with the king, expecting to find him there. They agreed to meet for a quiet midday meal after each of them finished their private meetings this morning.

"Renard?" she calls as she walks around the room and peers into the bedroom and informal study. Her guards follow her, sensing the queen's unease. She checks the desk to see if he left a note. If duties call him away from a planned meeting, he always leaves a note. The desk is completely clean.

Vivienne turns toward one of her guards. "I need you to find out where the king is. It's possible his meeting went longer than he anticipated, but he always lets me know."

The guard bows. "Your Majesty, I will see what I can find out and send word when I do." He bows again and departs at a jog.

The guard makes to the end of the hallway and is met by a group of knights with shields up around something he can't see.

"Ahem," the queen's guard says, clearing his throat.

The group of knights stop, and one splits from the group, stepping forward. "We need to make it to the king's chambers now. It's life or death!"

Still not sure of what is going on, the queen's guard moves out of the way so the group can pass. He's about to head back toward the king and queen's chambers when two of the royal healers rush past him. Cursing, he turns and follows them at a run. Something has happened.

The knight leading the group carrying the king pushes the door to the private chambers open and leads the way into the bedroom. The knights carrying the king gently slide him off the bench they were transporting him on. The healers enter the room followed by the queen.

She gasps when she sees the black arrow still protruding from his chest. "Is he…?" she whispers, afraid to say the word *dead* for fear it comes true.

"No, he's still alive, but barely. You need to gather your children and prepare them. We will do our best to save him. The arrow is very, very close to his heart," the head healer says solemnly to the queen.

Tears stream down her cheeks and she nods. "I will go find them. I pray the situation is improved when I return." She steps out of the bedroom and quietly pulls the door shut behind her. The knights serving as her guard stand waiting for her orders. "I need to find my children and explain to them the situation. We must do what we can to determine where the arrow came from. He was with the Wolf this morning. Is the Wolf also hurt?" She pauses, trying to think of everything that needs her immediate attention. "We must keep the news that the king is injured quiet for now. After I speak with the children, I want to meet with the council members currently residing in the palace."

A few days after her meeting with the empress, High Priestess Thérèse decides to do some research on the prophecy that has Angélique so worried.

Thérèse's desk and the two tables in her workspace are covered in scrolls and books. She's reading through a couple of prophecies that are from the same seer as the one Angélique read, but older. One mentions several of the same pieces with one part that is distinctly different.

> *The diamond can be found*
> *Three warriors will seek*
> *The horse will guide*
> *The Mouth will fight*

"The Mouth…where have I heard that term before?" Thérèse says out loud. She stands up and walks over to one of the tables and grabs a book titled *Sorcerers of the Ages*. Flipping through the pages, she stops when she reaches one with a very detailed drawing of a dark blue-black dragon.

At the top of the page, it says Waha, which means mouth.

"The Mouth is a powerful ice dragon with the ability to become a human ice sorcerer. Strengths include ice, resistances to water, air, and earth magic, man-made weapons. Weakness, lightning," the high priestess reads out loud. "Hmmm…" she murmurs. The book is over one hundred years old, which means if the Mouth in the prophecy is the same as Waha in the book, then the dragon is old and likely powerful.

Thérèse takes the book and the scroll with the prophecy and sets them carefully on her desk and begins to put everything else back in its place. If the empress asks for more information, then she will share with her the book and scroll.

It has been a week since the attack on the king. At the recommendation of the head healer, King Renard is in a healing sleep. The likelihood of him making even a fifty percent recovery is very slim. However, the healing sleep is buying the queen and crown prince time to figure out their next step.

Richard slams his fist on the table, causing the jar of quills to tip over. "I can't believe we are still no closer to finding out who shot him! We should be able to find out something!"

The Wolf, keeping his temper tightly leashed, glances at the queen before responding. "I know you are angry. We all are, but things like this take time."

"If Kass were here..." the prince starts.

This time the Wolf does growl. "Kass is not here. We must rely on the people we have in the palace to get our answers."

"Whose fault is it that he's not here? You let my father send them away on the stupid diplomacy mission!" the prince shouts. The queen looks like she's about to say something, and the Wolf shakes his head. The prince has been bottling up his emotions, as they all have—at least for now it's just the three of them.

"When your father recovers, you can take up your questions about the mission with him. It's always possible they will return any moment." At the Wolf's comment, all three of them turn toward the door, waiting in silence to see if it will open.

The doorknob turns and the door creaks open. Boots shuffle on the stone doorway before Lord Armand steps inside. The prince, the queen, and the Wolf let out their breath.

"Were you expecting someone else?" Lord Armand says, seeing their expressions.

The Wolf shakes his head and whispers, "Only wishing..."

"Well, this might help." Lord Armand drops a pamphlet of papers on the desk. The Wolf snatches them up before the prince. The first sheet is a sketch of the side of the palace and the tower he met King Renard in. The second sheet has writing on it in a different language. The Wolf is about to ask if Armand knows the language when he drops the piece of paper with a gasp. The prince, curious, picks it up. He looks at the words but doesn't recognize the language at all.

"Care to share what you know, Wolf?" asks the queen.

The Wolf sighs. "I can't read it, but I recognize it as the language that's used in Les Tropiques Eternels."

The queen gasps. "The country we're in negotiations with?"

The Wolf nods. "Yes, that one. Please hear me out. They also have a neighboring country, La Jungle Noire, that speaks the same language. I suspect it is someone from the neighboring country who wrote this. We have intelligence Ruschmann Blackwell formed ties with them and it's likely that his axmen and fire mage came from La Jungle Noire. La Jungle Noire is not very well known, but those who do know of it also know that it is the best place to find mercenaries, spies, and assassins for hire. We also know, thanks to some mages at Onaxx Academy, that magic portals are continuing to be used, and some of them originate in La Jungle Noire. In fact, High Mage Ivy sent me a note saying that a portal was opened immediately before the attack on the king. She was on the way to the palace to warn the king, but it was too late.

"Our biggest problem, though, is we don't have anyone in Etria who can read this language—or at least not that I'm aware of. Which means for us to know what it says we will have to use the mirror to communicate with Empress Angélique. While normally that would not be an issue, I am not sure we want to reveal to her and the people within her court that King Renard is severely injured. He is the only one who has been communicating with her through the mirror. She will know something is wrong if anyone else uses it," the Wolf concludes.

The prince hands the papers back to Armand, before tugging at his lip. "These papers are a lead. We now know the assassin is likely from La Jungle Noire. Let's see where this takes us and then decide if we need to ask the empress to translate."

Lord Armand bows and leaves.

"I should go help, now that we have a direction." The Wolf bows and hurries to catch up to Lord Armand before the prince can give him different orders.

195

Richard looks at his mother. "They still haven't given me all of the details of this diplomatic mission."

She smiles at him sadly. "Perhaps they believe if they give you the details, they are giving up on the king recovering. I'm sure if you knowing will make a difference, they will not hesitate to tell you.

"Richard, you must prepare yourself. Even if your father recovers, the likelihood of him being able to be more than a figurehead is slim. You are old enough, married, and with a child of your own. There is no reason for me to become regent for you. Becoming regent or king will require you and Sunette to have a public presence of unity and love. As a crown prince, your duties to be seen together are minor compared to as ruler of Etria. What you do behind closed doors is your private affair, but every time you step out of them you will be on display. So will Sunette and Harriett."

The prince replies, "I understand, Mother. I should go talk to Sunette." He heads for the door, but the queen stops him.

"Don't forget what was discussed in this room, specifically the nature of your father's illness, is a secret for now. No matter how tempting, you cannot share it with anyone." The prince nods and leaves.

When Richard reaches his office, he turns to his guards. "I need a few moments alone." The guards reluctantly agree after they check the office, and the prince slips inside and shuts the door. He sits down on the couch in front of the hearth and finally lets go of his hold on his emotions. Tears begin to stream down his face.

"Where are you, Kass? We need you here...I need you. I don't want to do this alone," he whispers through the tears.

Theo, Lewis, Urlo, and Hereward are practicing two on two with swords when they notice Prince Geff sitting at the edge of the practice ring.

Theo lowers his sword. "Let's take a break for a few minutes." The others nod and grab their water flasks.

Theo walks over to the prince, taking in the puffy red eyes and drawn expression. "Are you OK?" he asks quietly before sitting down next to Geff.

Geff looks at Theo and shakes his head. "No, I'm not…but I'm not supposed to tell anyone anything."

Taking a deep breath, Theo decides to risk the question that has been eating at him for a while. "Even Borus?"

Geff looks sharply at Theo. "Borus is…"

"Missing," Theo cuts in, finishing Geff's sentence.

"Umm…I'm not allowed to say that either…" Geff whispers sadly.

Theo gives Geff an awkward hug. "I'll let you be, then, since you can't talk about it. But I…we…" he says, glancing at the others who are now only a few feet away, "just want you to know that we are here for you and for Richard. If you ever need anything."

Geff nods and watches his four friends head back to the practice ring to continue. *I wish I could tell them everything.*

Borus, Kass, and Jules walk toward the tent of the high priestess. A dark brown horse with a light mane and tail is heading across the village at a trot, with a hawk on its back. Borus glances at Jules. "Is that the same horse from the beach?"

Jules nods. "Yes, it is. I was wondering where Sir Horse went."

The stallion slows down as he approaches the brothers. Jules walks over to him and offers his hand. The stallion licks his hand, then nuzzles his chest.

Kass looks at the hawk in surprise. "Skye?" The hawk clacks her beak and flies onto Kass's shoulder, promptly combing his hair with her beak. "I thought you were lost," Kass whispers. "The prophecy mentions a horse as a guide…I haven't seen any other horses," says Kass.

"You're probably right, Kass. We will know for sure if he is still here tomorrow," replies Borus. With a glance at Sir Horse, they step into the tent.

"Welcome, please sit," the high priestess says, gesturing for them to take chairs at her end of the table. Borus and Kass take the two seats on either side of her, with Jules sitting next to Borus.

"Tomorrow your journey will begin at dawn. Packs of food and the list of supplies you requested are being prepared now and will be in your tent when we finish here."

Empress Angélique summons Admiral Jean d'Antillon, the leader of her navy. She is waiting for him in her sitting room, wanting to keep the nature of the meeting private.

A gentle knock on the door, then a footman opens it. Admiral Jean d'Antillon is a small, wiry man. He has short, curly, dark-brown hair, brown eyes, and dark tan skin from his years on the ocean. The admiral bows deeply to Empress Angélique.

"Please come in and sit," the empress says warmly. The admiral waits for her to sit first before selecting a chair facing her.

"What may I do for you, Your Majesty?" he asks. There had been no indication in her summons about the nature of their conversation.

The empress replies, "I want you to take a ship to Lua Pele'ele."

The admiral sucks in a breath. Her request is not what he expected to hear.

"May I ask why?" he says.

"Yes, I will tell you why. The seer who died almost twenty years ago left a scroll from her last vision. There are things in that scroll that I have recently received confirmation have come to pass, which means if the rest of it also is accurate, we need to have a ship waiting at Lua Pele'ele." The empress watches the admiral, wondering if he will ask for additional information. He had been close friends once with the king of Lua Pele'ele.

Instead of asking for further explanation, the admiral says, "I will hand-select the crew for this ship and do as you ask."

"Do not forget to bring at least one healer," the empress reminds him. With a sad smile, she stands and holds out her hands. The admiral stands and takes her hands, kissing them. "I hope we will see each other again, Jean," she says quietly.

"So do I," he replies equally quiet. Releasing her hands, he bows and walks out.

14

FALL 609

Duchess Sunette takes her husband's hand and places it on her belly. "You're going to be a father again."

The prince smiles, but it doesn't reach his eyes. "That's wonderful news, dear. Mother will be thrilled to have another grandchild around."

Tears start to stream down Sunette's face. "I thought the news would help," she whispers. The two of them grew much closer in the months leading up to the birth of Harriett and immediately after. But once Richard found out about the Wolfensberger brothers being sent on some secret mission, he became distant. They barely see each other most days. The nursemaid assisting with Harriett keeps Sunette apprised of Richard's daily visits. However, they are carefully timed to avoid crossing paths with her.

The prince stares at the wall before glancing back at his wife. "Are you happy that we are having another child?"

Sunette sighs. "Yes. I love Harriett, and we are blessed to have a second child..." She hesitates. "I know you miss your friends, but Etria needs you…I need you, Richard." Sunette takes her husband's hand in hers. "Together we can get through this."

Richard covers their hands with his free one. "We will get through this."

The king's recovery is painfully slow. He is still bedridden but is permitted to sit up with assistance for one hour each day. Richard meets with him daily to learn everything he can that his father hasn't taught him yet about being king of Etria.

The rumors have begun to circulate around the palace and Ironhaven. The royal family is running out of time for the king to either make a public appearance or officially go forward with Richard's coronation.

"I just received confirmation from my contact in Ironhaven that King Renard is severely injured, but not dead," Lars quietly informs Roger.

"Not dead?" echoes Roger in surprise.

"Correct. The king's healers were able to use magic and heal him enough. My contact feels confident the king will still die but is unsure when."

"This is going to set us back," growls Roger.

Lars shrugs. "We have other pieces in place. Let's see how the next few months go. Then we can decide if we need to accelerate part two."

"What about the Wolfensberger brothers? I can't seem to find any information on their whereabouts. People like that can't just disappear without someone knowing something," Roger says, not sure if Lars is withholding information.

Lars shakes his head. "My contacts have not been very helpful with information on the brothers. I will keep trying. The last thing we need is them showing up and ruining everything when we finally are making progress."

The Wolf and Sir Gregory with fifty knights gallop toward the palace. Tied behind Sir Gregory is the man they believe is the assassin sent to kill the king. They got fresh horses that morning and are pushing them to their limits, wanting to deliver their prisoner to the king and praying he is still alive.

They've been searching for the assassin for two weeks. A few days ago, they finally got his trail and were able to capture him in the north near Alderth Castle. Per Richard's request, the Wolf still has not contacted Empress Angélique. He is hoping the prince will agree to contact her now, so she can question the assassin. Sir Gregory's attempt at interrogation resulted in the assassin refusing to speak Etrian. The Wolf is hoping to determine if there are more assassins.

"Empress Angélique was more helpful than I expected," murmurs Richard.

The Wolf shrugs. "She has been talking to your father for months to arrange the mission. They have a fairly good relationship. Or at least as good as two rulers of foreign countries can have."

At the king's request, the circle of individuals who know about the secret mission has broadened. Lord Armand, Sir Gregory, the Wolf, Richard, and King Renard were all present at the interrogation of the assassin that just concluded. The king has been tucked back into bed to rest and the assassin returned to his prison cell.

The prince gazes solemnly at each of the men in the room. Trusted advisors to his father and hopefully to himself as well. "We now know there is another assassin out there with the task of targeting the royal family. Since we were not able to determine who the target is, precautions must be taken to provide extra protection to all the royal family. The queen, princesses, and duchess will stay within the family quarters. I always want four guards with them when they are in a room and at minimum a full squad in the corridors. In addition to increasing interior security, I want to add more archers on the walls and double the number of men patrolling the outer wall. Until we can apprehend the second assassin, we cannot let our guard down."

The Wolf, Sir Gregory, and Lord Armand nod in agreement.

On a chilly gray morning, King Renard requests his oldest son and heir come speak with him. Prince Richard walks into the bedroom, where the king is sitting up in bed with pillows supporting him.

"Come sit." The king beckons and pats the bed. The prince reluctantly sits next to his father.

"I have already spoken to the queen. It is time for me to officially step down and for you to have the coronation ceremony. I know we keep hoping that I will be able to resume my duties. But it is clear that I have stopped improving." The prince looks at his father in alarm. "Don't worry, I'm not getting worse," the king reassures him. "I just am not able to run a kingdom in only one hour every day. We owe our people a ruler who is strong and capable." The king takes the prince's hand. "I'm tired, Richard...I need to take this final step. You have been doing a fine job so far. It is time you get the recognition you deserve."

The prince searches his father's face. "If this is what you wish, then I will begin the preparations."

The king nods. "One more thing before you go. Your mother told me your wonderful news! You must be thrilled to have another baby on the way."

"Thank you, Father," the prince says stiffly, then squeezes his father's hand and departs.

One son leaves and the other reluctantly walks into the room.

"You wanted to see me, Father?" says Geff.

King Renard looks at Geff sadly. "Yes...I know we have had our differences, but I want you to know that I love you, son. I hope that one day you will be able to forgive me."

Geff looks at his father with mixed emotions. "I love you too, but I am not ready to forgive you. Maybe if the Wolfensberger brothers survive this latest decision of yours, I will be able to forgive you." He gives his father a curt bow before quickly leaving.

Day 1 – The Quest

The three Wolfensberger brothers begin their trek to the top of the Black Volcano to fight the sorcerer and rescue the princess. Borus, with his now-shaggy short hair, holds his sword in his right hand. Kass's shoulder-length hair has more braids, beads, and feathers added by Keeaola, his bow and quiver are on his back, and Skye alternates sitting on his shoulder and flying ahead. Jules's long hair is tied back, making his missing ear clearly visible.

The map the high priestess has given the brothers is useful because it identifies specific landmarks they will pass. However, it is not drawn to scale, making it impossible to tell how far they must go to reach their final destination, the sorcerer's cave. The first landmark is a palm tree that is growing in the shape of an S.

"Look!" shouts Jules in excitement as he rounds a corner. Kass and Borus hasten their walk to reach Jules. There is a large palm tree on the right side of the path growing in the shape of an S.

"How peculiar," mutters Borus.

Kass nods in agreement. "At least we know the map is trustworthy...the first landmark on it is the S, and it's the first one we have come across."

"Good point," concedes Borus.

"Are the two of you done? We need to keep going," grumbles Jules, and he walks away from his brothers down the path.

An hour later the stallion shows up and takes a place next to Jules in the lead. They reach a fork in the road. Jules waits for his brothers to catch up. "There is no fork drawn on the map…which direction should we go?"

Kass and Borus look down each side of the fork. Sir Horse picks the left side and starts walking down it.

"Um, Jules…your friend is leaving." Kass points to the stallion that's almost out of sight. "The prophecy does say the horse is the guide…assuming he's the horse, we should probably follow him."

Borus jogs down the path after the horse, not wanting to lose him.

The stallion stops before the path curves out of sight and looks back to make sure they're following. When the brothers have almost caught up, Sir Horse tosses his head and continues walking around the curve.

The light is rapidly fading in the jungle. The S-shaped palm tree is the only landmark they have passed so far.

"Should we stop for the night or keep going in the dark?" asks Kass. Before they left the village, they had not discussed their plan beyond following the map and possibly the horse if it shows up.

All three of them look at Sir Horse. He snorts and goes about ten paces off the path, lies down, and goes to sleep.

Jules chuckles. "I guess we have our answer."

Back in the village, the high priestess summons Keeaola to her tent. Now that the brothers are on the quest, she wants to talk to the woman who found Kass. Keeaola enters uncertainly.

"Please sit," the high priestess says quietly. "Keeaola, I know we do not always agree—"

Keeaola snorts and then covers her mouth, turning beet-red in embarrassment.

The high priestess continues speaking as though she did not get interrupted. "The wisdom of our people for generation upon generation is here in this tent, within the scrolls behind us. There are hints in a few places about a man of our village who was cursed to become a dragon and cast out. Later references talk about an ice dragon, Waha, or the Mouth. Assuming it is the same dragon-sorcerer guarding the top of Lua Pele'le, then somehow over hundreds of years the man must have learned how to use strong magic.

"I hope you are right that these three golden-haired brothers are the solution to getting rid of the sorcerer once and for all. Twice we tried and failed to defeat him ourselves. Some of our very best warriors did not come home from those attempts. I struggle to believe that there is anything better about these strangers than our own people."

"Perhaps that is the purpose of the prophecy, to force us to put our trust in strangers. I don't know if I have ever heard of anyone capable of using magic the way the youngest brother does," Keeaola replies thoughtfully.

The high priestess considers Keeaola's words. Realizing it's something her brother, Kaihohonu, would likely be saying to her now, if he were still alive. "The only thing left for us to do is wait. If they are successful, they will return with the princess; if they perish, then…" She leaves it hanging.

Both women sit in silence for a while. Keeaola opens her mouth and then shuts it a few times, hesitant to speak.

"You may speak freely," the high priestess says gently.

Keeaola nods. "Very well. Did you feel the air shift the day of the storm?"

The high priestess narrows her eyes. "The air shift?"

The healer sighs. "I'm not really sure how else to explain it. When the sky went black it felt like the air got really tight, and then when the storm ended, the feeling went away."

"Hmm…that almost sounds like a time shift," murmurs Iukikina.

Keeaola gasps. "Those are real?"

The high priestess nods. "Yes, they are. I will have to check later, but I believe all of the time shifts that have been documented are when prophecies have been fulfilled. Such as that a year or more passed on Les Tropiques Eternels, when only a few days did here on the island."

There is a commotion outside of the tent and a head pops through the flaps. "Pardon the intrusion, but Lehua might have broken her arm and needs the healer."

The high priestess sighs and stands up. "You are needed by the village. Go see to Lehua, and I will search those scrolls."

Keeaola nods and departs.

A light snow is falling outside of Burmstone Palace, possibly the first snowfall of the year. Prince Richard and his wife are sitting in the room outside the nursery where their daughter, Harriett, is napping. There are two guards in the room with another two posted in the nursery and six outside the room. The second assassin still has not been found.

"You should read this." The prince offers Sunette a letter. Sunette opens it and reads.

> *Dearest Richard,*
>
> *We just received news of your upcoming coronation from Mother. Kabili surprised me by deciding both of us and our children—Johan and Danika—will be making the trip to be there for your big day. I cannot wait to see you again and to meet Harriett.*
>
> *Much love,*
> *Phaedra*

The letter floats to the floor. Sunette's eyes widen. "The entire Wanonian royal family is coming!"

Prince Richard nods. "It would seem so. Geff's trip must have made a significant impact for Kabili to make this decision." The prince takes a breath and then stares out of the window at the snow in silence before remembering Sunette is with him.

"Mother's plan is that my coronation will take place first, and as is tradition will be a public event. Yours will be a much smaller ceremony three days later."

"You do remember our baby is due late spring?" Sunette gently reminds him.

Richard shakes his head. "No, I didn't, I'm sorry. I've had so many other things on my mind. We're still hunting for the second assassin. The Wolfensberger brothers are still missing. These mysterious portals are still being opened, and the mage responsible hasn't been found…" His voice trails off.

Sunette takes her husband's hand and squeezes it. "You know I'm here if you need to talk."

Richard sighs tiredly and pats her hand. "I know, thank you."

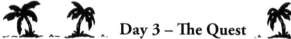 **Day 3 – The Quest**

Borus stands at the edge of the cliff, gazing at the massive waterfall plunging into the ocean. Kass taps Borus on the arm, trying to get him to move away from the waterfall so they can hear each other. Borus finally turns and follows him back around the curve in the path.

"I'm not sure about the bridge. I think we can make it, but can the horse? I do know that the likelihood of us surviving that drop over the waterfall is slim to none," Kass questions.

Jules studies the map. "I don't think we have any other choice. This is where it's saying to cross." He points where it shows the bridge and the waterfall. "I might be able to float the horse over if we run into a problem."

"OK, let's try it." Borus unsheathes his sword, and, using it like a staff, he tests the first plank on the bridge before stepping onto it. He continues until he's almost in the middle and then waves for Kass to come next. Kass starts across, hands gripping both ropes for balance. Skye flies above Kass. Jules watches for a moment before turning to the horse. Sir Horse looks at Jules, licks his hand, and then disappears. Jules looks around in surprise, wondering where it went. Then he hears a whinny. Jules looks at the other side of the bridge. The horse is on the other side.

"Strange," mutters Jules. He grabs the ropes and starts across. When Jules is about halfway across, Skye lets out a scream and flies in tight circles around Kass. Not sure what the hawk is doing, Jules takes another step. *Crack! Pop!*

The board Jules just put all of his weight on breaks in half, dropping him through the bridge. Startled, he grabs desperately for the ropes to keep himself from plummeting to the depths below. There's another sound, more like ripping, behind Jules. Jules struggles to pull himself up onto the bridge and glances back.

"Hurry!" shouts Borus.

"The bridge is not going to hold!" shouts Kass.

Scrambling, Jules shakily pulls himself up onto the next plank and, grabbing both ropes, starts walking quickly across the bridge. Three steps away from the edge there is a loud pop. As the last rope holding the bridge together gives, Jules fall backward. Borus throws himself at Jules, and they lock hands. Kass grabs Borus's feet and pulls both of his brothers slowly back over the edge of the cliff to safety.

When all of them are on solid ground, Kass lets go and rolls onto his back, panting. "Can you please not do that again?" he mutters.

"I promise we will do our best to not fall off any cliffs," says solemnly Borus before helping Kass to stand up.

Jules pulls the map back out, and they all study it.

"It seems like our next marker is a large boulder followed by a swamp." Jules rolls up the map and sticks it in his pack, taking the lead. The brothers walk for about half an hour and come upon a huge boulder.

"This must be the boulder," mutters Borus.

"Sure seems like it," agrees Kass. He steps around the boulder and comes to a halt. The path ends and is replaced by tall posts.

These posts are narrow and start short, gradually getting taller and taller until they reach the other side where the path is higher. The posts span an area of steaming and bubbling black liquid.

Jules looks at the horse. "Since we know you can teleport, I guess we'll see you on the other side?" He gives the horse a pat before climbing onto the first post. The posts are spaced out farther than they seem from the ground and require Jules to jump from post to post. He's completely drenched in sweat and breathing heavily by the time he reaches the other side. Borus and Kass quickly follow.

Borus trips as he comes off the last post and stumbles, falling forward onto his hands. *Riiiiip.* He stands up and looks around confused by where the sound came from.

Kass jumps off the last post and sees Borus's back and starts to laugh.

Borus whirls around. "What?"

Kass shakes his head and doubles over in laughter. Jules walks around Borus, inspecting him.

"Ah…you…um…you split open your pants…" he says, coughing to try to keep from laughing too.

Borus twists around, trying to see his split pants, and walks in a tight circle like a puppy chasing its tail, but he still can't see the rip. "You're sure?"

Jules nods. "Very sure. But…" He slings his pack off of his shoulder and digs around before pulling out an extra pair of pants. "These will fit you."

Borus raises an eyebrow at Jules and accepts the pants.

Prince Richard shuts the door behind him. He orders the guards to stand outside, wanting a few moments of privacy with his brother. The room he selected has no windows and only one door, so it's as safe as possible.

Geff sits down. "You wanted to talk to me?"

210

Richard paces. "Yes…King Kabili, our sister, and both of their children are coming to the coronation. The announcement comes unexpectedly, and I am not sure what to do since we are still trying to apprehend the second assassin."

"The coronation is still months away. Plenty of time to capture the assassin," Geff says reassuringly.

Richard pauses his pacing. "What if there is another one, too?"

Geff shrugs. "You can't spend life worrying about all of the what-ifs. That's not living. Until we know otherwise, we can only assume there is one more assassin. The best people possible are searching and it is only a matter of time before the assassin is captured."

Geff studies his brother. "Are you sure that is the only reason you wanted to talk? About the assassin?"

Richard sighs and throws himself into the other chair. "You know me too well."

Geff gives his brother a slight smile.

"I am also worried about the merchant ship and the diplomatic mission to Les Tropiques Eternels. The empress agreed to inform father and me if she receives any news, but we have heard nothing. Almost everyone wants to write them off as lost and dead. Father has been talking of hosting a memorial service for Borus, Kass, Jules, and Sir Oweyn when everyone is here for the coronation. While I know that Sir Oweyn was well known, I am not sure it is appropriate to have a public memorial for the brothers."

Geff sits there waiting as his brother speaks like he's talking to one of his advisors. Finally, Richard pauses and looks away. "I miss my friends," he whispers.

Geff reaches out and grabs his brother's hand. "I miss them too. I also believe in them and their ability to find their way home. Richard, they will come home."

Richard stays silent.

"You could talk to Sunette," Geff suggests.

Richard looks at his brother in surprise. "How can you say that?"

"Well…she is your wife and is soon to be queen. Why wouldn't you talk to her about some of your closest friends missing? You know, there is no rule that says that you and Sunette must be madly in love. What you do need is have a relationship of trust and respect. Even if she is just your friend. The way you are going on now, I imagine both of you are miserable."

Richard abruptly changes the subject. "With all the upcoming festivities, you are going to need to finally choose a bride of your own. I don't have a war I can send you off to fight to delay the decision anymore."

Geff grumbles, "I could go explore Les Tropiques Eternels?"

Richard wags his finger at his brother. "Sorry, if you want to do that you need to be at least betrothed. The traditions of the royal family dictate that if the two oldest children are male, both must marry and have children to ensure the continuation of the royal family. You need to do your duty, as I am doing mine."

"Duty sucks."

Richard chuckles darkly. "You have no idea, brother; you have no idea."

Day 5 – The Quest

"Stop!" Jules hisses. Borus and Kass look at him in surprise. "I can hear something," Jules whispers. They're almost to the top of the volcano. The path is narrow and steep with few places to hide.

"I can go look," Borus offers and slips up the path, taking care that his movements are slow and quiet.

Whoosh!

"Uh-oh." The horse bumps Jules and lowers himself. Jules climbs on.

The horse waits.

"Kass! C'mon!"

Kass pulls his bow off his back and a couple of arrows and then slides onto the horse behind Jules. The horse stands up and takes off at a run up the path.

As they reach the crest, they take in the scene before them. The area is mostly flat and open, rimmed in a high rocky wall of the topmost edge of the volcano. To the right the edge extends and creates a cave-like space. A huge blue-black dragon has Borus cornered against the rocks. The dragon is breathing huge columns of ice; Borus is dodging it, but barely.

Kass jumps off Sir Horse and fires arrows at the dragon, trying to get its attention to shift off Borus. Sir Horse charges toward the dragon as Skye screams and plummets from the sky, talons open, aiming for the dragon's head. Jules launches ice shaped like javelins at the dragon. Each one hits the dragon and shatters. The arrows are also just falling off the dragon without piercing its scales. Skye's strikes aren't doing any damage either.

"It's not working!" shouts Kass. Kass draws his sword and runs toward the dragon's tail, intending to try to chop it off. As he raises his sword, the dragon turns its head and slaps Kass with his tail. Kass flies through the air and slams into the rock wall at the back of the cavern.

While the dragon's attention is on Kass, Borus slips under its chest and slashes at its feet. Black oozes from the cuts. The dragon screams and rears up on its hind legs, swiping at Borus with its taloned front feet. The talons scrape across Borus's arms, creating long bloody gashes. He stumbles backward. The dragon swings its head and bashes Borus into the wall.

"Lightning," whispers a deep male voice. Jules whirls around, looking for the source. "Lightning," it whispers again. Jules rolls his eyes. Of course, he has forgotten. The prophecy says lightning, steel, and wood are needed to defeat the sorcerer.

Jules dismounts from the horse, wanting room to move.

"Sorcerer!" shouts Jules as he walks toward the center of the cavern. The dragon whirls toward him, hissing. The sky darkens and lightning flashes far away at first. Then the lightning strikes the ground in the cavern. The dragon sweeps its wings up to cover its face. The air around the dragon shimmers and in the dragon's place is a huge man in blue armor who looks much like the dragon he had been moments before.

"You! You think you are strong enough to take on Waha?" the sorcerer growls. He points his staff at Jules and a stream of ice shoots out.

Jules raises his eyebrow at Waha before sending a succession of lightning bolts at him. Waha hastily moves out of the way before creating a whirling shield of ice around himself. Jules throws some more bolts of lightning. They hit the shield with a sizzle. Looking around him, Jules gets an idea. He makes a twisting motion with his fingers and a small whirlwind begins to form. He adds water, ice, and lightning to it before sending the whirlwind toward Waha. The ice shield flickers and disappears, before reappearing.

The whirlwind continues to batter the ice shield, which continues to flicker. The sorcerer laughs evilly. "Is that the best you can do?" Waha takes a deep breath and blows. The whirlwind disintegrates.

"Psst!"

Kass groans and opens his eyes.

"Psst!"

Kass hears a sound again and sits up, reaching for his bow.

"Psst!"

His eyes finally adjust to the gloom around him, and he can see a white shape.

"Hello?" he replies.

"You're awake!" the voice says excitedly. "You need to get up. The mage with you needs help."

Kass looks toward the light and sees flashes of silver and blue magic. He stands up with some difficulty, then looks for his quiver but can't find it.

"Have you seen my quiver?" he asks hopefully. The white shape comes closer and then he hears the clinking of chains as she halts a few feet away. Kass realizes that the clinking is coming from the chains between her hands and around her ankle. As the shape comes into focus, he sucks in his breath. It's a filthy young woman; she has long hair, but most of her features are difficult to discern under the grime.

The woman sees Kass's blond hair, sucks in a breath, then whispers, "Three golden warriors…lightning, steel, and wood."

Kass gasps, realization dawning on him. "Are you the daughter of Empress Angélique? If so, my brothers and I were sent here by the high priestess in the village to defeat the sorcerer and to return you."

The woman nods and offers Kass some arrows. "I found these after you were thrown."

Kass smiles. "Just what I was looking for. Thank you." With that, Kass takes off toward Jules and the sorcerer.

Slurrrp. Borus cringes at the feeling of wetness on his face and his eyes fly open. Sir Horse is about to lick Borus's face again.

"No, you don't!" Borus growls, trying to shield his face with his arm. "Go help Jules. He likes you."

The stallion licks Borus again. Borus swears he can hear laughter, but there's no one else nearby other than the horse. Borus stands shakily and leans on the wall for support. Gingerly, he touches his face. His fingers get sticky; he pulls them away from his face and they're covered in blood.

The horse licks Borus's fingers and nudges him. Borus looks at the horse, then looks for his brothers. He can see Kass running out from the depths of the cavern. Borus pivots, looking for Jules, but his vision goes blurry. Borus closes his eyes then opens them again. His vision is clear. Jules is fighting the sorcerer in his human form, but it looks like Jules could be tiring.

Borus pushes away from the wall and takes a deep breath. His brothers need him. The prophecy says three golden warriors. Not one, not two, but three. Borus stands up straight and slowly makes his way toward Jules and the sorcerer.

Jules loses the hold on his ice shield. The shield drops, forming a puddle around his feet. As the shield drops, Jules sees Borus. Not wanting to let the sorcerer know Borus is approaching, Jules throws a series of lightning balls at the sorcerer.

"Give up! You're pitiful!" shouts the sorcerer, laughing as he absorbs Jules's lightning balls. Jules ignores the taunt and throws more lightning balls, hoping that by doing a low-energy attack he can keep the sorcerer's focus on him and conserve what remaining energy he has.

Jules throws a third round of lightning balls and is about to shout his own taunt when the sorcerer spins to look behind him and changes back into the dragon. When the sorcerer turns, Jules reaches deep into his magic and focuses on his brother's weapons. Imbuing them with lightning. Hoping that this is what he needs to do.

Borus is already swinging his sword when Waha changes into a dragon. Instead of cutting into a human arm, it glances off the side of the dragon. Cursing, Borus rolls to the side as the dragon swipes at him with its huge claws.

From the mouth of the cave, Kass nocks an arrow. When the dragon swipes at Borus, Kass releases the arrow. Skye plummets from the air onto the dragon's head. Just before the arrow hits the dragon, it flashes with lightning. The arrow pierces the dragon's back and sends small lightning bolts rolling across its scales. Skye releases the dragon's head before the lightning hits her. Kass fires a second arrow into the dragon's neck.

The dragon screams and tries to run at Kass as lightning continues to streak across its scales, causing it to spasm.

Borus slides underneath the dragon's belly unnoticed. He waits until Kass's second arrow hits. When the dragon rears and screams, Borus makes his move. He reverses his sword and jams it straight up into the dragon's belly.

The dragon screams again and convulses, changing back and forth between shapes. Borus leaves his sword and scrambles to get out of the way. His vision blurs and he sways. Jules rushes over and grabs Borus's arm to keep him from falling.

The sorcerer finally changes into human shape, and his body is still.

Kass walks over to Jules and Borus. "You OK?"

Jules gives him a quirky grin. "Depends on what you mean by 'OK.' We're alive."

Kass grins back. "Alive is great." Skye gracefully lands on Kass's shoulder.

Borus opens his eyes and stumbles backward.

"What's wrong?" Kass asks, surprised.

"H…hh…horse," Borus coughs, eyes wide.

"What about the horse?" asks Jules.

"Look!" Borus whispers and points.

The horse is standing in the middle of the cavern. Swirling golden dust surrounds him. The dust thickens so the horse is no longer visible and then thins out again, revealing an old man with white hair and almost-black skin in a white robe.

"Daddy?" they hear a woman scream.

Borus and Jules jump at the scream. Kass slaps his face. "Oh yeah, I found the princess!" he belatedly tells his brothers. The filthy woman in the white dress runs out of the cavern, embracing the old man.

The Wolfensberger brothers stand, watching the old man and young woman, not sure what they are witnessing.

"Who is the old man?" Jules finally voices the question they all have.

Borus shrugs. "No idea. I don't think the high priestess said anything about an old man."

Ten minutes pass, and the brothers are still waiting for an explanation. Kass decides to act. He walks over to the old man and the princess, sword loose in his hand. "Excuse me. Who are you?"

The old man releases the princess. "Please accept my apologies. This is my daughter Princess Émeline Manaudou. I am King Kaihohonu of Lua Pele'ele."

Kass stands there staring with his mouth hanging open. Jules elbows his brother. "You were the horse?"

The king nods. "Yes, I was the horse."

Jules looks at the king blankly.

Kaihohonu sighs. "Many years ago, Empress Angélique and I were in love. The people of Les Tropiques Eternels do not have the same beliefs or rules that Etria does for its ruler. The law of Les Tropiques Eternels permits the empress to choose if she wants to marry or have children and with whom. The husband of the empress does not become emperor; he is merely the consort. Status equivalent to an advisor, but the consort cannot rule.

"My title of king comes from my status amongst the people of Lua Pele'ele. The oldest male child of the high priestess is given the title of king of Lua Pele'ele. A man cannot be a high priestess. Because women rule in Les Tropiques Eternels, Émeline has her mother's name. After Émeline's birth I asked Angélique if she would marry me. However, Waha captured me and Emeline when we were visiting Lua Pele'ele. Waha is powerful and was able to trap me in my horse form. Because I could not shift to human, the traveling stones stopped working too. We never had the wedding."

"The stones should work now that you're not trapped?" Jules inquires, wondering if they can get home faster by using the stones.

"They should work, but you cannot use them," confirms the king.

"Why?" Jules asks warily.

"Both the empress of Les Tropiques Eternels and the king of Lua Pele'ele must give permission for someone to use the travel stones. Since the empress is not here, you cannot obtain permission from her. Don't worry, you will be able to go home. There will be a ship. As long as Angélique sent it."

The princess looks at her father, worried. "How would she know to send it?"

"The seer. She writes prophecies. I am confident she would have given your mother a path to find us if one existed. All Angélique has to do is find it," explains the king.

Borus steps closer to them, his vision having cleared again. "Do we have to walk all the way back down the mountain to the village?"

The king laughs. "Yes, we do have to walk, but there is a faster route. I will show you. There is also a nice spring-fed pond that we can each wash off in. Once you are clean, I can heal your wounds enough so you can make it to the village, and create clean clothing."

The princess wrinkles her nose and plucks at her dirty white robe. "The sorcerer would never let me out of his sight, even to bathe. I rarely would take the opportunity."

The king hugs his daughter tightly. "You won't have to worry about that anymore. You are safe."

Back in the village, High Priestess Iukikina says quietly to herself, "I should not have told the prophecy to the three brothers. They are too young and inexperienced for such a monumental task." Keeaola is setting up dinner and wisely decides to not comment.

"Instead, I should be trying to defeat the sorcerer myself. We are a strong people led by warrior women. There is no reason that by trying again we will not be capable of saving the diamond without the help of boys."

The priestess's quiet voice is cut off when the air gets tight in the tent, just as it had when the sky went black during the storm that brought the Wolfensberger brothers to the island. The high priestess and Keeaola stand there in the tent gasping for breath, when just as quickly as the air got tight, it releases them.

Just as the high priestess is about to comment on the air, there's a commotion outside.

"Keeaola, go see what is happening," the high priestess orders. Keeaola is just lifting the tent flap when she gets knocked over by Lehua running inside.

"Come quick! The king! The king!" Lehua says, then turns around and runs back out. The high priestess drops her fork and stands up, knocking over the chair in her haste. Seeing Keeaola on the ground, she pauses and offers the healer a hand up. Together they walk out of the tent.

King Kaihohonu of Lua Pele'ele, a muscular old man with short, curly white hair and chocolate skin, wearing a shimmering robe of gold, slowly walks to the center of his village. Screams and crying ring out around him as villagers rush out of the tents. Some of them reach out to touch him as he passes; others are praying.

Trailing behind her father is Princess Émeline. The princess has long reddish-brown hair and creamy brown skin; she is wearing a simple white robe and a thin gold crown on her head. When the first people see the princess, they fall silent. Everyone recognizes the king, but none of them recognize the woman behind him. The Wolfensberger brothers follow at a respectful distance behind the princess.

The king stops when he reaches the center of the village. The high priestess reaches the center at the same time. She gasps and falls to her knees.

"Ina, please," he says gently and tugs on her hands, urging her to stand.

"Is it really you, Kai?" the high priestess whispers, tears streaming. He nods. "Yes, it's me. Émeline is here too."

The princess steps forward and curtsies. "High Priestess Iukikina."

The high priestess wipes at her face and studies the princess. "She looks like Holokai."

The king is surprised by this comment and turns to look at his daughter. "I will have to trust you in this, sister. I was young when we lost Holokai. I remember small things about her—the sound of her voice, the touch of her fingers in my hair."

Iukikina smiles sadly. "You're right. I was almost fifteen and you were barely five when she died and returned to Lua Pele'ele. But enough of that. Come inside."

The high priestess takes the king's arm, and they walk together into her tent.

Émeline turns back to look at the brothers. "Are you coming?"

"Can we come? Last time we were here, the high priestess did not seem to like us very much," replies Borus.

Émeline shrugs. "I don't remember her, but my father seems to. I think we should all go inside. You said she promised you could go home if you completed the quest. At the very least, she needs to send you home."

Borus, Kass, and Jules follow Émeline into the tent, and the flap falls shut behind them.

The king and high priestess continue to have a quiet conversation. Kass is growing impatient.

"Excuse me," he says so his voice will carry across the tent. The king and high priestess stop talking. "High Priestess, my brothers and I made an agreement with you. If we defeated the sorcerer and rescued the princess, then you would send us home. We clearly accomplished that. So, can you please tell us how to get home?"

The high priestess looks at her brother, who is also her king, then back at Kass. "There is a ship that will be waiting for you. However, you cannot go home yet. You need to escort the princess back to Les Tropiques Eternels."

Kass angrily takes a step forward. Jules grabs his arm to keep him from doing something they will all regret.

"I will take you to the ship, but I will be traveling through the stones myself to so that the empress can prepare for your arrival," the king explains.

"Tonight, you will sleep here and in the morning be on your way. Now, I know you are weary. The three of you should go clean up, eat, and rest," the high priestess says firmly, dismissing the Wolfensberger brothers.

On a balmy fall evening in Pont des Baleines, the tall dark travel stone blazes with light. The guard assigned to watching the stone, Léonie Moitessier, jumps in surprise. She levels her pike, hoping she won't have to use it. The stone continues to blaze with light as a shadow forms within the light. It begins small—only a tiny dot—and grows until it's the size of an average person. Léonie watches, undecided. She's not allowed to leave her post until her assigned time is over. However, she is not sure if she should call for help.

The light begins to fade and the shadow gains definition. A tall, chocolate-skinned man with short, curly white hair and golden eyes steps away from the stone. His robe is shimmering gold and around his neck is a gold chain with the ancient symbol of Lua Pele'ele.

With her pike still aimed at this strange man, the guard hesitantly speaks. "State your name and purpose."

The man looks at her in sympathy. "You are young and inexperienced. I'm sure the empress will forgive your actions. I am King Kaihohonu of Lua Pele'ele."

There is a clatter as the pike falls to the ground and the guard drops to her knees. "Your Majesty, please forgive me."

The king sighs. "You will be forgiven if you tell me where I can find Angélique."

The guard gasps at the familiarity the king is using with the empress.

"I do not have a lot of time. Directions please," the king says more firmly. The guard reluctantly tells him what he needs to know and watches as he departs.

After being told by numerous people where Angélique is, all incorrect, King Kaihohonu decides to follow his instincts and look in her private garden.

He opens the gate quietly and sees Angélique sitting on the grass with her back to him. He sings quietly, changing the words of the song he wrote long ago.

Long ago when they were young
Long ago before they were gray
A girl found a boy
They would run
They would laugh

Angélique turns around, tears streaming down her face. Her voice barely a whisper she sings.

Long ago when they were young
Long ago before they were gray
A girl found a boy
They would sing
They would dance

Kaihohonu steps up to Angélique and holding her hands, his voice joins with hers.

Long ago when they were young
Long ago before they were gray
A girl found a boy
By crossing through the forbidden magic stones
A boy found a girl

They fall silent, embracing.

Twenty guards with High Priestess Thérèse come running into the garden. The first guard stumbles to a halt, seeing the empress embracing the strange man. The other guards run into the first one and fall into a disorderly heap.

"Your Majesty, get out of the way!" shrieks the high priestess as she calls upon her magic.

Angélique whirls around, pulling Kaihohonu behind her. "*No!* I am not under attack. Stand down immediately," the empress shouts furiously.

The high priestess extinguishes her magic, and the guards get themselves back into a line again.

"Who is this man?" demands the priestess.

"I will answer your question, but if you ever speak to me like that again, you will be executed," replies Empress Angélique coldly. "This is the king of Lua Pele'ele, King Kaihohonu. He is the father of my daughter, Princess Émeline."

The color drains from the high priestess's face. She almost attacked a king.

"Your services are no longer needed, Thérèse. Guards, please escort her back to her tower and find Lady Odette," the empress orders.

The Wolfensberger brothers, the princess, and the admiral are all on the ship heading out into the ocean. Borus is standing next to Jules at the railing on the side of the ship.

224

He shudders and looks at Jules. "You're sure there are no storms coming? I am not sure I like that we are once again on a ship trying to get to Les Tropiques Eternels."

"I told you already, there are not even clouds in the sky for miles around us. Unlike last time, the admiral knows where he is going. Remember, he told us he's made this exact voyage many times for the empress. Stop worrying." Jules turns and walks to the bow of the ship, gazing out onto the ocean.

Borus sighs and watches Jules walk away before realizing that they still don't know how long they have been gone for.

Émeline stands next to Admiral Jean d'Antillon as he expertly guides their ship through the water.

"You know my mother?" she asks hesitantly.

He nods. "I do know her. She is a very strong woman and ruler. She had to be to survive the loss of both you and your father. I know you were with the sorcerer for a long time and are bound to have questions. Please ask me anything. I will do my best to give you the answers you seek."

"Did Mother have any more children?"

The admiral shakes his head. "No. There are some at court who still do not approve of her choice. However, our laws do not require an empress to marry or even have a consort. An heir must be female but can be a blood relative or an individual the current empress finds to be best suited to the position."

Émeline looks at him in surprise. "You are close to her?"

He smiles sadly. "Yes, one of the few people she has been willing to confide in since you and your father disappeared. Over the years, I have been her warrior, advisor, and friend. I know you don't know me, but I feel I should give you some advice. These golden warriors who saved you from the sorcerer. If you seek out their friendship, they will give it to you. I know their type and it can be difficult to gain their trust and friendship, but once you do, it will be forever.

I see now why their king sent them, and we will forever be in his debt for that decision."

The admiral and princess gaze over the railing, watching the brothers. One of them is telling a joke and the other two are laughing. They are relaxed.

"How will we get them home?" she asks.

"I will offer to sail them back to Etria once the empress has the opportunity to meet with them. Their trip was originally intended to open negotiations for trade between both countries."

The princess nods in understanding.

Angélique and Kaihohonu stroll arm in arm through the imperial gardens. The ship carrying their daughter and the men responsible for her rescue is due to arrive in a few hours.

"Angélique, as ruler of Les Tropiques Eternels, you owe Etria deep gratitude for rescuing Émeline and me. It is critical you make an appropriate decision on how to thank them as a ruler, not as a mother."

"What do you mean?" the empress asks.

"King Renard has two male heirs. From what I understand from the Wolfensberger brothers, the oldest is married. The younger of the two, Prince Geffrey, is not," Kaihohonu says quietly.

"You're not suggesting what I think you are?" she replies, shocked.

"Yes, I am. Émeline is the appropriate age. You told me the original desire was to create a trade agreement with Etria. What better way to secure that than through the joining of the countries with a marriage union?"

Angélique yanks her arm away from Kaihohonu. "How can you say I should give away my daughter when I just got her back! Our people do not require marriage. How can you expect me to force her into something I refused myself?"

Kaihohonu shakes his head. "You forget...you did agree to marry me, after Émeline was born, but then Waha took her and trapped me in my horse form."

226

Angélique glares at him.

"This is why I said you need to consider what I am saying as an empress, not as a mother. What you also must consider is if you do not offer a suitable thanks to Etria, will they even be willing to establish trade agreements? If the answer is no, then what does that mean to the future of Les Tropiques Eternels?"

Angélique paces. They are already falling into their old habits. Kaihohonu being the voice of reason, cutting through her temper, and giving the empress the chance to consider all options.

"What if...what if I send her to Etria with the brothers, offering her as a wife to the prince, but add conditions? Such as if they accept, she will come here while preparations are being made for the wedding so I can make up for lost time."

Kaihohonu nods. "Very reasonable. One other thing I forgot to mention...I am going to raise another one of the magic stones."

"You can do that?"

"Yes, I was taught how a long time ago. I can make one that connects us to Etria, at Burmstone Palace. I just need you to do so."

Three days after King Kaihohonu arrived through the magic stone, the admiral leads the freshly washed brothers up to the empress's throne room. Before the steward opens the doors, the admiral turns and faces the brothers. "Remember, she is the empress, equivalent to your king."

The doors open.

The steward announces, "Admiral Jean d'Antillon!" The admiral walks at a stately pace up the green aisleway and bows.

"Sir Borus Wolfensberger, Sir Kassandros Wolfensberger, and Squire Julien Wolfensberger, from Etria!" announces the steward. The brothers enter in the order they are announced with several paces between them.

Empress Angélique sits on her throne on its raised dais. To her right, a smaller yet equally ornate chair holds her daughter, Princess Émeline. Standing at her left is King Kaihohonu.

She studies the golden warriors as they enter the throne room and slowly approach her. Borus is in the lead. Kass, the tallest of the three brothers, is next with a hawk sitting on his shoulder. Bringing up the rear is Jules, the air around him crackling with energy.

"The youngest is a squire?" she quietly inquires.

Kaihohonu, equally quiet, responds. "A knight-in-training, he is also a master-level weather mage."

The empress's lips form an O in surprise. The weather magic explains why she can feel the energy around him.

"Welcome to Les Tropiques Eternels. I know this trip did not go as anyone planned and for that I am sorry. However, it is because of your bravery and dedication that I now have my daughter and her father here at my side. Only the truest of warriors would have been capable of defeating Waha. I will be forever in your debt."

Borus is about to speak when he catches King Kaihohonu's eye. The king shakes his head.

The empress continues, motioning for the women standing to the side of the room to come forward. "As a token of my gratitude, I present you with these items."

The first woman comes forward and kneels in front of Borus, presenting him with not one, but two swords. He takes them and is surprised by their weight. He was expecting them to be heavy, but they're not. He bows deeply. "Thank you, Your Majesty."

The next woman comes forward and kneels in front of Kass. She is holding what appears to be a piece of armor. Kass takes it and then realizes what it is. Lightweight, but incredibly strong, with leather padding on the shoulder. It is a shoulder guard so that he can be protected, but Skye can still perch, and he has the flexibility he needs to shoot his bow. Skye flutters into the air as Kass bows before resettling herself on his shoulder.

The third woman comes forward and kneels in front of Jules, offering a staff with a large sapphire at the top. Jules takes it, running his hands over it, then hears a click. The wood slides off, revealing a sword. Jules grins. It's perfect.

"Thank you." He bows, still smiling. King Kaihohonu winks at him.

The brothers shuffle their feet, wondering if they are going to be dismissed.

"There are two more matters we need to discuss." The empress takes a deep breath before continuing. "The first is that when you return home, you will be taking my daughter, Princess Émeline, with you and presenting her to your king. I am hoping to join both of our countries through marriage. Second, I know you are eager to get home. King Kaihohonu is preparing to create a new travel stone that will permit travel between Les Tropiques Eternels and Etria. To go home, you will be traveling through the stone instead of by ship."

Borus murmurs quietly to Kass, "We're going to travel through a stone? I think I'd rather go on a ship again."

Jules hears the comment and shrugs. "From what I've read, it's painless to travel that way, and very quick. We can get from here to there in a matter of minutes, not days."

The empress clears her throat. "It will take a week for all of the necessary preparations to be made. I know you want to get home as soon as possible, but creating a magic stone is not a simple process."

The brothers bow in unison. The empress stands and departs through a side door. The brothers sigh in relief.

"We'll be home in a week!" Jules exclaims.

"Yes, just one more week," agrees Borus. They turn and head out of the throne room toward their rooms.

"Do you think it's odd that she didn't tell us if there's any news from Etria? Or that we still don't know how long we've been gone for?" Kass inquires.

Borus shrugs. "Considering I don't think King Renard ever tells the Wolf all of the details even though he's one of the king's most trusted advisors…no, I don't think it's odd. She rules a country. We're merely visiting knights. The empress doesn't owe us anything, no matter what she says."

15

WINTER 610

There is a pounding on the king's study door. The prince stops talking to the king and motions for the guard to open the door. Sir Gregory and the Wolf burst into the room. The Wolf is carrying a sack. He drops the sack onto the desk in front of the king. The lacing comes open, revealing hair. The king jumps backward.

"What on earth!" he shouts, then covers his nose as the stench reaches him.

Richard starts gagging. "Ugh!"

"There's your second assassin," declares the Wolf, his eye glittering with triumph.

"At least, what's left of him," chimes in Sir Gregory with a wicked smile. The guard who opened the door hastily covers the head and the sack with a blanket, trying to diminish the smell.

The prince takes a drink of water and clears his throat. "Did you get any information from him?"

Sir Gregory nods. "Yes, we didn't need a translator this time. There are no other assassins to worry about. It was just the two."

"Why the head?" the king asks, carefully trying to avoid breathing through his nose.

"I thought it would be safer. A head can't escape," the Wolf explains.

The king shudders and pulls his chair away from his desk before sitting in it. "I will be able to rest more easily now knowing my family is safe. The coronation is quickly approaching. Our visitors will start to arrive tomorrow. It will be nice to be able to return to our usual activities."

Sir Gregory and the Wolf look at each other than at the king. "Your Majesty, Your Highness. We are needed elsewhere, good day." Both bow and leave.

"Well...what wonderful news. We can now relax with the assassin taken care of and make sure everything is perfect for your coronation," the king says with a smile.

Prince Richard looks at his father and whispers, "It's not perfect without Kass."

The king looks at his son, confused. "Did you say something?"

The prince shakes his head. "No. I too am needed elsewhere, Father. I'll see you tonight at dinner." Richard bows and leaves.

"Your plan failed!" shouts Roger, lunging toward Lars, sword drawn.

Lars hastily brings up his sword to block. "You are young and inexperienced. What you consider failure, I consider a bump in the road," growls Lars as he pivots and strikes at Roger.

"A bump? Both of our assassins are dead and none of the royal family is dead." Roger speeds up, viciously going after Lars. Lars struggles to block the sword, and it slices his arm. Lars stumbles backward and Roger leaps forward with his sword point at Lars's throat.

"What are you doing?" hisses Lars.

"I'm going to clean up your mess. I won't kill you yet, but if you screw up again…" Roger leaves it hanging. He lowers his sword.

Lars rubs his hand on his throat, thinking, *When did Roger become the person in charge?*

The queen, furious, pulls her daughter aside. "You cannot wear black to your brother's coronation. That is inappropriate, Ellandre!"

Ella glares at her mother and shouts, "Then I'm not going!"

The queen and princess stare at each other until Ella finally looks away.

"You may finish with the princess now," the queen says, motioning for the seamstress to continue. While the seamstress is measuring and placing pins, the queen peruses the bolts of fabric. The coronation and celebration are meant to spotlight her oldest son and daughter-in-law. The rest of the royal family, therefore, should be attired in muted colors. She decides on a pale dove-gray silk with pink trim for Ella and a shimmering light gray-purple silk for herself.

When the seamstress is done with Ella, the princess leaves, and Sunette comes in for her turn.

The queen walks over and embraces her daughter-in-law. "How are you feeling?"

Sunette gives her a strained smile. "The nausea is gone, but Harriett is crawling all over the place and getting into everything."

Vivienne chuckles. "I remember those days. Richard will be wearing the deep-blue silk. Are you going to have your dress in the same or did you have a different idea?" the queen asks.

Unlike Ella, Sunette is permitted to have a say in her coronation attire. Sunette touches the different bolts of deep-blue fabric, a bolt of almost sheer gold fabric catches her eye. "What if we do the deep blue silk, and then on the sleeves, have some of the gold coming through slashes in the blue?"

The queen considers, then nods. "I like it. Let's show the seamstress."

The evening before the coronation ceremony, a group of young men are gathered in a room deep within Burmstone Palace. Guards are stationed outside and can hear frequent bursts of laughter.

Richard clears his throat. "I know we're having fun, but before we break this up there is a more serious matter I want to discuss with everyone here." Silence falls across the room as Theo, Urlo, Hereward, Kristoff, Lewis, Percy, and Geff all turn toward the man who will be their king by the end of tomorrow.

"There have been questions, spoken and unspoken, about Borus, Kass, and Jules. I know they have been absent for a long time. I am sorry that you have been kept in the dark. This summer they were sent to establish a trade agreement with Les Tropiques Eternels and on the way there, the ship wrecked," Richard explains quietly.

Murmurs go around the room. He raises his hand.

"I do not know if they are alive or dead. However, when I am king, I will allow you to volunteer to go on a search for them. We can start planning this within the next few days even."

As his friends take time to digest the new information, Richard looks around the room. Realizing how lucky he is to have close friends who are more than just knights.

Theo looks Richard straight in the eye. "Thank you for finally telling us. We will definitely be taking you up on the offer."

Richard nods. Geff grins. "OK, enough of this serious stuff. Want to play one more round of cards?" The others laugh and Geff deals the cards again.

Today is a sunny and warmer than usual winter morning at Burmstone Palace.

234

"Everything is ready and perfect," Queen Vivienne says excitedly to her husband and king.

King Renard smiles at her. "Good."

"The plan is that you and I will enter first, followed by Geff, Phaedra, and Ella. We are all going to be sitting to the side of the dais for the ceremony. Richard and Sunette will enter; when they reach the end of the seats, Sunette will join us and sit. Richard's ceremony will be front and center. Once Richard is crowned, he will leave, and the rest of us will follow in the reverse order of how we entered.

"Once we get out of the hall, you will sit down in the wheeled chair and be taken to the celebration. Our family, except Richard and Sunette, will already be in the room when guests are arriving. Richard and Sunette will have a grand entrance." Vivienne smiles, remembering some of the grand celebrations they have had over the years. She hopes her children are able to enjoy this one as much as she has enjoyed them in the past.

The king gasps suddenly.

Vivienne turns to him. "Are you OK?"

The king squeezes his eyes shut tightly and slowly reopens them. "Yes, I'm fine."

Vivienne studies him a moment longer, not sure if she believes him.

"It's time for us to start getting dressed, then," she says gently.

Ella sneaks in the door as someone she doesn't know comes out. She's hoping to catch her brother alone. His back is to her. "Richard," she says quietly.

The prince turns toward her. "Hey, little sis. You look lovely."

Ella blushes. "Thanks. I guess Mother was right about the dress." Richard looks at her, not sure what she's referring to. "Never mind. Don't worry about me, today is your big day. King Richard!"

Richard rolls his eyes. "I really hope you will just call me Richard, or brother. I am not going to be any different at the end of the day than I am right now."

Ella shrugs. "I hope so. I don't want you to change, brother. You're perfect just the way you are." She grabs him in a hug. "I need to go before I get in trouble. I was supposed to be finding Phaedra, not coming here."

Richard hugs her back and lets her go. Shaking his head, he straightens out his coat and checks himself in the mirror. *I wish you were here, Kass,* he thinks, then squeezes his eyes shut, forcing his thoughts back to the details of the coronation ceremony.

The coronation ceremony is beautiful and boring. Relief fills Ella when her brother, newly crowned King Richard, exits the hall.

During a break from dancing, Ella is sitting next to her father when he starts coughing. She grabs a cup of water as a server comes by and offers it to him. King Renard takes the cup but starts coughing again and it drops, shattering.

Vivienne rushes over. King Renard is still coughing. His handkerchief covering his mouth is turning bright red. Ella looks around frantically. Richard and Sunette are dancing and occupied. Her sister is not. Ella stands up and runs over to Phaedra. "Come quick! We need a healer."

The king's guard have been called and King Renard is carried out of the banquet room. The queen and both of her daughters are following closely behind.

"What about Richard?" Ella whispers.

The queen shakes her head. "No, he is busy and where he needs to be. We can take care of your father."

The slow song ends. Geff looks around, debating if he should accept another dance or not. He realizes his mother and father and both sisters have departed. The prince bows to his dance partner and walks away from the dance floor heading toward the empty chairs and the guard standing near them.

Geff can feel something weird in the ground. *Now what?* he thinks. He sees the Wolf and makes a beeline toward him. "Grab a few men and come with me, something is going on outside." The Wolf looks at the prince in surprise and nods. He quickly goes around the room tapping on the shoulders of a few select individuals, Sir Gregory and Lord Armand among them. They meet the prince outside in the courtyard. Next to the prince is a stack of weapons.

"How?" asks the Wolf. The prince shakes his head, not wanting to waste time.

"Something is going on. Out here. Grab your weapons. We need to check it out," the prince orders.

The knights draw the swords and with the Wolf and Sir Gregory in the lead and the prince at the back of the group they cautiously advance down the pathway.

The air pulses around them. About ten feet in front of the Wolf, the ground starts to vibrate.

"Get ready!" the Wolf growls. The ground in front of them splits and a hole forms. A large stone the size of two men emerges from the ground. There are glowing symbols carved into the stone.

Sir Gregory takes a step toward the stone, sword at the ready. Nothing happens. He takes a few more steps. When he is within arm's reach of the stone, he pokes it with his sword. Still nothing.

He turns and looks back at the Wolf. "Now what?"

The guards carrying King Renard finally make it to the king's quarters. The royal healer is waiting for them. They quickly settle the king on the bed. His coughs continue and the amount of blood is increasing. The healer examines the king and shakes his head sadly.

"We can help keep him comfortable, but there is nothing else I can do. His heart and body never recovered completely from the assassination attempt."

The king gasps, struggling to breathe. He grabs wildly for Vivienne's hand. She sees what he wants and takes his hand in hers. Ella and Phaedra take his other hand.

"I...love...you," he says breathlessly, then closes his eyes, and with one last raspy breath is gone.

"Father!" screams Ella.

Her mother whispers, "Goodbye, my love." Tears streaming down their faces, the three women mourn.

A brilliant white light engulfs the stone behind Sir Gregory. He spins, ready to strike whatever comes through.

A tall person emerges. Sir Gregory brings his sword to the intruder's throat.

"Identify yourself!" he orders in his commander voice.

The person steps toward Sir Gregory, causing the tip of the sword to nick his throat.

"I am Sir Borus Wolfensberger of Etria," Borus replies loud enough to carry.

Sir Gregory lowers his sword. "Borus?"

Suddenly, Sir Gregory is shoved out of the way as Prince Geff rushes to his friend and pulls him into a tight hug. "Where have you been?"

Borus is about to reply when the light from the stone intensifies. "I need to move, more are coming." Just as Borus steps to the side, Kass steps out of the stone. Kass trips on Borus's foot. Sir Gregory reaches out to steady him.

"Who else is coming?" Sir Gregory asks, curious.

"Jules...and a surprise guest," replies Borus mysteriously.

Kass and Borus move farther out of the way as Jules steps through and off to the side.

Prince Geff hugs each of them in turn. "I can't believe you're alive! We all thought you were dead when the wreck washed up on the Sapphire Coast. You've been gone for over six months! Speaking of which..." Geff stops talking when the light on the stone flashes again. This time a woman comes through. As she steps away from the stone, the light disappears.

Borus, still in shock from Geff's revelation of how long they've been gone, shakes himself and steps forward and bows formally. "Prince Geffrey of Etria, may I present to you Princess Émeline of Les Tropiques Eternels and Lua Pele'ele."

The princess steps forward and curtsies the precise amount due from a princess to a prince. Jules is next to Geff and elbows him when he just stands, staring.

Geff coughs and bows. "Your Highness," he says and offers her his arm.

Glancing over his shoulder, Geff indicates they should follow him. "Princess Émeline, I would like to introduce you to my brother, King Richard."

Borus gasps. "King?"

The Wolf steps in and speaks quietly and quickly to Borus, Kass, and Jules, as they follow the prince and princess back toward the celebration. "Yes...I promise I will catch you up on everything that has happened since you left. For now, rest assured King Renard is still alive. We must hurry up and follow Geff."

Borus is dying to ask more questions but decides to wait until later.

The newly crowned king is dancing with his wife when there is a commotion at the entrance to the ballroom. He glances around and realizes his parents and siblings have not returned yet from wherever they went. He signals the musicians to stop playing and the guests clear off of dance floor, the leaving the king and his soon-to-be queen alone in the middle of the room. Everyone's attention is on the main doors.

The Wolf slips through the doors and whispers quietly to the steward before disappearing back out the doors again. The steward bangs his staff on the floor to get everyone's attention. The guests continue to talk quietly among themselves until the steward speaks. "Your Majesty and guests. May I present Sir Borus Wolfensberger, Sir Kassandros Wolfensberger, and Squire Julien Wolfensberger."

The three brothers slowly walk into the suddenly silent room. King Richard struggles to compose his face as he is flooded with so many emotions. Whispers start to swirl around the room.

"They're not dead!"

"Where have they been?"

The steward bangs his staff again and clears his throat loudly.

"Your Majesty. May I present Prince Geffrey of Etria, escorting Princess Émeline of Les Tropiques Eternels and Lua Pele'ele."

The crowd collectively gasps. Then the whispers begin again.

"Who is she?"

"Les Tropiques Eternels is so far away."

"How did she get here?"

The steward makes eye contact with the king and bangs his staff for a third time, as silence once again falls on the room. The king speaks. "It is my honor to welcome you, Princess Émeline, to Etria. Please join our celebration." Richard bows and offers her the princess a hand. She delicately takes his hand, and he leads her onto the dance floor.

The orchestra plays a slow song. Richard dances with the princess, glad for a moment to talk to her. "I hope your journey was not too difficult to get here?"

Émeline gives the king a smile and shakes her head. "It was not much of a journey. My father created a new travel stone. So, we walked through a stone in Les Tropiques Eternels and a few moments later were in your courtyard."

The king looks at her in surprise. "A magic traveling stone? I've heard of magic portals, but the stone is new to me."

The princess stays silent for a few moments. "Hopefully you don't mind, but you now have a traveling stone. From my understanding, it is not possible to uncreate them. It is possible to prevent someone from traveling through them though."

Richard is about to ask her another question when one of the doors at the back of the room is thrown open. A distraught Phaedra comes in, looking for her husband, King Kabili of Wanonia. Through the open door, loud wailing can be heard.

Richard sees his sister's pale face and drops Princess Émeline's hand. "Excuse me!" He rushes away to his sister's side.

King Kabili reaches her at the same time. "What's wrong my dear?" Kabili says soothingly.

"He's dead," Phaedra replies in a monotone voice.

"Who is dead?" Richard asks in alarm.

"Father," she whispers before burying her face in Kabili's shoulder as sobs rack her body.

Reeling from the news, struggling to contain his emotions, Richard turns, looking for someone who can help. The Wolf is standing just behind him. Richard debates but decides he needs the guests to leave more than he needs to be tactful.

Richard is about to open his mouth when the Wolf, who has heard everything, shakes his head. "Consider it done. Go take care of your family."

The Wolf steps away from the royal family and walks into the middle of the empty dance floor. He takes a deep breath to settle himself.

"Attention!" he shouts in his battle voice. The room becomes silent instantly as the guests look at him in surprise. The Wolf rarely speaks to anyone at formal occasions like this.

He clears his throat. "I regret to inform you that tonight's festivities must end earlier than we anticipated. Thank you all for coming. Please leave!"

Using hand signals, the Wolf orders the guards to usher people out. Within a few minutes, the hall is completely empty, except for the Wolf standing in the middle of the silent ballroom.

COMING SOON

THE
BEAR'S CLAW

BOOK THREE OF THE THREE BROTHERS TRILOGY

ELIZABETH R. JENSEN

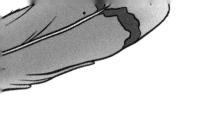

ACKNOWLEDGMENTS

Thank you to my friends and family who have been supporting me throughout this new and exciting direction—becoming a published author. I could not do it without you. To my amazing editor Pam, I'm so glad I found you! And last but not least, my cover artist Melissa, once again you brought my vision to life.

ABOUT THE AUTHOR

Elizabeth R. Jensen is an award-winning finalist in Children's Fiction and Arabian horse breeder in Atlanta, GA. Elizabeth has a bachelor's degree in animal science, a master's of business administration and a master's of organizational leadership. In elementary school, Elizabeth was introduced to creative writing in an after-school poetry class for gifted students. Since then, she has continued to write poetry. The Hawk's Flight is her second novel.

CPSIA information can be obtained
at www.ICGtesting.com
Printed in the USA
BVHW032212071222
653746BV00010B/75